DETECTION
UPSTAIRS, DOWNSTAIRS
AND IN MY LADY'S CHAMBER ...

"A Sort of Miss Marple?" by H.R.F. Keating
It is too, too worrying when Queen Elizabeth II discovers she is missing her wedding ring ... until she decides to emulate her favorite fictional detective and sniff out the sticky fingers who purloined so important a personal possession.

"A Black Death" by Edward Marston
In the reign of Edward III, a Welsh pretender to the crown plots to eliminate his British nemesis, the Prince of Wales, but the best laid plans may go awry when a suit of black armor proves to be a red herring for a would-be assassin.

"Balmorality" by Robert Barnard
Turnabout is fair play when there are all kinds of cheating going on during a country weekend at Balmoral, and Bertie, still not quite King, intends to even the score in a very high-stakes game of poker, croquet ... and passion.

"A Day at the Races" by Edward D. Hoch
Edward VII has, as one of his fondest wishes, a longing to see his horse win the Ascot Gold Cup, but this outing to the track will have him *not* seeing the famous 20-carat gold trophy, for someone has swiped it ... and it's up to his hefty highness to get it back.

AND MORE HIGH CRIMES
AND UPPER-CRUST CASES FROM
TODAY'S TOP MYSTERY AUTHORS

S0-AXS-072

ROYAL
CRIMES

~

EDITED BY
Maxim Jakubowski
and
Martin H. Greenberg

A SIGNET BOOK

SIGNET
Published by the Penguin Group
Penguin Books USA Inc., 375 Hudson Street,
New York, New York 10014, U.S.A.
Penguin Books Ltd, 27 Wrights Lane,
London W8 5TZ, England
Penguin Books Australia Ltd, Ringwood,
Victoria, Australia
Penguin Books Canada Ltd, 10 Alcorn Avenue,
Toronto, Ontario, Canada M4V 3B2
Penguin Books (N.Z.) Ltd, 182-190 Wairau Road,
Auckland 10, New Zealand

Penguin Books Ltd, Registered Offices:
Harmondsworth, Middlesex, England

First published by Signet,
an imprint of Dutton Signet,
a division of Penguin Books USA Inc.

First Printing, August, 1994
10 9 8 7 6 5 4 3 2 1

PUBLISHER'S NOTE
These stories are works of fiction. Names, characters, places, and incidents either are the product of the authors' imagination or are used fictitiously, and any resemblance to actual persons, living or dead, events, or locales is entirely coincidental.

Contents

Introduction

The British Royal Family.

Who are they really?

Who needs them?

Well, these are certainly two questions you will not find an answer to in these pages of mystery. This is principally a book of entertainments on a subject more usually covered by tabloid newspapers, glossy magazines, and tell-all indiscreet biographies. As a Briton (despite my Polish-like name), I sadly realize that my chances of appearing in a future honor's list (a quaint British ritual whereby titles and sundry initials are bestowed upon one by the reigning monarch at the behest of the Prime Minister of the day, for services rendered of a sometimes esoteric nature) will forever be compromised by my association with this gently subversive collection, but, as Cain pleaded so eloquently in days of old, I just couldn't resist. The Royals on a crime spree! Too much of a temptation, and I'm not even an anti-royalist!

Past, present, and even future, the assorted members of Britain's hallowed Royal Family keep on exercising a curious fascination in a million different ways. The opposition between private and public image, the glitz and circumstance and the private sadness behind, all grist to the imaginative mill. And an ideal ground for speculation for crime and mystery writers.

Fifteen British and American crime writers took up the challenge, and the result is a delicious cocktail of sedition, mystery, mischief, and affection. Many are historical, others more daringly contemporary, but all the stories we've collected provide intrigue and entertainment.

Six of our contributors are American, although three of them live in England, and it is interesting to compare the difference in approach between our master criminals, depending on which side of the great pond they live on and origin. But all come up with fascinating angles and particularly ingenious variations on the royal theme.

Bob Barnard, from deepest Yorkshire, was even inspired to pen two separate blue-blood mysteries, including an ironic nod to Peter Lovesey's Bertie books. Keep your eyes peeled for the joke! Other writers have proven more serious, but the pouring of blood and the solving of puzzles has never been so regal.

And already many of our crime writers are waiting for the signal to shoot, poison, execute, and exterminate other dynasties in a future volume. Sleuthing pharaohs, thieving czars, scheming Grimaldis, and other dubious foreign royals are crowding at the gate. Well, my patriotism cannot allow crime to remain the exclusive property of the British Royals, can it?

—Maxim Jakubowski

About the Authors

ROBERT BARNARD is one of the most popular English mystery writers, with a multitude of novels and short stories to his credit. A favorite panelist at American mystery conventions, he writes full-time and lives in Yorkshire, following an academic career which took him to Australia and Norway. His latest novels are *A Fatal Attachment* and, as Robert Bastable, *To Die Like a Gentleman*.

MOLLY BROWN is one of the mystery and science fiction fields' rising stars. An American living in London, she has won the British Science Fiction Association Award for best short story of 1991, and her crime stories have appeared in many leading anthologies. Inspired by her royal story here, she has since begun her first historical novel, featuring Aphra Behn and Nell Gwyn, *Invitation to a Funeral*.

GWENDOLINE BUTLER is the author of more than fifty books. Her main series character is John Coffin, who featured in her Silver Dagger winner *Coffin for Pandora*. She has also won the Best Romantic Novel of the Year award and an Ellery Queen Short Story Award. She also writes as Jennie Melville, featuring woman detective Charmian Daniels in her books.

PAUL DORRELL was a young British writer for young adults whose first crime stories had appeared in recent anthologies. Sadly, he died of AIDS shortly after completing his story for *Royal Crimes*.

EDWARD D. HOCH is a past president of the Mystery Writers of America. He is one of the genre's most prominent short story writers, with nearly eight hundred stories to his credit, as well as thirty books. An Edgar winner for "The Oblong Room," he currently edits *The Year's Best Mystery and Suspense Stories*, and his stories have appeared in every single issue of *Ellery Queen's Mystery Magazine* since May 1973.

GRAHAM JOYCE's first two novels have been much-acclaimed horror novels, the latest of which is *Dark Sister*. He lives in the Midlands and is considered a rising British fiction star.

H.R.F. KEATING is the creator of Inspector Ghote, one of crime and mystery's most popular sleuths. A past chairman of the Crime Writers' Association and the Society of Authors, president of the Detection Club and twice a winner of the Gold Dagger award, his latest novel is the first in a new series, *The Rich Detective*.

MICHAEL Z LEWIN is an American mystery author who has lived in England's Somerset for many years. He is the creator of private eye Albert Samson and police lieutenant Leroy Powder. He has twice been nominated for Edgars. The "Z" stands for Zinn, which is his mother's maiden name.

PETER LOVESEY is a past chairman of the Crime Writers' Association and recent winner of the Anthony award for his novel *The Last Detective*, which has since been followed by *Diamond Solitaire*. He has featured Bertie, Prince of Wales, as a sleuth in three novels and is the leading British exponent of the historical mystery novel.

SHARYN MCCRUMB won the Edgar award for her wonderfully titled *Bimbos of the Death Sun* (since succeeded by *Zombies of the Gene Pool*). Equally at ease with comedy thrillers and evocative regional mysteries, she has been nominated three times for the Anthony and twice for the Agathas, winning the latter award for her story "A Wee Doch and Doris."

EDWARD MARSTON is the pseudonym used by British writer Keith Miles for his popular series of historical mysteries set in the world of the Elizabethan theater. His latest Marston mystery is *The Mad Courtesan.*

JESSICA PALMER is an American writer now living in England. Her first horror novel, *Dark Lullaby,* has just been followed by *Cradlesong.*

MIKE RIPLEY is the creator of the Angel series, featuring a lovable London cab driver cum sleuth. He is also the crime reviewer for London's *Daily Telegraph,* a television scriptwriter, and the foremost beer expert among Britain's crime community. He also writes for *Mystery Scene.*

KRISTINE KATHRYN RUSCH is editor of *The Magazine of Fantasy and Science Fiction.* She lives in Oregon and has burst like a comet onto the mystery and SF firmament over the last few years, with an awesome body of work, encompassing short stories and challenging novels, including the *The White Mists of Power.*

MARK TIMLIN, the tallest man in British crime fiction, writes the fast-paced Nick Sharman series, which is set in his native South London. His latest Sharman novel is *Ashes for New.*

The Monster of Glamis

by Sharyn McCrumb

HRH The Princess of Wales

Balmoral
August 1992

My dearest Wills,
   Mummy has a longish letter to write you, although
you won't get it for years and years, as I'm going to
leave instructions with someone clever whom I *really*
trust. (*Not* Robert Fellowes! He may be your Auntie
Jane's husband, but he is also "Brenda's" private secretary, and to me he is neither kith nor kind!) (I realize
that you will be reading this years from now, so you
may not know that "Brenda" was the magazine *Private
Eye*'s name for HM, your granny. I think I shall continue to call her that in this letter. Much safer really.)
   I thought I'd better put all this down so that you'll
know what happened, in case there's something you
can do when you become King. I do hope you will believe what I tell you in this letter, and investigate the
matter very, very carefully yourself. Courtiers cannot
be trusted to tell you the truth, Wills! It is most important.
   This week at Balmoral seemed the best time to write
an account of what happened. Heaven knows there's
nothing else to do here in the wilds of Scotland! I can't
think why Queen Victoria ever wanted to buy it, but
apparently the madness was hereditary, because her descendants adore the place. Every morning everyone
goes out with their beastly guns, stopping at noon to

gobble sandwiches, and coming back at teatime caked
with mud. Once they actually asked if I wanted to go
with you boys and act as a beater, frightening the little
birds out of the hedges. I said I thought not. I can be
quite stubborn when I choose, you know, Wills. Anyhow, it's damp and dreary outside, and even more
dreary inside, with nothing to do but jigsaw puzzles
and listen to that family go on about their horses' ailments. No one will miss me, because I never say anything anyway, so I came away to write to you.

Funny to think of you as a great grown man reading
this. I simply cannot picture it, or picture *me* having to
drop a curtsey to my own darlingest King Wills. So
you must pardon me there in the future as you read this
for addressing you as a nine-year-old boy, but that is
what you are as I write this. You and Harry have gone
pony-trekking with the Phillips children, so I shall be
quite alone for hours to write. It will take hours, as
I've never been much hand at composition, so do bear
with me if I ramble. I'm not clever, you know. Not
with books. I daresay I'm clever enough in other ways.

Your Auntie Fergie (the Duchess of York) was always said to be the clever one, but it was me whom
she came to two summers ago when she found the papers and wondered what it all meant. It was here at
Balmoral that it happened, as a matter of fact. Things
weren't so dreary here then, because she was such a lot
of fun. Sarah and I had each other to talk to, and once
we even took the family cars and raced each other
round the back roads of the estate. We got a proper
ticking off for it, too! It was a bit after that—I was in
my rooms doing ballet exercises when Sarah turned up,
with that impish grin she always has. She was wearing
a heavy green woolen jumper and corduroy trousers—
good colors to offset her red hair, but not flattering for
her rather bulky figure. Inwardly I shuddered, but I
was too glad of her company to risk offending her with
well-meaning criticism. She was raw from having got
too much of the other kind.

"Hullo—ullo," she said, waggling her fingers at me.

"Stop trying to get a flatter tummy. You'll only make me look worse in the tabloids."

I made a face at her, and went on doing pliés. "You're welcome to join me," I said. "It wouldn't kill you, you know."

"No, but look, do stop for a bit. I've found something," said Sarah. "Something actually interesting. Come and see."

I thought it was a ploy to get me to stop practicing, but she seemed so earnest that I left off, and plopped beside her on the sofa. "What is it now? Did you come upon a stash of wine gums?"

Sarah shook her red curls, and her eyes glowed with that look that always meant mischief. "I've been snooping!" she whispered, glancing about to make sure that no one was hovering.

"All clear," I told her. "We're off-duty at Balmoral, so there aren't so many servants underfoot. If you want guaranteed privacy for hours, though, try ordering a sandwich. Now, what have you been up to?"

"I've been poking around. You know how dreary it gets, waiting for teatime. And I happened to go into the box room that holds junk. You know, old vases, spare fishing rods—and I came across a trunk labeled MARY R, and I thought I'd have a look inside, to see why they stashed it. I could guess, of course."

"I can guess, too," I said, stifling a yawn. "You mean Queen Mary, Her Majesty's grandmother, I take it, not the ancient Tudor one? Then it's hats. I've seen pictures of her in those hats. Dreadful. Was that it? A trunkful of ghastly hats?"

Sarah's eyes widened. "You mean you haven't heard about old Queen Mary? The old guard still whispers about it. Diana, she took things!"

"Oh, I knew that. It was common knowledge. Once in my grandfather's time she came to Althorp, and the servants had spent hours packing away every little object d'art and knickknack in the house. She didn't pocket them, though. She asked for them, and wouldn't take no for an answer, so of course one always knew whither one's treasures had gone, but the gifts were not cheerfully given."

"And they dare to call me Freebie Fergie," Sarah said, scowling. "At least people give me things because they want to. Nice tax-deductible dresses and trips; I don't go to people's houses and nick the bric-a-brac!"

"One mustn't be too hard on her, Sarah. She grew up terribly poor, in a grace-and-favor apartment at Kensington Palace with bill collectors forever trying to dun her father, Prince Francis of Teck. I suppose she became rather mercenary. Her little hobby does make life awkward for the rest of us, even though she's been dead for thirty years. Has anyone asked you about the teapot yet?"

Sarah was rooting around in our fruit basket, hoping that you and Harry had overlooked a banana. You hadn't. "What teapot?"

"The one from Badminton House in Gloucestershire. Queen Mary spent the war there, and when she left, a few of the Duchess of Beaufort's possessions went with her. The Beauforts are always trying to corner one of us and asking us to have a look round for the family trinkets. They're particularly keen to get back a silver teakettle on silver gates that belonged to the duchess, but I know you didn't find that in the trunk."

"No." Sarah had settled for an orange and was peeling it with a look of intense concentration.

"That particular teapot is on the Queen Mum's breakfast tray every morning. Hard luck to the Beauforts. What did you find in the trunk, then?"

"Oh, the usual sorts of things. Old silver brushes, and gloves, and yellowed handkerchiefs, but there were a few jade carvings that looked quite old, and one of those carved wooden puzzle boxes. I had one as a child."

"A jewelry box?"

"It could be," said Sarah. "There is a brass plate on the top that says DUNGAVEL HOUSE. The box is about eight inches long, made of different kinds of wood inlaid in strips, and it opens to reveal a compartment that you can put things in. But the trick is that if you push a certain slot on the side, a hidden compartment opens up beneath the first one."

"And did you find any jewelry?" I asked. I wish Sarah wouldn't wear rubies. It clashes dreadfully with her coloring.

She shook her head. "No. Just some papers."

"How tiresome for you." I yawned. "Did you bother to read them?"

"Of course, I did. They were addressed to the Duke of Hamilton at Dungavel House."

"Oh, a Scottish peer. Surely you don't mean that he and Queen Mary—"

"Lord, no!" squealed Sarah. "They weren't love letters, Diana. They were an official communique to the duke from the Third Reich, dated 1941."

I lost interest at once. I always found history quite stupendously boring. "I daresay Oxford might like to see them, or the British Museum for one of their moldy collections."

Sarah's eyes danced. "Oh no," she whispered. "Not these papers! I'd rank this lot as yet another unexploded bomb from the war. They contain an offer from Adolf Hitler, proposing to put Edward VIII on the throne of Russia."

Sarah insisted on explaining it all to me, as if I wouldn't know that Edward VIII was Queen Mary's oldest son, the Family's "Uncle David," the one who abdicated to marry that woman from Baltimore, and sent the Crown into such a tizzy that the word "divorce" still gives them palpitations. It cost poor Meg her romance with Peter Townsend in the fifties, and pretty well ruined her life. People were always muttering about Edward VIII whenever Charles and I had a row, so I should jolly well know who he was by now. He left off being King in 1936, and went to France, leaving his younger brother, Bertie, to take the throne of England. I couldn't see why Adolf Hitler would want to offer Uncle David another throne, though. Rather uncharacteristically thoughtful of him, I said. Still nothing came of it, because the Russians kept their communist leaders for years and years, and Uncle David and Wallis Simpson kept on knocking about the world partying and staying in expensive hotels for decades until they both went ga-ga, so I couldn't see what Sarah was looking so fluffed up for.

"What difference does an old letter make?"

"Quite amazingly dim," sighed Sarah, tapping her head, and looking at me in a sorrowful way. The sort of look I got from Charles when I asked if one of his modern paintings was done by Pablo Casals.

"Rubbish," I said. "The letter was written fifty years ago by a now-defunct government. Uncle David's dead. The Soviet Union is a hodgepodge of little states. The Nazis are just a bunch of old war movies now. *The Great Escape. The Dirty Dozen.* So what?" Another thought occurred to me. "Why did they address the message to the Duke of Hamilton, anyhow? Why not to the King?"

Sarah looked pleased with herself. "What's the only thing you know about Dungavel House?" she prompted me.

"It's in Scotland, so it's cold and damp."

"No. It's been converted into a prison now, as a matter of fact, but in 1941, Rudolf Hess bailed out of his plane on the grounds there. You *have* heard of him, haven't you, Diana?"

"Vaguely. Some sort of spy, wasn't he?" I shrugged. "Anyhow, don't tell me you knew all this off your own bat. You've been mugging it up in the library, haven't you?"

"One or two encyclopedias," Sarah said. "I knew it was important, and I wanted to get it all straight. Rudolf Hess was Hitler's Deputy Fuhrer. In May 1941 he stole a plane, flew to Scotland, and asked to speak to the Duke of Hamilton. Apparently, they had met at the 1936 Olympics in Berlin."

"I thought we were at war with Germany in 1941," I said. I've always hated trying to remember dates.

"We were. Hess claimed that he was acting on his own initiative, and that all he wanted was to negotiate a peace between Britain and Germany."

"That sounds rather noble. I don't suppose anybody was grateful." I was pretty sure that I'd have heard of him if he'd won the Nobel peace prize.

"Ungrateful is understating the case," said Sarah. "This is where it all gets madly interesting. The Duke of Hamilton did go and talk to him, but after that, the government shut Hess up in the Tower of London for the duration of the war. He was the last prisoner ever kept in the Tower of London, in fact."

Sarah's frightfully good at crossword puzzles. You can see why. Four letters: *last prisoner wishes to trade Tower for Cassel,* that sort of thing. "Was the job offer to Edward VIII part of Mr. Hess's peace plan?" I still couldn't see why it mattered, but it was still hours till teatime, so I humored her.

"No. It was never mentioned. No one would have dared." She could see I wasn't following her. "Look. The offer was that Edward should have the throne of Russia upon the following conditions: that Britain should ally with Germany, and that Britain should help Germany invade and defeat Russia."

"Offer refused, of course."

"Yes, of course, but here's the thing: the secret offer was made on May 11, 1941. Germany invaded Russia in late June. Britain did not warn the Russians of the coming invasion. According to these papers, Hess told our government about the invasion plans, but we did not pass along the information to the Russians, our allies. Well, not our allies yet, but not our enemy, either. They had declared themselves neutral. Yet we didn't warn them."

"Why didn't we warn them?" I tried to work it out for myself. "We didn't like the Russians frightfully, did we? They had a revolution during the First World War, and killed off the Czar and all the Royals, who were relatives of our lot."

"Close relatives. The Czar and George V were first cousins, and could have passed for twins. Their mothers were Danish princesses. So I don't suppose anyone in Britain actually liked Stalin and his government, but that isn't why they withheld the information about the Nazi invasion."

"Are you sure? It wouldn't be the first thing the family's done for spite. Remember how they refused to make Uncle David's wife a *royal* duchess, just because they loathed her?" I can't remember battles or dates, but titles and family trees do make a fair bit of sense to me. It's all people ever seem to talk about.

"I know exactly why we didn't warn the Russians about the invasion," said Sarah dramatically. "It's because we would have had to show the Russians the paper that Rudolf Hess was carrying—in order to prove how we knew. And we couldn't show them the paper because it also proved that Edward VIII was a traitor."

I was very shocked indeed. And indignant. Imagine being a collaborator with the Nazis and not having the tabloids crucify you! Sarah can't even wear polka dots without getting narky stories run, and they go on about my shopping until I could scream, but here's a Royal who actually did something frightful and—not a word! Unfair, I call it. Beastly.

"Do you really think the government would have protected Uncle David even at the risk of offending a wartime ally?" If so, I thought, things have certainly changed for us Royals.

Sarah frowned. I could tell that she was thinking about all the lectures she'd got from the palace watchdogs, and all the ticking off for the most trivial of reasons. "Well," she said at last, "he was the King."

"Not then he wasn't," I pointed out. "By 1941, he'd already abdicated, and was being a royal nuisance, ringing up the new king, and trying to tell him how to run things. And the Queen Mum, who was Queen Consort then, hated him. She still practically spits his name, because she thinks his abdication shortened her husband's life—all the extra responsibility of being king. Edward hated her, too. He called her the Monster of Glamis, because she was so mean about his dear Wallis. I don't think the courtiers or the government would have lifted a finger to get him an extra ration coupon, much less risked national security to save him from his own silly blunders."

"It's true," said Sarah. "All of Edward's staff would have left royal service, because the new king would have wanted people whose loyalty he could trust. The new courtiers would have been in their jobs *because* they opposed Edward VIII. So, no, the government wouldn't have kept it a secret."

We looked at each other, realizing the truth of it at the same time. "But the family would!" Even if they loathed him, they'd have kept the secret to keep the rest of them from looking guilty by association.

I went back to my ballet exercises, and Sarah began to pace up and down, as we worked it out. "The government was never given these papers," Sarah announced. "They were never told about them. Hess landed in Scotland, said his piece to the Duke of Hamilton—"

"And Hamilton notified the family instead of the government!" Of course he would have. He was a duke. *My* father would have done the same.

"Douglas Hamilton was a Scottish duke," said Sarah. "All the more reason. The Queen was the daughter of a Scottish earl. Of course, he'd warn their majesties about the family scandal."

"They wouldn't tell the government, would they? No. It would make the whole family suspect."

"People thought there was far too much German blood in the family as it was," said Sarah. "Remember that everyone had to change their surnames during the First World War. The Saxe-Coburgs became the house of Windsor; the Battenbergs became Mountbattens, and—I forgot—who did the Cambridges used to be?"

"Teck, I think. That was Queen Mary's maiden name. Her father was a German prince, you know."

Sarah gave a low whistle. "They dared not let the secret out, did they? Britain might have dumped the monarchy then and there."

I nodded. "So they took the papers, but they turned Hess over to the government. Why didn't he tell what he knew to Churchill?"

"I don't know. Maybe he did, and he wasn't believed. But I doubt it. I wonder what became of him?"

I shrugged. "Too bad the encyclopedias here are so out of date. What are you going to do with the papers? Destroy them?"

"No," said Sarah. "I think I'll keep them. They might come in handy someday."

Kensington Palace
October, 1992

I shouldn't have let Sarah keep those papers, but I don't see how I could have prevented her. I was never any good at talking her out of mischief. I even helped her poke people with umbrellas at Ascot once. I thought people would never shut up about that. I did wonder what had become of Rudolf Hess, though. It was tricky thinking of people to ask. They might want to know why I was interested. Your grandfather, Prince Philip, would know, of course, but he's terribly touchy about the subject of Nazi Germany. His sisters were married to German soldiers, and they weren't even invited to his wedding in 1947, so I thought I'd better not broach the subject with him.

I waited until we got back to London, and I was trotted out for a formal reception. I had to make small talk with diplomats and generals, and I thought that might be an intelligent thing to ask instead of "Does your wife polish your medals for you?"

I picked a doddery old fellow, who looked old enough to remember Napoleon, and worked the conversation round to the war, and then I said, "By the way, General, do you happen to know what happened to Rudolf Hess?"

He got a funny look on his face, and for a moment, I thought I was doomed, but then he harumphed, and said, "Officially, you mean."

That set me wondering. "After the war," I said. "I know he was in the Tower of London until then."

"Oh, that. We turned him over to the Americans and

the Russians, and they put him in Spandau Prison in Berlin."

I smiled prettily. "And when did they let him out?"

"Never did. He committed suicide in there a few years ago, at the age of ninety-something. Good riddance, Nazi bugger." The general peered at me curiously. "Are you thinking of resitting your O-levels, ma'am?"

I gave him the downcast eyelash look that people take for shyness, and murmured, "Oh, no, General. It's just that I thought he went on to become a ballet dancer in the sixties." That's the sort of remark people expect me to make, and I got away with it and drifted on to the next guest. I had hoped to find what he meant by "officially," but I'm not allowed to dawdle with any one guest. Besides it might have made him suspicious.

When the party was over, I barricaded myself in the bathroom, and rang up Sarah. "Found out what happened to Rudolf!" I told her, reciting the general's account of Hess's life imprisonment.

"Life?" said Sarah in disbelieving tones. "That seems a bit stiff for someone who sat out most of the war in London. And on a peace mission, too. And he lived to ninety, and they didn't let him out?"

"It's an unforgiving world," I said. "When did Wallis Simpson see the inside of Buckingham Palace? Not until her husband's funeral."

"That was family spite," said Sarah. "Government memories are shorter. I still say it doesn't make sense."

"Well, the general did say something else. When I first asked him what had happened to Hess, he said, *'Officially?'* Now what do you suppose he meant by that?"

"It suggests a secret. Perhaps we should ask a few more generals."

"No," I said. "I don't want anyone to notice. I'll ask my hairdresser. He always knows everything."

Althorp
December, 1992

Bear with me, Wills. I know this is a longish letter
about ancient, ancient history, but Mummy does have a
reason. And it took ever so much longer to find it all
out than it will take you to read. Besides, I should
think by now that you'll be doing the government
boxes, so you should be used to reading longish wran-
gles about government intrigue. But this is special.
This is family.

It's Christmas time now, but I couldn't bear to spend
another holiday at Sandringham pretending we're all a
happy family now that the separation is official, so I
came home to spend the season with your Uncle
Charles, Earl Spencer. I miss your Auntie Sarah more
than ever, but I dare not talk about her to anyone. This
has been the worst year of all of our lives, with Sarah
and Andrew splitting up, and the problems between
your father and me coming to light and ending in separation, and now the fire at Windsor. If I've learnt anything these past twelve months, it's that I must never
let anyone see this paper. Nothing I do is safe. Not
even a telephone call. Poor Sarah. For all her clever-
ness, she trusted the system far too much. I only hope
that when you are the system, Wills, you can fix
things.

I was right about my hairdresser. He knows abso-
lutely all the dirt, and he *never* tells tales to the press.
I just adore him. I must admit, he was surprised when
I asked him about Rudolf Hess.

"Rudolf Nureyev, Your Royal Highness?" he murmured, tucking a curl into place.

"No. It isn't a ballet question," I told him. "I mean
the Nazi fellow who crashed in Scotland on a peace
mission during the war. I heard that there was some
sort of rumor about his case."

He thought for a moment, while he combed. "Seems
like there was a bit of talk when he died, back in the
eighties, ma'am. While this side bit sets, let me nip
over to the other booth and ask Nigel. Loves war mov-

ies, does Nigel." A few minutes later he was back, combing again. "Nigel says you must be referring to the theory that it wasn't Hess at all in the prison."

"Who was it?" I asked, turning my head at just the wrong time, and getting a hair-pull. "Ouch!"

"Beg your pardon, Your Royal Highness. Nigel says that it's been rumored for years that the fellow in prison didn't look like Rudolf Hess, and didn't seem to remember people and details from his life before the war. Apparently there are all sorts of bits of proof that the fellow in the German prison wasn't the chap who landed in Scotland in 1941. Nigel says he could find you an article on the Hess mystery if you liked."

"No, thank you," I said quickly. "It was only something I heard at a party. I'm not really interested." I didn't want any rumors to surface about my inquiry. I had a feeling that Mr. Hess was a very dangerous topic.

I told Sarah so when I visited her at Sunninghill Park later that week. Andrew was off at sea in those days, and Eugenie was still an adorable little baby, so I looked in on Sarah when I could spare the time. She was terribly lonely. That day I made her come out for a walk in the garden so that we wouldn't be overheard. Sarah received my news of the substitute Rudolf Hess with satisfaction, but no surprise.

"That explains why Hess didn't tell the government that the ex-king was a traitor," she said. "After the real Hess told the Duke of Hamilton about the offer, his papers were confiscated, and someone else was brought in to impersonate Hess. The government never saw the real Hess at all."

"Why not just kill him and present the authorities with a corpse?" I asked.

"Because a Scottish farmer had captured Hess when he parachuted. He was taken alive, you see. If he subsequently died, it might have been suspicious. Instead, he was hustled to London and put in the Tower for four years. Or *somebody* was!"

"Who would agree to go to prison as a Nazi?" I asked, but Sarah gave me one of those meaningful looks, and said very firmly, "Her Majesty's Bobo. Queen Victoria's Mr. Brown. Princess Anne's body-guard."

I knew what she meant. The Royal Family has al-ways had a few adoring, utterly faithful servants who would do anything for their favorite Royal. They spend their entire lives in royal service, and become the clos-est of confidants. I supposed that in Queen Mary's day there may have been even more servants who would have felt it their duty to sacrifice their very lives for the good of the Firm.

"I don't suppose the servant realized that it would be forever," Sarah said thoughtfully. "Probably he as-sumed that it would be just until the war was over. He'd have been assured of a royal pardon, but of course the government wasn't told about any of it, and they handed him over to the other Allies, and then there was no saving him. He had to play out his role to the death."

"A royal servant impersonating a German?" I said.

"Use your loaf, Diana! Half the family *was* German. I'm sure they had servants from the old country. There was always a German governess in tow. There were probably other retainers from there as well."

"Wouldn't someone miss a royal servant?"

"Not if he had a relatively minor position. Footman or—"

"Gardener!" I suddenly realized that we were talk-ing about Scotland. "A servant at Balmoral. It's so re-mote, no one would know what went on there. Is it far from Dungavel House?"

Sarah considered it. "A hundred miles perhaps. They could have done it in a few hours, I think. One tele-phone call to Balmoral from the Duke of Hamilton, and it could all have been arranged by morning."

I began to pull leaves off a branch of rowan. The wind felt suddenly cold. "But what did they do with the real Rudolf Hess, Sarah! Surely, you can't think that he agreed to become a gardener at Balmoral?"

"No. But I don't think they killed him. It's not the family style. We tend to shut people up when they're inconvenient, at least at first. Richard III and the two little princes. Brenda the First imprisoning Mary Queen of Scots."

I giggled at "Brenda the First." Sarah is awfully jolly, but I'm always afraid she'll slip and say something like that in public or to the press. Then heads would roll!

"I wonder if there's any way of finding out what they did with the real Rudolf Hess?" said Sarah.

I shivered. "Are you sure you want to know?"

I don't know exactly where Sarah got the information about the family secret, but I do know *when* she got it. It was in January of 1991, just before she left for a trip to the Everglades Club in Palm Beach, Florida. I know that she had been looking into old record books on Balmoral, and researching family history, and she did publish the nonfiction book about the royal ancestors, but I think that book was just an excuse to cover up her real inquiries. I wasn't seeing much of her by then, because she'd become rather too impulsive for safety, and besides I had more than enough troubles of my own. But just before she left for the United States, she sent me a coded package to my secret postal address in Knightsbridge (there is no privacy at the palace, with all those prying eyes!).

Even then, Sarah was unusually careful. There was no message from her, and no explanation. All the package contained was a souvenir guidebook of Glamis Castle. That was the Queen Mum's girlhood home in Scotland, so at first I thought it was another of Sarah's jokes, so I paged through it to see if she had put any funny little drawings in the illustrations, or perhaps written crude remarks in the margins—but she hadn't. The book was perfectly ordinary. I couldn't see what she meant by sending me such a thing, so I put it away in my desk at Kensington.

Later, of course, I must have read it twenty times. When I realized that the woman who came back from Florida, the one who got drunk on the plane and threw sugar packets, was not Sarah Ferguson, Duchess of

York. The family knew about the substitution, of course, but the resemblance was nearly perfect, and by then Sarah's public appearances had been curtailed, so that she didn't go out much. No one ever gets very chummy with a Royal, anyhow. "How do you do, ma'am?" is about the sum total of anyone's acquaintance with us. Except for the servants and courtiers, but I warned you already that one cannot trust *them*. Believe it.

I stayed away from the imposter Fergie after that. I didn't want anyone to think that I suspected. I knew too much, you see, and it would be dangerous to let them find out that I knew. I think poor Andrew minded very much about losing his wife and having to put up with that imposter, but the family's word is law, so he had to go along and pretend that the stranger was Sarah. He didn't have to pretend for long. A few months later the "Duchess of York" took a holiday on the Riviera with a silly-looking Texan, and a photographer conveniently snapped some scandalous photographs that finished the Yorks' marriage. After that "Sarah" left Sunninghill Park, left the family, and left public life. I think the family hopes people will forget about her. I wonder where the imposter will go when the furor dies down—back where she came from?

Not that it matters. What really concerns me is the whereabouts of poor Sarah, who knew too much. She must have tried to use her knowledge of the family secret as leverage in some battle with the family. Sarah was just impulsive enough to have done such a foolhardy thing. But I know where she is, just as she knew where the real Rudolf Hess ended his days.

I don't know what she did with the Hess papers, though. I suspect that the family never found them. When the fire broke out at Windsor Castle, and Andrew was the only family member present, I did rather wonder, but I'm not sure I even want to know where those papers are. They've done enough damage as it is. And at least I know what has become of poor Sarah.

Glamis Castle is in Scotland, a few hours north of the Duke of Hamilton's estate. In the guidebook I finally found the message Sarah was trying to send me. It is on page six: "The secret chamber, about which are woven many legends, is thought to be located deep in the thickness of the crypt walls on the left as you face the two small windows at the end. In this room it is said that one of the Lords of Glamis and the 'Tiger' Earl of Crawford played cards with the Devil himself on the Sabbath. So great were the resulting disturbances that eventually the room was built up and permanently sealed. . . ."

I've done quite a bit of reading on Glamis Castle, birthplace of the Queen Mother, and home of Macbeth. There is a secret room, behind walls that are three feet thick. From the left side of the castle one can see the narrow windows high up the wall of rosy stone. They say there is no way into that room, but there must be. Someone took food in to Rudolf Hess for however long he lived there, before he took his secret to the grave. I'm sure the family sees that its prisoners are well treated. They are not cruel people; only single-minded.

If you are reading this, Wills, you are now the King, and you must make them do as you say. Take people that you trust and go to Glamis Castle. Your cousin Simon will be the nineteenth Earl of Strathmore and Kinghorne by now. I wonder if he will know the family secret? Anyhow, you must find that secret room, and if your Auntie Sarah is still alive, you must get her out.

Mummy is counting on you.

> With lots of love to my own dear King,
> HRH Diana, The Princess of Wales

A Statesman's Touch

by Robert Barnard

"Mais c'est incroyable!"

The hotel manager looked down toward his beautifully shod feet with an expression more of distaste than of disbelief. The head porter who had summoned him thought to himself that if you find a trickle of blood seeping under the door of one of the bedrooms into the corridor, it is not altogether surprising to discover a corpse behind the door, or to find that the corpse was murdered. But, as an intelligent man, he held his peace.

"It's that man Radovan Radič," said the manager, his mouth twisting as he looked down at the body with the gaping wound between its shoulders.

"A Bulgarian, wasn't he?" the porter asked.

"Serbian, I believe. But Serbian, Bulgarian, Hungarian—they're all the same. Brutes!" He looked around the spare, ill-furnished room, one of their cheapest. "I only know of this creature because the police were around asking about him last week."

"Illegal resident?"

"Worse, much worse. Apparently he was a thoroughly unsavory character—all sorts of activities, including blackmail. He had been touting letters from Marie of Romania."

"Ah—to Prince Stirbey?"

"No, not that old story. Something more recent. They thought it possible he was an agent of the King of Serbia, but on balance they thought he was acting for his own ends. I was all for throwing him out onto the street at once, but the Sûreté begged me not to. Here they could keep an eye on him, they said. I wish now that I had insisted, but when the Sûreté begs ..."

"Of course. In our position one obeys. Who have we in the hotel tonight?"

"Ah, that is the question."

It was indeed. The Hôtel George IV, formerly the Impérial, situated on the Avenue Decazes, had carved for itself a minor but vital role in the diplomatic comings and goings of that year 1919, the year of the Peace Conference. Paris was awash with kings, statesmen, and mere politicians, not to mention the attendant diplomats, secretaries, and the inevitable newspapermen. Behind the ceremonial and the open negotiations there mushroomed a myriad process of secret diplomacy, and behind that there mushroomed encounters of a more personal nature. The George IV catered, discreetly, for any assignation, whether political, romantic, or frankly sexual, which the participants wished to keep from the gaze of the public or of rival statesmen. The hotel's system of backstairs access and private corridors was unrivaled in the French capital, and the manager was formidably discreet. He already regretted the renaming of the hotel, which had been done in the hope of profiting by a confusion with the new and magnificent George V. But the hotel had found a quite different and much more lucrative identity and would have benefited from a more anonymous name. That very morning an English visitor had commented cheerily that the only connection George IV had had with France had been his delusion that he led the allied troops at the Battle of Waterloo. The manager's demeanor had been glacial. It was the height of bad taste to mention the Battle of Waterloo in Paris.

He now enumerated the hotel's more sensitive guests, strictly in order of rank.

"The King of Spain is in Suite 15 with a woman who is not his mistress."

"Madame Grigot would raise hell if she knew."

"Quite ... Alfonso XIII—such an *unlucky* number. I'm surprised his mother chose the name."

The head porter caught his drift.

"Spain remained neutral during the course of the war," he remarked.

"Very profitably neutral. His Majesty was a noncombatant, at least on the field of battle ... I think, you know, that we need take no special steps where His Majesty is concerned."

The head porter nodded sage agreement.

"Then there is the President of the United States. He is in Suite 7 with the prime minister of Italy."

"There is no question of—?"

"No, no. Out of the question. The President has no such inclinations. Mrs. Wilson would never allow it. They are engaged in extremely sensitive discussions concerning Italy's new borders in the Tyrol. They will have to be informed."

"Of course."

"And then there is the Prime Minister of Great Britain ..."

"Ah yes. Mr. Lloyd George."

The head porter of the George IV naturally managed "George" more or less in the English manner, but "Lloyd" came out as "Lo-id." He was, nevertheless, extremely familiar with the name.

"Yes. With a most attractive woman of a certain age. I escorted them personally to Suite 12, his favorite suite. The Prime Minister's patronage is of course an honor to the hotel. . . ."

"Naturally."

"Though it is not an honor we can proclaim. . . ."

"Except discreetly."

"Exactly. We proclaim it discreetly. Mr. Lloyd George must of course be told before the police are summoned. . . . Who else? The Belgian ambassador, the Latvian chargé d'affaires, the Australian foreign minister, all with ladies. They can be informed. For the rest, diplomats, members of various parliaments—they must take their chance. We will inform them if we can, but before too long, for our good name, we must summon the Sûreté. *Mon Dieu!* They said they wished to keep an eye on him! What an eye!"

And leaving the head porter on guard outside the door, with instructions to inform any curious guests that there had been an unfortunate accident, the manager hustled off in his stately fashion to alert his guests.

In Suite 15 the young dancer whose name was unknown to him lay under the King of Spain and thought rapturously that it really was something, to be pleasured by a king. The pleasure was undisturbed by any call from the hotel management.

In Suite 7 the President of the United States of America put down the telephone and rose.

"Mr. Prime Minister, this has been a most interesting and productive meeting, and we have made real, very real progress, but I regret that it must come to an end."

The President's interpreter, who looked like a Mafia boss but who was in fact a Harvard professor, rose to his feet, but the Italian prime minister remained seated and looked petulant.

"But Mr. President, I wish to protest about Merano—"

"I'm afraid that there has been a murder in the hotel—some scruffy little Balkan muck-raker. It would greatly harm me in the American press if it were thought that I were making secret deals—coming to unofficial understandings—with a foreign power. No doubt the Italian press feels similarly strongly."

It didn't, but the Italian prime minister got to his feet.

"Of course. And my king is very touchy about his prerogative in matters of foreign policy."

"Ah, I think I have met your king. A very small man, I seem to recollect."

"But touchy accordingly. You are right, Mr. President, we should be gone."

"Why don't you stay, Giuliano? You could go through what we've already agreed on. No scandal in your being here."

And the President and Prime Minister opened the door on to the backstairs corridors and scuttled out. In minutes they were in two taxis which the manager had summoned for them, speeding back to their respective hotels.

In Suite 12 the British Prime Minister was more relaxed than the American President.

"Yes, I'm alone." He flicked his tongue around his lips. His companion for the night had just returned from her maid's room and had said with a coquettish smile, "Ten minutes!" He could hardly wait. "The lady is preparing herself," he told the manager.

"Mr. Lloyd George, I am desolated to have to tell you that there has been a murder—"

"A murder? In this hotel?"

"Yes, indeed. A Balkan adventurer of the most dubious kind."

A Balkan adventurer? Do you mean a gigolo?"

"No, no. A Serbian with a criminal bent. Perhaps it is best for you not to know the details."

"Perhaps it is."

"So I wondered whether you and the most charming lady would wish to . . . remove yourselves from any intrusiveness on the part of the police?"

"Hmmm . . . You have not yet called the police?"

"No, indeed. I informed you first, Mr. Prime Minister."

"Obliged to you. Hmmmm. I have a certain . . . experience in handling tricky matters of this kind."

"Your statesmanship is known to all, sir."

"Leave it with me for ten minutes or so. I may be able to advise you how to handle this. Suggest something to . . . to safeguard the reputation of the hotel."

"Of the hotel, of course, Mr. Prime Minister."

In his office on the ground floor of the George IV the manager fumed at the well-known hypocrisy of the English. To pretend that he was thinking of a solution to the hotel's crisis when all he wanted from the period of grace was . . . what he had come for in the first place. How truly perfidious was Albion!

* * *

In Suite 15 the nameless young dancer, once more under the King of Spain, was deciding that it was even more extraordinary than she had thought, being pleasured by a king.

In Suite 7 Professor Giuliano, master now of a luxurious suite, wished he could have taken advantage of the well-known freedoms of the Hôtel George IV. But with police in the offing that was hardly on the cards. With a sigh he returned to the maps of Southern Europe which had been occupying his master and his guest. He took hold of the carafe of barley water that Mr. Wilson had been drinking, then changed his mind and poured a glass of the Prime Minister's French champagne. As he sipped, he looked down at the maps on the desk and a new expression came over his face.

In Suite 12 Mr. Lloyd George took up the phone.

"Mr. Manager? Suite 12 here. Now, you said this Johnnie was Serbian, did you not?"

"Yes, Mr. Lloyd George. What I believe we are now to call Yugoslavian."

"Well, we shall see about that. But it's a good point. Got any of his fellow-countrymen on your staff, have you? Or anyone else from the Balkans? Very quarrelsome people, the Eastern Europeans. Or even a North African might do."

"I believe there is someone in the kitchens—let me see, I think there is somebody from Croatia."

"Capital. Part of the new kingdom."

"I seem to remember he is one of the meat chefs."

"With the skills of a butcher, then? Even better. I wouldn't mind betting his passport is not in order."

"It does often happen that people will work for less if we . . . turn a blind eye."

"Quite. Well, offer him a good sum of money—what's a thousand pounds in francs?—and tell him to disappear."

"Ah, you mean—?"

"It will be unimaginable riches to him. He'll take himself off and become a rich man in his own country. You don't need to do anything more. Tell the police he's disappeared, and they'll jump at it. Crime solved with no effort. Suspicious foreigner—everyone's happy. They won't trouble anyone else if the solution's handed to them on a plate."

"I do believe, Mr. Prime Minister, that you're right."

"Of course I am. And there'll be no scandal attached to the hotel. We all want that, don't we? Let me know how things go."

As he put down the phone, the door to the bedroom opened, and a vision in rustling silks swept through.

"My *dear*!" said Mr. Lloyd George appreciatively.

The men from the Sûreté behaved in a way that at first bordered on the surly.

"This is the man Radič," said the inspector, looking at the body on the floor with disgust.

"It is. I wanted to throw him out."

"We told you to keep an eye on him."

"You said that you would keep an eye on him."

"That's what we meant. My God! With this man's record it could be anyone—and possibly one of the highest in Europe. Or of course one of their hire-lings . . ."

"It occurred to me—" began the manager.

"Yes?"

"Did you not say that the man was possibly in the pay of the King of Serbia?"

"It was one of the possibilities."

"And has he not recently proclaimed himself king of a country called Yugoslavia?"

"Lord knows. Who understands what goes on down there? I have an idea you're right."

"It is a very quarrelsome part of the world."

"They're always at it. Love, war, love, war."

"It is, after all, where the late conflict began."

The inspector nodded sagely.

"It is. If the archduke were alive today, so would a hell of a lot more people be."

"Exactly. So I wondered if someone of one of the other nationalities that the king has annexed to his new kingdom, perhaps in a quarrel with this unsavory character . . ."

The inspector considered.

"You have someone from the region staying in the hotel?"

"Staying here? Heavens above, one was enough! It is, I believe, a poverty-stricken hole. But in our kitchens . . ."

"Ah. Someone without papers, no doubt."

The manager gesticulated.

"His papers *seemed* in order—"

"Who is this man?"

"He is one of the assistant meat chefs—a lowly position."

"I think we must talk to this man. What nationality did you say he was?"

"I believe Croatian."

"Who knows where these places are? But it is down there somewhere. Lead on, Mr. Manager."

Preceded by the manager, the policemen trooped along dingy corridors, up staircases, and then more staircases until they came to a long, low attic that served as a sort of dormitory for the lower members of staff. Watched surreptitiously by Turkish, Portuguese, Bulgarian, and Algerian eyes, silently beseeching that their papers be not asked for, fearful of being sent back from the squalor that they lived in to the greater squalor they had come from, the little army marched nearly the length of the dimly lit room.

"Ah, see!" said the manager, greatly surprised. "He is gone!"

The bed was neatly made. From the rough cupboard beside it all trace of the occupant had been removed.

"This, evidently, is our man. Come, Mr. Manager, and give us all the details on him that you have."

The little army turned, walked the narrow space between the rows of beds, and began the long trek down to the manager's office. As the door to the attic closed, there could be heard a great sigh of relief in several languages.

* * *

In Suite 15 the admiration of the nameless dancer had gradually turned to rage. This was too much! How many times was it now? She had lost count. Bang, snore, bang, snore, bang, snore. She felt like a leaky bicycle tire. This was being treated like a common prostitute. And at the end she wouldn't even get paid, probably. Come the dawn and it would be "Adieu, ma petite" and that would be that. *Le roi le veut.* Well, she'd had enough. What had been an honor had become a tedious hassle. Fortunately, the king was now in a snore phase.

She got up, but before she put her clothes on, she peeped out of the door. The first things that met her eye were the backs of two stalwart gendarmes bearing something covered with a sheet away on a stretcher. Turning her head, she saw two more gossiping at the other end of the corridor. Police in the hotel! An inconspicuous departure would be quite impossible. She sighed. Better stick it out.

On the bed the snores lessened in volume. The king stirred.

In Suite 7 Professor Giuliano contemplated his handiwork. The map the President and the Prime Minister had worked on lay to his left hand, a red line stretching halfway across the thigh at the top of the leg of Italy, breaking off when their work had been interrupted—the new border between Italy and the defeated Austria. At Professor Giuliano's right hand was a duplicate map, unused in the negotiations, on which he had drawn a new red line, mostly identical, but which now veered north at a crucial point, to put on the Italian side Merano and a rich area of Alpine villages, woods, and grazing lands. He took the map on his left and the suite's heavy table lighter over to the grate and set fire to a corner. When he was satisfied it was entirely burned, he went back to the desk and poured himself another glass of champagne. Being born in New York did not mean he was not still a patriotic Italian. He smiled with professorial self-esteem;

it was a brilliant stroke, worthy of his father, the Mafia boss.

As the first rays of dawn struck the Avenue Decazes, the phone rang in Suite 12. The British Prime Minister had always impressed on the manager that, should anything of importance arise, he should always be rung. "If I am busy, I simply don't answer," he had said. Now he was already dressed and in the sitting room while his companion completed her morning toilette in the bedroom

"Mr. Prime Minister?" said the manager. "I thought I should tell you that, thanks to your brilliant suggestion, everything went like a dream."

"Glad to hear it. All it needed was a touch of statesmanship."

"The police accepted absolutely my interpretation of the unfortunate event and the man's disappearance."

"Of course they did. Less trouble."

"The man will by now have evaporated, and the case is in effect closed."

"Splendid."

"The police have now left the hotel, and you and your charming guest can leave without arousing any impertinent curiosity."

"Excellent. I think I hear her coming now. Call two taxis, will you?"

The door from the bedroom had indeed opened, and sailing through, dressed for her morning activities, came the lovely woman of a certain age who had shared the Prime Minister's night. He gazed at her appreciatively: splendid figure, regal carriage, gorgeous clothes and hat. Odd to think of her as granddaughter of that dumpy little woman. She, like him, would from now on be caught up in the great public events of the time. Poking through the too-small evening bag, he saw the reddish brown tip of a hat pin; typical of her and her kind always to be prepared for an emergency!

"I've just had a call from the manager," he said. "The emergency's over. The police have gone."

"Excellent," she said. "I have a very full morning of engagements. Civil of him to let you know."

"Naturally, he did," said Mr. Lloyd George, swelling to his full adiposity. "I advised him how to go about things."

"I do love a clever man."

"And I *am* the Prime Minister of Great Britain."

She paused before disappearing through the door.

"And *I* am Marie of Romania."

A Black Death

by Edward Marston

Only one arrow was needed. Plucked from its sheaf, it was fitted to the bow-string with deft fingers, then drawn steadily backward with its head pointing up at a slight angle. When the longbow was bent to its full extent, its target was measured in an instant and its tilt adjusted accordingly. The arrow was released with a fierce surge of power, and it explored the air in a rising trajectory until it located its victim. Descent was swift, silent, and deadly. Heavy armor was no protection. After a flight of over two hundred yards, the arrow came hurtling out of the sun like a white-hot brand and pierced the camail with contemptuous ease. It cut into the throat of the rider with such force that it knocked him backward from his horse and stilled forever the proud war cry on his lips. The assassin was pleased with his work.

He had killed the Prince of Wales yet again.

Meurig was born with murder in his heart. His earliest memories were of death and deprivation. His first instinct was to seek revenge. Meurig had been dispossessed. He was cheated out of his birthright by an accident of nature and robbed of his eminence by a cruel twist of fate. He was the grandson of Rhodri, brother of Llywelyn ap Grufydd, and so his lineage should have been impeccable. But his mother lacked the wedding ring that would have gained him an honorable place among the descendants of the princes of Gwynedd. Royal blood pulsed through his veins, yet he was not recognized as a rightful claimant to his father's rank and estate.

More humiliation followed. He was raised in England, in the very country which had ground his own beneath its iron heel. He was forced to live among the enemy. Born on the wrong side of the blanket and brought up on the wrong side of the border, Meurig was tormented by a sense of loss. He was estranged from his own land and cut off from his own language. His crown had been snatched away from him. Hatred and rebellion mingled in his breast. He needed someone to blame and someone to kill.

His chosen victim was Edward.

Wales had good cause to rue that name. It was Edward I who had conquered the land with such vicious finality and who built a series of huge castles to keep it in subjection. It was his son, Edward II, born in one of those same castles at Caernarvon, who became the first Prince of Wales and who thus symbolized the fate of the defeated nation. And when Edward II was murdered by foul conspiracy, it was *his* son, Edward III, who seized the throne and continued the oppression of the Principality. Meurig loathed them all, but there was one Edward for whom he reserved real animosity.

Edward, Prince of Wales.

The eldest son of Edward III had other honors bestowed upon him. At the age of three, he became Earl of Chester; at the age of seven, he became Duke of Cornwall. But these were irrelevant titles in the fevered mind of Meurig. What rankled with him was that Edward of Woodstock became Prince of Wales at the age of thirteen. He supplanted Meurig himself. He was guilty of a royal crime—the theft of a crown.

For Edward was the anointed prince of a land that he had never visited. He held sway over a people whose customs he did not respect and whose language he did not understand. His title gave him added status and a greater income, but Wales gained nothing in return. Through his envious eyes, Meurig saw it all very clearly. Edward did not just commit a royal crime. He epitomized it.

Destiny linked the two of them from the start. Meurig and Edward were the same age, the same build, and the same coloring. Both were skilled in arms, and both had a noble bearing. Each was a natural leader of men. The resemblance ended there. While Edward, Prince of Wales, had a glittering future before him, Meurig had only a lifetime in the shadows ahead. The young Welshman wanted to burst into the light and free his nation from the yoke of the tyrant. There was only one way that he could achieve his ambition. Meurig, the true heir of Gwynedd, had to vanquish the usurper. One Prince of Wales had to be destroyed by another.

An accomplice was needed. Meurig soon found him.

"How will you kill him, Meurig?"

"In single combat."

"With sword, with dagger, with lance?"

"With my bare hands, if need be."

"Why not put an arrow between his eyes?"

"We must fight on equal terms."

"He gives Wales no equal terms."

"Edward will be slain by me," said Meurig grimly. "But I will be a just executioner."

"Stab him in the back!"

"I have to think of my honor."

"Poison the English *mochyn*!"

Idwal was a short, stocky young man with a mop of dark hair falling down to a matted beard. He was a distant cousin of Meurig's on the maternal side and gave the latter total respect and obedience. Royalty had brushed Meurig and left its mark indelibly upon him. Idwal was glad to serve the next Prince of Wales. He never tired of discussing methods of disposing of the incumbent holder of the title.

"Beat his brains out with a boulder."

"Leave it with me, Idwal."

"Ride him down with your horse."

"I will decide."

"Remember how they killed his grandfather," said Idwal with a wicked grin. "Use a burning poker!"

They were only sixteen when they first began to plan the assassination. Eager to quit England and to perfect his military skills, Meurig had come to France to join a band of roving mercenaries. He was part of a small force of Welsh expatriates—Idwal among them—who were willing to fight for money until the time came when they could fight to liberate their country. Meurig provided a focus for their patriotic impulses, and he quickly rose to a position of command. It was a prince-dom of sorts.

He served in Spain, Alsace, and the Swiss cantons. He cut down the enemies of a Breton paymaster before selling his allegiance to the Duke of Anjou. Battle only served to sharpen the edge of his ambition. Every blow he struck was for the honor of his country. Every man he killed was Edward, Prince of Wales. Every time he fought, he avenged a royal crime.

"We must raise an army, Idwal."

"How?"

"We must hire a fleet."

"When?"

"We must invade Wales and drive out the English."

"Where is the money for all this?"

"It will come," said Meurig. "It will come."

And Idwal, like all the others who sat around the camp fire, believed him. Their captain inspired confidence. He gave them a vision and purpose to carry them through their grisly existence. They were hired murderers, but they had hope in their hearts. Nothing could stop them now. They came to believe that they were invincible.

Then the final enemy struck. It came from the east, and it brought devastation in its wake. The disease was so savage in its effect and so widespread in its attack that it seemed as if the Day of Judgment had arrived. Whole towns were brought to their knees and whole villages emptied of their inhabitants. Nothing could escape the Black Death. It killed evenly among high and low, it snuffed out the lives of holy men just as easily as those of heretics.

Meurig led his company north at full gallop, but they could not outrun the disease. By the time the Welshmen reached the coast, a third of their number had died in hideous ways. By the time their ship sailed, another ten had fallen to the invisible foe. Others expired at sea, others again survived the voyage to find the plague waiting to welcome them ashore. Meurig's dreams were shattered. He and Idwal were left with a mere handful of soldiers.

It was time to fight with different weapons.

"Kill for the English!" Idwal was disgusted.

"We have no choice," argued Meurig. "We will not get close to the Prince of Wales unless we join his army."

"It is a betrayal."

"Edward is the one who will be betrayed."

"We swore an oath to fight *against* him."

"He will not expect an attack from within his ranks."

"Let us burn him alive in his tent!"

"Mine is the surer way, Idwal."

"Drive a stake through his black heart."

"It may be slow," said Meurig, "but it will be sure."

And Idwal eventually came to accept the wisdom of the advice. There was a long wait. The war with France was languishing and the Prince of Wales—now hailed as a hero after the battle of Crécy—busied himself with visiting his estates and distinguishing himself in knightly pursuits at a series of tournaments. Meurig was not idle. He and Idwal kept their skills in an excellent state of repair. While Edward was jousting for applause, the two Welshmen were practicing at the butts with their longbows or exercising their sword-arms. Peace wearied them, but their common purpose still smoldered.

"How will you kill him, Meurig?"

"Like a prince."

The chance finally came. War with France was resumed. The Duke of Lancaster led an army that landed at Cherbourg and struck out toward Brittany. Edward, Prince of Wales, went deep into Aquitaine to attack from the south. An important part of his army was a troop of mounted archers. Meurig and Idwal rode behind the man they despised.

Edward cut a striking figure. His black armor was

beautifully made to fit the contours of his body, and it covered every inch of him. His helm was surmounted by a royal lion. His jupon, sleeveless and tight-fitting, displayed the quartered arms of England and France. A straight-bladed sword with a large hilt hung from his left hip. Seated astride his horse, he looked the very flower of chivalry.

Even Meurig and Idwal were impressed at first. What sustained their rancor throughout the years was the idea of a Prince of Wales. Now they were confronted by the reality, a courageous knight who was loved and trusted by his men. But the assassins soon saw another side to the flamboyant young hero in the black armor, for he did not mount a direct attack on the French army at all. His policy was to destroy and to terrorize. Edward led a series of *chevauchées*, daring raids on towns and villages, looting and burning with indiscriminate brutality before riding on to his next prey. The chivalric commander was fighting like the most depraved mercenary. Meurig and Idwal hated him even more.

They watched and waited, but their opportunity did not come. Their leader was too alert and too well-guarded. It was the intercession of the French that helped them. King Jean assembled a huge army and rode south to do battle. Edward could not avoid the encounter and quickly sought a good defensive position. He chose a wooded slope some two miles south of Poitiers. Meurig could at last move in for the kill.

"They say there are thirty thousand Frenchmen!"

"Those are but rumors, Idwal."

"Their army will massacre us."

"Think on our sworn duty."

"I am not ready to die yet, Meurig."

"The Prince of Wales is."

"We have to fight a battle tomorrow."

"Kill Edward and there may *be* no battle."

Idwal listened intently, and the persuasive tongue of his master soothed him once more. The plan was bold enough to try and cunning enough to succeed. A royal crime would at last be avenged on behalf of their nation. On the eve of a battle between England and France, it was Wales that would strike the decisive blow. Idwal scorned danger. He was not prepared to die in the service of a foreign power, but he would willingly lay down his life for his country.

"Wait for my signal," ordered Meurig.

"I've waited these ten years."

"Take up your station with great care."

"I'll merge with night itself."

"Have your bow ready."

"It is cut from the finest yew."

"Choose your sharpest arrows."

"They will fly straight and true."

"Pray that they may not be needed," said the other. "If it please God, I will dispatch him myself."

Meurig had no doubts on that score, but he still believed in having a second line of attack. If his dagger should miss its mark, then Idwal's arrows might yet succeed. One way or another, a great ugly stain on their national pride would be removed.

The eager Idwal pressed for important details.

"How will you kill him, Meurig?"

"With cold steel."

"Cut his foul throat."

"I'll strike at his heart."

"Feel no pity."

"I do not, Idwal."

"Show no mercy."

"There is none to show."

"Butcher his body," urged the other with sadistic glee. "Hack it to pieces and drench the ground with his blood."

Meurig shook his head solemnly. "I will accord a royal corpse all due respect. We are not barbarians, Idwal."

"Edward has fought like one in these wars."

"He will die as a true soldier."

"He will die. Let us agree on that."

Meurig nodded. "He will die."

The two men embraced, then parted to rejoin the others. They were soon hammering stakes into the

earth so that their sharp points stuck up at an angle to
give a hostile greeting to any attackers. The English
army would fight on foot. The mounted archers had
tethered their horses in the safety of the trees.
Crouched behind their barricade, they would discharge
their arrows at an enemy whose size was swelled by
each new report. Fear spread through the ranks, but
Meurig and Idwal worked calmly on. They stalked a
different foe.

It was the Sabbath, but this was no day of rest.
While soldiers of both parties went about their business, the Church bestirred itself and made a vain attempt to avert bloodshed. Cardinal Talleyrand de
Perigord shuttled to and fro between the armies with
his robes flapping in the wind as he tried to maneuver
the two sides toward a peaceful settlement. Edward did
not seek battle with the French host. Hopelessly out-
numbered and completely surrounded, he was in such
a desperate situation that he offered huge concessions
to King Jean—even the return of Calais and Guines—
but nothing short of abject surrender would content the
French.

The cardinal warned, argued, cajoled, and pleaded,
but it was all to no avail. He resorted to the power of
prayer, but it could not alter the course of history. Two
armies were preparing to fight the Battle of Poitiers to
a bitter conclusion. Nothing could stop them now.

Edward strengthened his defenses still further, then
toured his camp to put heart into his men. There was
no hint of dread in his manner, no touch of weakness
in his voice. He had never lost a battle and did not intend to lose one now. Even Meurig was forced to ad-
mire his brave defiance. Edward turned a frightened
army into a confident force. Soldiers who were re-
signed to defeat now dared to believe in victory. The
charisma of their leader had worked its magic.

There were tactics to be discussed and battle plans
to be finalized. Edward consulted with his commanders
long into the night, then he withdrew to his pavilion to
snatch a few precious hours of sleep before the conflict. Meurig bided his time, then moved swiftly into

action. The royal chaplain was about to put on his vestments when the Welshman slipped soundlessly into his tent. One thrust of the dagger sent the chaplain to his Maker. His body was summarily stripped.

Dressed as a priest and walking with the measured tread of the sacred, Meurig went off to his unholy task. As he picked his way through the camp, he gave a signal to the watching Idwal. Guards were on duty outside the royal pavilion, but they did not obstruct the prince's chaplain. Nor did they observe the shadowy figure who crept up in the undergrowth and lurked behind some bushes only thirty yards away. Sentinels were posted all round the camp, but they were on the lookout for French soldiers and not for Welsh assassins. The plan was working.

As Meurig came into the pavilion, however, he saw something that rocked him back and made him reach for the dagger that was concealed in his sleeve. The Prince of Wales was standing before him, armed and ready for battle. They faced each other at last. The encounter for which he had yearned was finally taking place. But as Meurig took a threatening step forward, there was no response from Edward. And the latter did not even flinch when his chaplain jabbed at him with a dagger. Then Meurig realized that he was confronting an empty suit of armor.

It stood tall, dark, and proud in the flickering light of the torches. Meurig was moved. So this is what it meant to be Prince of Wales—to reside in a sumptuous pavilion and to lead an army into battle in a magnificent suit of armor. With a covetous hand, he stroked the helm and the camail that was laced to it to protect the chin, cheeks, and neck of royalty. His fingers rippled over the chainmail, then met the sculptured smoothness of the breastplate.

The craftsmanship was quite breathtaking. Meurig was only a mounted archer who fought in a nailed jerkin of filled leather above a mailed shirt. He wore a plain bascinet on his head, not a work of art like the helm before him. There were no superb iron gauntlets for his hands. All that he had was a bracer to guard his left arm and catch the string when an arrow was released. Jealousy stirred within him. Here was his true inheritance.

A cough from the adjoining chamber alerted him to his purpose, and he resumed his role as the royal chaplain. Parting the rich hangings, he stepped through into the inner part of the pavilion. Edward, Prince of Wales, lay sleeping on his couch with only his page in attendance. The latter saw no more than he expected—a visit from the chaplain at the approach of dawn to pray for God's help in the mighty struggle ahead. Meurig exploited the element of surprise. Whipping his dagger from his sleeve, he raised it up and brought the hilt smashing down on the page's skull to knock him senseless. The page fell to the ground in a heap.

Meurig smiled. The Prince of Wales was at his mercy. All he had to do was to push a blade between some ribs, and a lifelong promise would be fulfilled. Destiny beckoned. The ghosts of his princely ancestors urged him on. He lifted the knife, but it froze in his hand. Meurig could not move.

Doubts assailed him. Should he not wake his enemy so that he could kill him in a fair fight? Should he not make Edward understand that a royal crime demanded royal recompense? After ten years of planning, the assassination should surely have more to it than a momentary plunge of steel. What honor was there in a squalid murder? Meurig wrestled with the irony of the situation. He had killed an imaginary Prince of Wales a hundred times, but he could not now dispose of the real one.

Screwing up his courage, he raised the dagger high in the name of Wales, but something stayed his hand yet again. Edward opened his eyes. He came out of his dream to gaze up at his executioner for a fleeting second before lapsing back into a drowsy slumber. Meurig was chastened. That brief glance between them contained a whole world of recognition. In the eyes of his victim, he saw valor and integrity and pride. He saw the one man alive who could lead his army to victory on the morrow against impossible odds. He saw the cold arrogance of power and the unmistakable glint of royalty.

He saw kinship.

Idwal watched anxiously from his hiding place with a nervous hand clutching at his beard. What had happened inside the pavilion, and why was it taking Meurig so long? They had rehearsed the murder endlessly in a thousand discussions. Had the plan gone awry? Was Meurig standing in triumph over the corpse of his victim? Or had he made his escape through the rear of the pavilion? What if his disguise had been detected? Had he been slain by guards, or was he being held to face trial and execution? Why did he not step out of the pavilion?

The answer eventually came. Meurig had faltered. On the last few, vital steps of a ten-year journey, he had tripped and fallen. For it was not a royal assassin who strutted out into the night air. It was the Prince of Wales in full armor. There was no moon to shed its light on the scene and no fire to cast its glow, but Idwal knew what he saw—Edward of Woodstock, the scourge of his nation.

A Black Prince who deserved a black death.

Only one arrow was needed. Plucked from its sheaf, it was fitted to the bow-string with deft fingers then drawn steadily back. With a hiss of derision, Idwal sent it off on its fatal errand. The most famous suit of armor in Christendom was no match for the skill of a Welsh archer. Whistling its way into legend, the arrow shot out of the darkness with the future of a nation riding on its flight. It pierced the camail with vengeful force and sliced out the throat of its victim. Idwal barely had time to watch his quarry fall to oblivion before he himself was hacked to death by a dozen English swords. His life was forfeit, but a sense of deep satisfaction went with him to his grave.

He was not the only man to die happily in the darkness. When they lifted the visor of his helm, they found that Meurig was still smiling with regal joy. He had regained his rightful crown after all. He had risen to power among the lords of the house of Gwynedd. He had vindicated family honor. One royal crime answered another. By stealing a suit of armor, he won back the country of his heart. Edward might still awake to glory. He might still lead his army to heroic deeds in the forthcoming Battle of Poitiers and plant the English flag more firmly on French soil.

But Meurig ended his life as the Prince of Wales.

A Day at the Races

by Edward D. Hoch

The word spread rapidly that Edward VII would be coming to Ascot that afternoon. It was not especially surprising news, because the four-day Royal Ascot traditionally attracted the horse-loving monarch from nearby Windsor Castle. On this cool June Tuesday in 1907, however, there had been some doubt. The crucial vote in Commons on Henry Campbell-Bannerman's resolution restricting the power of the House of Lords was due in a matter of days, and there was talk that Edward would be meeting soon with the Russian foreign minister.

Nevertheless, as the hour of the first race approached, the stocky, gray-bearded figure of the king was seen to alight from one of the horse-drawn landaus used to transport the Royal Family from Windsor. The crowd voiced some disappointment that his wife, Queen Alexandra, was not in the party, but the customary cheer went up as Edward entered the Royal Enclosure.

Held over four afternoons in late June, the Royal Ascot was England's most glamorous horse-racing event. For women hats were obligatory, and the only men without formal morning dress, including top hat and tailcoat, were the uniformed police officers assigned to control the crowd and protect the Royal Family. On a table on the lawn behind the grandstand, the racing event's top prize—the Ascot Cup—was on display. Thirteen inches high and six inches in diameter, the 20-carat gold cup weighed four and a quarter pounds. It would be awarded on the final day of the races, but right now it was being guarded by a policeman and by a representative of the firm that had made it. They stood at either end of the table as King Edward and his retinue passed by.

"A magnificent prize," Edward commented to Sir John Ingram, who had accompanied him that day. "My horses have won the Derby and the Grand National, but never the Ascot Gold Cup."

"Your time will come," Sir John assured him. "Perhaps even this year."

"Not this year," said Edward with a shake of his head. They turned into the Royal Enclosure. Off across the course they could see some of those in attendance picnicking and drinking champagne before the first race.

"They'll want you to present the trophies to the winners," Sir John Ingram said.

"Blast it, I suppose they will! I generally get Alexandra to do it for me."

They went up the steps to the Royal Box, and Edward settled down in his seat. He had a perfect view of the race course, and it was only a brief stroll to the unsaddling enclosure where the winners would be honored. He'd done it before, and in Alexandra's absence he supposed he could do it again. Meanwhile, there was the view to appreciate—all this prime horseflesh and all these lovely women in their elaborate finery.

"They'll want you to ride up the course before the first race," Sir John reminded him.

"Yes, yes," Edward replied, stroking his beard. There was nothing he liked better than a day at the races, unless perhaps it was a day on his yacht.

From the king's seat in the Royal Enclosure he could not see the table he'd passed earlier, where the Ascot Gold Cup was on display. The two guards, Chief Constable Raymond Wiggins and company representative Jeffrey Smight, seemed bored with their task of warning people away when they tried to reach across the ropes and touch the trophy.

It was just before the first race, when the crowd had pressed forward for a glimpse of King Edward ceremo-

niously traversing the course in his landau, that a
young woman fell to the ground under the ropes.
"Here now," Jeffrey Smight said, reaching down for
her. "You have to stay outside the enclosure."

"I was pushed!" she insisted in a loud voice. "Get
your hands off'n me!"

"What's this, miss?" the constable asked, coming to
lend a hand.

"I fell down an' he grabbed me!" She scrambled to
her feet, avoiding their hands. Her flowered pink hat
had come off when she fell, and now Constable Wiggins bent to retrieve it.

"Thank you," she muttered, adjusting the hat in
place as she turned to disappear into the crowd.

"What's this?" Jeff Smight suddenly exclaimed.
"Where's the cup?"

Wiggins whirled around and stared in disbelief. "I
. . . It's gone!"

The velvet-covered table was empty. Somehow the
gold cup had been snatched away, almost from under
their eyes.

"Stop that woman!" Constable Wiggins yelled.
"Stop her! She stole the cup!"

Several bystanders quickly grabbed the young
woman in the flowered pink hat before she could break
free of the crowd. But it was obvious at once that she
carried no treasure of a material nature within the folds
of her dress or cape. Wiggins fastened a beefy hand on
her wrist nonetheless, as if she represented his only
link to the missing cup.

"I'll have to report this to my employers at once,"
Jeffrey Smight announced. "The gold in that cup is
valued at thousands of pounds."

"Wait a bit," the constable insisted, turning to his
prisoner. "What about it, young lady? Did you pass the
cup to a confederate?"

"I don't have your bloody cup!" she insisted, but her
choice of language had already made it obvious that
she was not the typical Ascot spectator. "I never
touched it. I think it fell off the table."

That caused both men to look down, but there was

no golden cup on the trampled grass. "What's your name, miss?" Jeffrey Smight asked.

"Daisy Blaine."

"Who is escorting you today?"

"I'm here with my brother. We got separated in the crowd. I don't know where he is now." She tried to pull her wrist free of the constable's grasp. "Let go! You're holdin' me too tight!"

Two other police officers came running up, attracted by the commotion. "What's the trouble, sir?" one of them asked.

"The Ascot Gold Cup's been stolen. I'm taking this woman into custody as a witness." He glanced out at the track, where the king's horse-drawn landau was just completing its stately procession. "I suppose someone will have to notify His Majesty."

The task of bringing the news to the Royal Box fell to Sir John Ingram. He'd been watching the procession from the rail in the unsaddling enclosure, and as he started back he was intercepted by Constable Wiggins. He listened intently to the constable's account of the bizarre theft, if that indeed was what it proved to be, and went to inform Edward.

"The Ascot Gold Cup," he announced to the monarch, who had just resumed his seat in the Royal Enclosure.

"What about it?"

"Someone seems to have stolen it. Or at least it has disappeared."

Edward was perplexed. "We passed it on the way in. Weren't there two guards on the scene?"

"There were, Your Highness. Somehow their attention was distracted for a moment and the cup disappeared. A young woman fell by the table and had to be helped to her feet—"

"I see." Edward, obviously displeased by this cloud over an otherwise splendid day, thought for a moment, and then said, "Have the officer in charge brought to me here. I'll see if I can't get to the bottom of this matter."

Ten minutes later, just as the favorite had won the first race handily, Sir John returned with Chief Constable Ray Wiggins. The monarch let his eyes scan this man who stood before him, dark cap in hand, looking just a bit stout for his uniform. "Tell me what happened, Constable."

Wiggins nervously recounted the events of the afternoon, climaxing with the disappearance of the cup. "We were both distracted," the officer admitted. "And the crowd was, too. Everyone was looking toward the track as your carriage went past, and then this woman fell and naturally Smight and I went to her assistance."

"Smight?"

"Jeffrey Smight. He represents the company that made the cup."

"Of course," Edward said with a little nod. "Go on."

"The young woman was apprehended before she could escape, but clearly she did not have the cup on her person."

"Might she have passed it to one of the other spectators?"

"A possibility, but a remote one. Neither of us saw her touch the cup at any time, and our eyes were naturally on her from the moment she fell. She herself says the cup toppled from the table to the grass, though we did not see this either."

"You did not see very much, Constable."

"No, sir," Wiggins admitted quietly, shifting his feet nervously.

"What is this young woman's name?"

The constable consulted his notebook. "Daisy Blaine, sir."

"Has Scotland Yard been notified?"

"Certainly, sir. They have a team on their way from London."

"Do you have any suspicions, Constable?"

"Irish troublemakers, Your Highness."

Edward chuckled. "I hope not! The queen and I are scheduled to make a visit to Dublin Castle in three weeks' time."

Sir John leaned forward to whisper a suggestion.

"Perhaps you would want to see Jeffrey Smight as well."

"Yes, yes! But first bring me this woman, Daisy Blaine. And John, place a wager for me in the second race, will you? Smith's Pride to win. The usual amount."

The young woman named Daisy Blaine was ushered into the royal presence a few moments later. She wore a flattering pink dress and hat and carried a light cape over one arm. The day had grown a bit warmer, allowing the removal of some outer garments. She gave the hint of a curtsy, obviously unsure of herself, and said, "It's a pleasure to meet you, King."

Edward masked a smile. "Is this your first visit to Ascot, my dear?"

"That's it. I come with me brother."

"And where might we find him?"

"He's prob'ly gone off without me by now."

"That's a very nice dress you have on."

"He bought it for me."

"Your brother?"

"Ah . . . yes."

"Did he ask you to fall down in front of that table with the gold cup on it?"

"No, I slipped on the grass! Really I did!"

"You didn't take the cup and slip it to him in the crowd?"

"How could I? Them two was watchin' me e'ry minute."

"The constable and Mr.—?"

"Smight."

"Of course. Miss Blaine, where do you think the Ascot Gold Cup is right now?"

"I got no idea," she said with a shrug.

He gave her a final smile. "Thank you for your help. I hope you enjoy the remainder of your day at Ascot."

Sir John Ingram returned to the Royal Box as Daisy Blaine departed. "Bad news, Your Highness. Smith's Pride ran fourth."

"Bad news, indeed. Get me this fellow Jeffrey Smight, will you?"

"Scotland Yard will want to handle the actual investigation," Sir John reminded him.

"Of course, of course, but maybe we can make their job a bit easier."

Smight was a rugged young man, still in his thirties, who looked out of place in his formal morning suit. As he entered the Royal Box, he touched the brim of his top hat and smiled. "Pleased to meet you, Your Majesty."

"What can you tell me about this business, Mr. Smight?"

"Probably no more than Constable Wiggins. It happened while you were having your procession, sir. This young woman fell down, and while we were helping her, the cup disappeared."

"Could anyone just reach over the ropes and touch it? When I passed by earlier it seemed to be out of reach."

"It was! No one could reach it from outside the ropes, and I didn't see anyone with a fishing net trying to snare it." He smiled at that, then turned serious again. "Really, Your Highness, I can't imagine how it could have happened."

"The crowd was looking away, at the track," Edward reminded him.

"But this young woman, Daisy Blaine, was facing the cup, even as she fell. She claims she saw it topple to the grass. If we believe her, the earth must have swallowed it up."

"Certainly your firm has insurance on the cup."

"Of course, but it's a great blow to us to have it stolen like this, while on public display."

"Perhaps I can help retrieve it," the monarch said. "Go now."

Jeffrey Smight departed, going down the steps of the Royal Box with a hand to the brim of his tall hat, as if protecting it from a sudden gust of wind.

"A baffling crime," Sir John said. "Do you wish to place a wager on the next race, Your Majesty?"

"I believe I'll skip the next one, Sir John." He stood

up suddenly and called out to the police guards to the Royal Enclosure. *"Stop that man!"*

Sir John and the other members of the royal party were startled by his outburst, none more so than Jeffrey Smight, who turned to glance back at Edward. Perhaps there was guilt on his face at that moment, as the guards moved in to obey the King's orders.

"What is this?" Sir John asked. "Why are you detaining him?"

"Because Jeffrey Smight has stolen his employer's Gold Cup."

"Stolen it? But where is it?" Sir John demanded as Edward marched down the steps to confront Smight.

"Where? Why, it's under his hat!"

With those words Edward lifted the topper from Jeffrey Smight's head, revealing the missing cup inverted like a golden dome upon his brow.

It was Chief Constable Wiggins who came to the Royal Box after Jeffrey Smight had been taken into custody. "Begging your pardon, Your Majesty, I heard about what happened and I was wondering how you found the missing Gold Cup. I never suspected Smight for a minute!"

Edward stroked his beard, feeling pleased with himself. "Oh, it was a simple enough matter. That young woman, Daisy Blaine—you only had to hear one sentence out of her mouth to know she didn't belong here at Ascot. Someone hired or asked her to get dressed up, come here, and create a diversion, which is exactly what she did. At that exact moment most of the crowd was watching my procession down the race course. Her fall diverted your eyes and any others not watching the track. The cup fell to the grass as she said—and vanished!"

"So it had to be one of us, Smight or me."

"And when Miss Blaine knew Smight's name, I was pretty sure it was him. The cup, six inches wide by thirteen inches deep, would hardly fit into a pocket or under a jacket. But it would fit nicely under one of the top hats every man here is wearing—every man except those in uniform like yourself, Constable. Your cap is much too small to conceal the Gold Cup. Besides, you had the courtesy to remove it when you visited me here earlier. Smight did not remove his top hat, but only touched the brim. When he left me, he actually held that brim to keep the hat—and the cup—firmly in place as he descended the steps. Inverted, as he wore it, the six-inch-diameter bowl came down over his hair and scalp by a few inches. The rest of the thirteen-inch height fit snugly under the rather tall top hat he was wearing. Working for the maker as he did, he had plenty of opportunity to test the fit of the cup under the proper hat."

"That's amazing," Constable Wiggins said, a trace of awe in his voice. "But why didn't I see him do it?"

"Your attention was diverted by the young woman, just as he'd planned. He simply knocked the cup to the soft grass, quickly covered it with his top hat, and returned hat and cup to his head."

"How did he manage to keep something that heavy on his head for so long?"

King Edward smiled. "It's not difficult with a little practice. I believe it weighs about the same as my coronation crown."

Bring Me the Head
of Anne Boleyn

by Kristine Kathryn Rusch

The memory comes to her in fragments. Her mother's hand, cold, oddly shaped, the long sleeve hiding the extra finger, grips Elizabeth's tiny arm. Her mother tugs her into a corner, against the rough stone walls in their wing of the palace. "Take this," her mother says. Elizabeth looks up, but she cannot see her mother's face.

Men are running down the corridor. Her mother stiffens. Elizabeth shivers in the castle's chill. "Take this," her mother repeats. Something heavy falls into her palm. Elizabeth grabs it. Her mother releases Elizabeth's hands. The men have arrived. Her mother pushes her away. The men surround her mother.

"Go, Elizabeth," her mother says, but Elizabeth stands in the corner and stares at her palm. Her mother has given her a golden ring that would fit over three of her fingers, with a flashing ruby in the shape of a falcon, her mother's symbol. The ring is pretty.

Elizabeth looks up. Her mother cries out, but Elizabeth cannot see her. Her mother's face is gone forever.

Twenty-two years later, Elizabeth stands in the same corridor. Now she notices details she missed. A suit of armor, as tall as she is, guards a corner. Long tapestries cover the sweating stones. The corridor smells damp, as if the chill never leaves this place. If she closes her eyes, she can see the men, their features as distinct as the lines between the stones, but she cannot see her mother.

The ring. Elizabeth has forgotten about the ring, until now. The last thing her mother said to her, the last thing her mother gave her, and she had not seen it since the day the guards hauled her mother away.

It doesn't matter. Elizabeth is Queen now. All the years imprisoned in her own home, the years in the Tower, walking daily by the scaffolding, all of the lies, don't matter. She is Queen. She will remain Queen until she dies.

She tightens her fists, like the three-year-old child she was that afternoon in the corridor. No one will take her away. No one will imprison her again. No one will own her again.

No one will behead her.

"We are Queen," she whispers. "We are Queen."

But she does not believe it. In this corridor, she is Elizabeth Tudor, daughter of the adulterous Anne Boleyn. A bastard child, denied her right to the throne by an act of her sister's Parliament. A woman, unfit to rule.

This corridor has drawn her, two days after her coronation, like a siren singing in the waters. The last time she stood here, she lost something precious.

She is not sure what it is.

Elizabeth Regina is not a pretty woman. But at twenty-five, she is tall and strong and can outthink the men around her. She is ruthless. She knows, someday, she will order people to their death as easily as her father did.

She must be hard, or die.

This morning she thinks of her father as she sits on his throne, her counselors around her, bobbing like whipped dogs. Sir William Cecil, fat Nicholas Bacon, and Sir William Parr, brother to her father's widow, still wear their coronation finest. They do not tell her everything because she, as a woman, will not understand. She has spies who inform her of things the counselors will not. They will not outsmart her. They cannot.

The throne room is cold. The entire castle is cold.

All of England is cold. Beyond these walls the land is covered with blood. Her sister tried to make England Catholic again—returning property to its pre-Henry ownership, and making England bow to the pope. The landed gentry would not give up their rights to former church land. The countryside is scarred, ripe for the taking. France and Spain know this. They watch England like hawks watch a mouse. Their heads never turn, but their eyes are always moving, waiting for Elizabeth to make one mistake, waiting for the ax to fall.

In her dreams the ring slides around her wrist. She wears it to the execution. She kneels on the pillow and leans into the block. The wood is cold against her neck, pushing her Adam's apple into her throat. Before her is a peasant's basket made of twigs. She looks up. The executioner wears a hood. He must have no head at all. He is a swordsman from France, like the one hired to kill her mother. Elizabeth wants to say something brave, but she cannot. Her mother's hands close around her throat. *You have such a very little neck!* Elizabeth cringes. Her mother's last words still reflected her vanity. Elizabeth does not want to seem vain. So she says nothing. The sword glistens as it falls. She feels a snap. Her head bounces into the basket—and then someone whisks it away.

The banquet hall is large. The tables form an open square. Jugglers stand in the middle. Their performance is mediocre at best. She saw better as a child. The mutton is warm, and the ale inviting. But she doesn't touch it. Spirits will muddle her already confused mind.

She has not had the ring in over twenty years. She cannot remember having it after her mother died. But the ring does not concern her.

What she thinks of is her mother's head.

By morning they will have opened her mother's grave. She and her trusted assistants will go down to the grave site and examine the body. When she sees the head, severed from the neck, the nightmares will stop.

They must.

She has more important things to think of. She must control her courtiers. She has a meeting with the bishops. Philip of Spain wants to see her. During the week she must inspect the fleet.

She cannot lose sleep over events twenty years past. For if she does not think about now, she will step on the chopping block. Her head will tumble into a basket, and she will be whisked away.

Forever.

Elizabeth climbs the steps to her chambers. Her purple brocade is heavy, the stiff, ruffled collar biting into her neck. Her mouth is sore from smiling for hours. The banquet was interminable. She will be happy to sleep.

As she steps into the narrow, tapestry-filled corridor leading to her chambers, a man steps out of the candlelit gloom. He bows at the waist. He is slender; his tights fit well, and his tunic is a rich velvet. Sir Robert Dudley, whom she has just made Master of the Horse.

"Milady," he says as he rises.

She taps him with the small gold fan she clutches in her left hand. "I am your liege," she says.

"Forgive me, Highness." He captures her hand as he bows again, kissing it with a flourish. She resists the urge to pull her hand away. She remembers this, as if it has happened before: a man bowing over her mother's hand; her mother's fluted laughter echoing through the corridor. "I wish to speak to you, alone."

"We are alone." She suppresses a sigh. She hates the stupidity of clandestine politics.

"Highness," he says, his hand still imprisoning hers, "I wish to ask your hand in marriage. I—"

She tugs her hand from his. "Sir, you forget yourself— and your wife," she says. Then she laughs, the sound an echo of her mother's joy. "Besides, I entertain no proposals before bedtime."

"Ah, but, lady," Dudley says, "those are the best kind."

The morning dawns gray and cold. Elizabeth wears a heavy cloak as she stands beside the open grave. Her mother's grave was to have been secret, but they have had no trouble finding it. A light mist falls, bathing everything in a filmy light.

Her advisors stand around her, all men who have been loyal to her since her father died. They have had late-night discussions about ways to get the country to accept another Tudor Queen. Already the Parliament is working on the Act of Supremacy, which will abolish papal power and will bring that power home to England. She will cause no unnecessary deaths—her father's downfall—and she will not be seen as a zealot, which was part of her sister's.

The advisors stare into the grave. Two men lean over the side, with winches braced against the marble. They have been struggling for an hour now to lift the heavy lid.

Perhaps her mother isn't even buried there. Her father wanted to destroy her mother's body when he discovered her adultery and incest, actions her mother denied. But his pain did not last long. He had married Jane Seymour before Elizabeth realized that her mother was dead.

The rain becomes a downpour. She raises her cloak, but the wind blows it off her head. An advisor steps across the open grave. "Highness, there is no need to stand in the rain. We will summon you when the coffin is opened."

She wipes the water from her face. In her twenty-five years she has never stood before a grave. She doesn't like it; it makes her think of her own mortality, of the lord who spoke to her the night before.

If she dies without an heir, the crown will pass from the Tudors. Her father spent his own life—and many other lives—securing a rightful heir. Is she failing her duties as Queen if she does not do the same?

* * *

She enters the palace through the kitchen. Women, their brown robes dragging on the dirty floor, bend over large ovens. The kitchen smells of bread. A fire burns in the oversized hearth. Cooking pots hang above it. A large grate stands before it, so no one turns too quickly and sets her skirts on fire.

Elizabeth scans the faces—a habit she has had since childhood. She sees one that makes her start. It is an old face, with a wart on one cheek and wrinkles that cascade down the skin like tear tracks. But she still recognizes it, like the edges of a dimly remembered dream.

"Nurse?"

The women all turn at the sound of her voice and curtsy, remaining crouched with their heads down until she bids them to stand. She takes the hand of the old woman who had been her nurse so many years ago.

"How long have you served in the kitchen?"

"It be since yer mum, milady, died, Highness."

Elizabeth tucks the old woman's hand under her arm. "Come with me," she says.

She takes the old woman up the back stairs. They go through a hall of portraits—all Tudors. Her father never tolerated any other family portrayed in the hall— and stop in a small sitting room.

Elizabeth perches on a gilt-edged chair. She bids Nurse to sit in one, too. Nurse sits gingerly on the edge.

"Do you remember my mother?" Elizabeth asks.

Nurse frowns. Elizabeth can see the fear.

"Please?" Elizabeth says. "It is all right to discuss her."

Nurse nods and looks down at her red, chapped hands. "Yer mum, she was a lady, Highness. She treated us all good. She laughed a lot, she did, until the end, and she loved ye, sneaking into yer room at nights to give ye sweets."

Elizabeth clutches a memory only fleetingly—a tall woman, smelling of perfumes, standing over her bed, handing her candies.

"My mother had a gold ring with a ruby set in the center."

"Her wedding band it was."

"She gave it to me before she died, and I don't have it. Do you know where it went?"

Nurse becomes still, as if she thinks Elizabeth is blaming her. "I got sent away soon as them guards came, mum. I did not take no ring."

"I know," Elizabeth repeats gently. "She gave it to me. But I no longer have it. I wonder if you—or any-one from the time—knows what happened to it."

"You was wearing it last I saw," the nurse says. "And your father, the king, throws a high holy fit. That was what sent me to the kitchens. But I'll look, High-ness, and I'll ask. Maybe someone knows."

"Thank you," Elizabeth says. She stands. Nurse stands too. "Now, come with me. You do not belong in the kitchens anymore. You will wait on ladies again, as you did before."

Nurse curtsies, but not before Elizabeth sees her eyes. Nurse is still frightened. Like Elizabeth she does not believe any of this is true.

The rain has become a drizzle. It is almost twilight. Elizabeth wears her wet cloak. They have opened the coffin, and they sent for her.

Someone has built a tent over the grave's open mouth. The rain seeps through the fabric, but does not fall as harshly as it does outside. Elizabeth steps into the shelter, her kid slippers sinking in mud. She does not look down until she is in line with the grave itself.

Her mother has no body, only a skeleton. The hands tell her she is staring at Anne Boleyn. The extra fingerbones rest on her mother's chest like a sign.

Her mother wears simple black, with no jewelry at all. Odd that the dress survives, but the skin does not. Elizabeth makes herself look to the head of the coffin. There, off to one side, sits the skull, staring at the body as if it cannot believe it is separate.

The skull wobbles in her vision. Then it fades, and she sees her mother for the first time in twenty years.

Long black hair cascading down her back. Dark red lips and snapping brown eyes. Her mother is smiling, laughing, head tilted toward another man's, looking to be kissed.

Elizabeth takes a step backward. She recognizes the face more than she remembers it. She sees it in the mirror every morning.

Her mother's face is her own.

She places the skull next to the mirror in her chambers. The wavery glass catches the edge of the skull, so that when Elizabeth applies her own makeup, she will see and remember.

A knock echoes in the stillness. Elizabeth frowns. She has asked not to be disturbed. She glances at her dressing room door, wondering if she should disturb her ladies. But something tells her not to.

The knock echoes again. She goes to the door and opens it herself. Nurse stands there. She averts her gaze and curtsies when she sees Elizabeth.

"Highness, ye might want to come with me. I have found yer ring."

Elizabeth brings two ladies-in-waiting in case this is a trap. They go down a dusty back staircase. The stones are chipped and crumbling. Dirt falls from the railing. Elizabeth suppresses a sneeze. Nurse leads, a hand above her head to push away cobwebs, the other holding a torch.

The staircase opens in a large basement room. Nurse lights the torches near the door. Elizabeth steps inside. The ladies wait by the stairs. Five dust-covered glass cases line the walls. She goes to the first and stops when she sees a crown twinkling in the firelight. Other jewels lie beside it.

"The second case, Highness," Nurse says.

The second case holds another crown, this one made of light silver with diamonds adorning its face. Elizabeth remembers it on her mother's head during those nights when she brought sweets to Elizabeth's room. Emerald necklaces encircle the crown. Ruby bracelets lie beside it. And, in the center of one of the bracelets, Elizabeth's ring.

Two memories collide: She is hiding in her father's chamber, listening to him speak, something she loved to do. He and his advisors are talking about her mother, using words she doesn't understand. Finally, her father laughs. "She has made it easy then," he says. "Leave me. And don't come back until you bring me the head of Anne Boleyn."

A fear starts in Elizabeth's belly, a fear that comes back after her mother dies, when her father sees the ring. He snatches it from her fingers. "Did you give this to her, Nurse?" Nurse says nothing. "Mummy did," Elizabeth says. "Mummy?" Her father mocks. "Mummy is dead." His hand closes around the ring. "And this is mine."

He took it from her. He stole it from her as he had stolen her mother, as he had stolen her life. It is her revenge to stand here, among the jewels owned by his dead wives, and rule the country he hoped to give to a son.

She does not need to fear him anymore. He is dead. He shall never hurt her again.

She opens the case and snatches the ring. She slips it on the third finger of her left hand. She is her mother's daughter, flirtatious and bright. She is her father's daughter, ruthless and cold. She is the marriage of the best of them, and she will outdo them all.

"These are not safe here," she says. The wealth of the kingdom lives in these glass boxes. "You will stay until I send someone down here to move them."

Nurse nods. Elizabeth reaches out a hand adorned by her mother's gold wedding band. "We are grateful," she says.

Nurse curtsies. Elizabeth whirls and goes back up the steps. Her ladies follow. She twists the ring. She has come full circle. She is Queen of England now— her mother's dream, her father's fear.

She is Queen, and Queen she shall remain.

Forever.

A Sort of Miss Marple?

by H.R.F. Keating

The enjoyment afforded to Her Most Excellent Majesty Elizabeth the Second, by the Grace of God, of the United Kingdom of Great Britain and Northern Ireland and of Her Other Realms and Territories, Queen, Head of the Commonwealth, Defender of the Faith, Sovereign of the British Orders of Knighthood, Captain General of the Royal Regiment of Artillery, etc., etc., by the works of the writer Agatha Christie has been often recorded.

Her grandmother, indeed, the late Queen Mary, had a standing order for each new Christie title and passed on her partiality to, in turn, her daughter-in-law and her granddaughter. A younger Queen Elizabeth has been photographed extending a white-gloved hand to the author's white-gloved hand at the premiere of the film *Murder on the Orient Express*, smiling down with a look of something very like complicity. While the author once said the two most exciting events of her long life were her acquiring her first car, a bottle-nosed Morris from the advance on her fourth book, and being invited to dine at Buckingham Palace.

What is not so well known—possibly because it may never have happened—is the occasion when Her Majesty took on for a short time the very mantle of Miss Marple. It all began one late night in the private apartments of the Palace . . .

Something over an hour after Her Majesty had gone to bed, she woke. An intruder? Once again? Bloody revolution at the palace gates? A usurper armed to the teeth? None of these things. Simply the need for a pee.

Even monarchs' urinary systems can behave oddly on occasion.

A few quick steps from her at-this-time lonely bed, across the dressing-room and into her bathroom. And there, by what chance she never knew, her eye happened to fall on the miniature Meissen bowl into which she was accustomed as soon as she considered herself "off duty" to put her rings, delighted in these latter days to be able to slip them off and relieve certain mildly arthritic twinges. And at once something about the little bowl struck her as being wrong.

For several moments, still sleep bemused, she stood looking at the glitter of gold and diamonds in the tiny piece of Meissen. Then she realized. Her wedding ring was not there among the others.

She glanced at her hand. No, quite unadorned. She looked all round the bathroom. Could she, in a moment of forgetfulness, have put that ring down somewhere else? She found nothing. She went back into the dressing-room. No gold ring glinting in any obvious places. She felt down the sides of the armchair facing the television set in which she sat last thing in quiet and comfort when no duties of hospitality kept her up late into the night. Nothing.

Back into the bedroom. Was it possible she had failed to take the ring off with her others? And it had then slipped from her finger to be lost among the bedclothes? Hardly. But nevertheless she rolled back the blankets—she had never had had any truck with new-fangled duvets—and searched assiduously. Nothing. Peer under the bed. Nothing.

She sat down on the bed's edge and tried to reconstruct all her actions from the first moment she had taken off her rings. It had been—she could pinpoint it almost to the minute—at just a little before ten-thirty. That was when *Newsnight* began on BBC2, and, if she could, she watched that, always just before it began allowing herself the luxury of slipping off her rings. And, yes, she could distinctly remember doing that last night.

So the wedding ring must have been there at ten-thirty, and the door of her bathroom had been under her own eyes up till eleven-fifteen when the program ended. Then Meadowcroft, her personal maid, had come in and asked if she was ready to go to bed. She had undressed, taken off her make-up, and brushed her teeth. Meadowcroft and her assistant, little Smithers, had taken her clothes and left, and she had gone into the bedroom. By, say, eleven-thirty or a few minutes after. So between then and—she glanced at the pretty little Louis Seize clock on the mantelpiece—a quarter to one the wedding ring had vanished. What had happened? What could have happened?

She reviewed the situation. Could some unauthorized person have got into the dressing-room while she was asleep and on into her bathroom? There had been, of course, some years ago that funny man she had woken to find sitting on the end of her bed. On that occasion, she remembered with a smile, she had invoked almost at once old Miss Marple. What would Miss Marple have done? She would have remained calm. So she in her turn had remained calm. And the whole business had had a satisfactory outcome.

But since that night there had always been a police officer stationed where he could see the whole corridor leading to her bedroom suite.

Right.

She slipped on her dressing-gown, went to the door of the dressing-room, opened it cautiously, looked out. And, yes, there on his little gilt chair was a reassuringly large police officer.

He saw her. Scrambled to his feet. Looked as if he was not sure if he was meant to be seeing her. Actually turned a dusky red under the light of the chandelier above him.

She beckoned.

He came up, managed a duck of the head that stood in for a bow. Had he seen anyone enter her rooms after her maids had left?

"No, ma'am. I've seen no one at all. Only the two maids coming out, as per usual."

"Thank you."

Back to bed. But not to sleep. Not even to lie down again. Altogether too much on her mind. Suspicions. Nasty suspicions. Very nasty suspicions.

She looked at the little Louis Seize clock again. Five to one. Not really all that late. She reached over to the house telephone on the table beside her and pressed the single number for the duty equerry's rooms.

"Pastonbury-Quirk here."

"Ah, Robin. Were you asleep?"

"Oh, ma'am. It's you. No. No, I wasn't asleep. Er—No. No, I was just sort of finishing off the *Times* crossword. Is there something I can do?"

"Well, yes, there is. Or there may be. Could you come along to my dressing-room?"

"Of course, ma'am."

Two minutes later there came Sir Robin Pastonbury-Quirk's discreet knock on the outer door and he came in, looking, for all the fact that he must be almost forty, like a schoolboy who somehow had got into rather too grown-up clothes. Hair seeming to be kept in control by a lavish dousing of water. Face changing moment by moment from white to a rosy pink and back again. Overlarge hands with an air of having only just been scrubbed free of inkstains with pumice stone. Arms and legs never quite where they ought to be.

But underneath the awkwardness and a tendency to blather there lay, as Her Majesty knew well, a first-class mind, logical, observant, and equipped with a ferocious memory for detail. In short—she smiled to herself inwardly—Hercule Poirot made English. Or, since for all his intelligence Robin Pastonbury-Quirk was not a genius—genius something hardly needed in an equerry—perhaps he was more dear old Superintendent Battle, Agatha's other occasional sleuth. Unfoolable, undeviating Superintendent Battle, made a lot less fatherly.

So without hesitation she explained in detail what had happened. And then she went on to confess to her Battle-sleuth-alike the suspicions, the nasty, inescapable suspicions that had come crowding into her mind.

"You see, Robin, this is the awful thing. I was where

I could see my bathroom from the moment I had put that ring into the little bowl there I keep them in right up until my maids left, and from then onward the police officer on duty outside had my door under his eye."

Nice Sir Robin blushed his quickly-come, quickly-gone blush.

"Are you beginning to think one of your two maids must have taken it?"

"But that can't be. It can't be. I mean, Meadowcroft has been with me for more than twenty years. I'd trust her with anything. And, all right, little Smithers hasn't been on the domestic staff very long. But you know what care we take about anybody new. Well, you've summarized the inquiries yourself often enough. As far as is humanly possible all newcomers are guaranteed honest, and besides I like the girl. She's obviously so proud to be doing what she does, and she's so willing. And, what's more, I flatter myself I'm not so easily deceived."

"I should say you're not, ma'am."

Sir Robin was fervent. No other word.

"So, well, what are we to do? I hate the thought even that one of those two may be guilty. I've tried telling myself it just can't be. And yet, I know, I shan't be able to see either of them ever again without a tiny niggling thought at the back of my mind that somehow she may have stolen that ring. And it will be tremendously valuable, of course, simply because it belonged to us."

She frowned.

"But I'm not going to put it all into the hands of the police," she said. "I couldn't do that. Not to either of them."

"Well, ma'am, it strikes me that there's one thing that must be done straightaway. That is— Well, that is, if you don't mind not going to— That is, if you don't mind sort of staying up a bit longer."

"Of course not, Robin. You want to make a search yourself. Quite right. And I want you to. If the ring does turn up somewhere, no one will be more delighted than myself. So off you go. Look everywhere."

"Well, yes. I mean . . . Well, I would have to go into your bedroom. Sort of heave up the bedclothes . . ."

"Of course you will, Robin, though perhaps you'd better wash your hands first if you've been doing the crossword. Mine get perfectly black after reading *The Times* in the morning. Do use my bathroom. And look everywhere in there, too, while you're about it. Don't stand on ceremony."

Blushing pink and yet pinker, Sir Robin Pastonbury-Quirk plunged into the bathroom to begin his search. But in the end, even after he had rummaged from top to bottom of the royal bed, he had to admit complete failure. Her Majesty's wedding ring, which she had taken off just before ten-thirty the evening before and to which it seemed only her two maids had had access, was beyond doubt nowhere in her own suite.

"I really think, ma'am, I've exhausted every last possibility," her slimmed-down Superintendent Battle said eventually.

"I'm sure you have, Robin. And to tell the truth, I've been aching to get back to bed for the past half hour."

"Oh, good gracious, I've kept you— But I sort of felt I had to, well, be thorough."

"Of course you did, and of course you had to be. But let's leave it now for tonight. We'll think what's to be done in the morning. You are still on duty then?"

"Oh, yes, ma'am. My tour runs from noon today—or actually yesterday now, I suppose—till noon tomorrow. So in any case I'd be coming to discuss the Program straight after breakfast. But even if I wasn't I'd— Well, I'd jolly well want to try and put it all right . . . It's really too bad that you feel you can't . . . Well, it's just a beastly bad show."

"Thank you, Robin. It's nice to feel I can always count on you. Good night now."

"Oh, yes. Yes. Good night. Good night. I'll leave you to get back to— Well, yes."

* * *

But in the morning, after Sir Robin had outlined the day's Program and drawn attention to the possible snags—"I'm afraid you'll sort of have to cut the managing director there short, apparently he's a terrible gasbag and he'll make you late for the Motor Manufacturers' luncheon" "No problem"—they had come to discuss the extraordinary event of the night before. And still there seemed to be no way out. The wedding ring had disappeared. Only the two maids, Meadowcroft and Smithers, were suspects.

"Look, Robin, this is what we'll do. Who takes over from you as duty equerry?"

"It's Henry Fairmile, ma'am. But—"

"No, listen. As soon as Henry comes on duty, I want you to make inquiries—no need to say: be discreet—about both Meadowcroft and little Smithers. Find out if for some reason either of them has a sudden need for money. I know Meadowcroft has a nephew she's very fond of. Perhaps he's got himself into some sort of a scrape. Or Smithers may have a young man who's not all he might be. I'm sure you'll be able to manage that."

Robin Pastonbury-Quirk was opening his mouth to assure Her Majesty, with perhaps rather more fulsomeness than was strictly necessary, that he would do as he had been asked when the door behind them opened.

"Good morning, Mama."

She turned.

"Oh, good morning, dear. Is there anything you want? I was just asking Robin to do something for me."

"No, no. No hurry. Finish off what you were saying and then I'll have a word."

"Right, Robin. Are you all clear now?"

"Oh, yes, ma'am. I'm sure I'll manage. Be sort of discreet, but—"

"Sort of!"

It was an explosion from behind them.

"Golly, I've done my best to cure my own staff of using expressions like that, but it's a bit much to find yours doing the same thing. *Sort of, sort of,* what an appalling way of using the English language. Such sloppiness. Intolerable."

"I'm awfully sorry, Your Royal Highness. I'll really make sure I don't say it again."

"Well, I should bally well hope not."

She looked at her son with carefully concealed ruefulness.

Really, she thought, I do sometimes wonder how he'll turn out when I pop off. Such a black and white way of looking at things. Still, it won't be my worry . . .

"All right then, Robin. Come and see me just after Henry's paid his final call tonight. I'm sure I can rely on you."

"Oh, yes. Yes, indeed. You know, I'd sort— I mean, if I ever let you down I'd— Well, I'd feel terrible."

Exit of abashed equerry.

That night, after Sir Henry Fairmile had paid the duty equerry's customary brief visit to see if Her Majesty had had any last-minute thoughts, Superintendent Battle (as she had come increasingly to think of him) arrived in his turn. But he brought no new evidence.

"No, honestly, ma'am, I've made jolly stringent inquiries, and neither of them, neither Meadowcroft nor that little Smithers girl, has anything against them. Meadowcroft's nephew is in a regular job and getting good pay, and there's no hint of any gambling or anything like that. And, no, young Smithers hasn't got a boy friend. Apparently she's always deploring the fact to her fellow maids, though actually, to be brutally frank, one can well see why. Not the most prepossessing of young women."

"Oh, Robin, what a thing to say. I know she's no beauty, but that doesn't stop a young girl acquiring followers. Though, I must say, looking at things the other way round as it were, I've often wondered why you haven't acquired a wife. All those flirtations with the ladies-in-waiting, and nothing ever coming of them."

Robin Pastonbury-Quirk blushed.

"Well, yes, ma'am, there is that. But— But, well, I

really did make the most tremendous inquiries about little Marilyn Smithers, and she absolutely doesn't have anybody who might want money from her."

"Marilyn. Is that her name? Do you know I had no idea. You are a good detective, Robin."

Further blushes.

Well, she thought, I hope I've managed to put that right. I really oughtn't to have teased poor Robin like that, only he does in some ways ask for it.

"Yes," she went on, with some haste, "it's extraordinary really how easy it is to forget that one's maids are anything else than one's maids, that they have another existence outside the household that's just as real as their lives in it."

"Oh, yes, ma'am, perfectly true, perfectly true. Jolly acute of you to see it."

He looked at her, shining-eyed.

My Miss Marple persona, I suppose, seeing what's really what. It does pop up every now and again. And sometimes at quite the wrong moment. I remember at the Coronation, sitting with that fearfully heavy crown on one's head, and suddenly thinking about her, thinking like her. Miss Marple, of all people. When I was meant to be having solemn thoughts about the task I was inheriting. And most of the time I was doing that too, of course.

And, damn it, both sets of thoughts in my mind were equally proper. Tremendous hypocrisy, really, to pretend the me that, just sometimes, is Miss Marple is somehow less than the me who is the monarch. When I'm her, I'm not a sort of, to borrow that useful expression, Miss Marple. Any more than I'm a sort of monarch when I'm opening Parliament. I'm really fully both.

And, what's more, I'm sure everybody can be two things at once, both equal. Wherever they seem to come in the social scale. Whoops. Back to Meadowcroft and little Smithers—Marilyn, what a name—and I suppose the only thing left now is for me to find an opportunity of having a word with each of them. See if the Meadowcroft or the Smithers who's something else

besides one of my personal maids had any other reason
to take my wedding ring, which young Superintendent
Battle didn't find out about.

Only ... Exactly what kind of a word am I going to
have? I can't even suggest to either of them that they
took the ring. It's just that sort of suspicion about an
innocent person that I must try to rid myself of. It
would be too unfair to say anything, to Meadowcroft
or to Smithers. Certainly, that's what Miss Marple
would have insisted on. She was always absolutely
firm about that.

Miss Marple. Yes, that's what I've got to do. I've
got to be my Miss Marple self.

So how would she approach the subject? Oh, and I
know. I know at once. Shrewd old Miss Marple would
have just one question to ask. It would seem to be a
question about something entirely irrelevant, and yet it
would be the key to the whole mystery.

But what on earth can my Miss Marple question be?

Late that evening, while Meadowcroft was gathering
together the clothes worn for the day's final engagement and Smithers had gone to fetch a new tablet of
soap after Meadowcroft, the eagle-eyed, had spotted
that the one on the bathroom basin was almost used up,
Miss Marple got a chance to put the question she had
at last hit on.

"Oh, Meadowcroft, I've been meaning to ask
you . . ."

"Yes, ma'am?"

"I was wondering if you might care to have a photograph that we have signed, as a memento of your
time with us and an expression of our gratitude for all
you've done?"

Meadowcroft was at once overcome with embarrassment.

"Oh, ma'am, that is good of you. And there's nothing I'd like more."

Then her face resumed its habitual expression, a
faint suspicion that something somewhere was out of
place.

"But I hope there won't be no question of mementos for many a year yet, ma'am. I'm not near retirement. Not by a long way."

"No, no, Meadowcroft. I trust you'll be with us for a good many years still. It's just that something put the idea into my head, and I thought I'd ask you while it was in my mind."

"I'm sure it's very good of you, ma'am."

So, Superintendent Battle, when you next come to chat with Miss Marple, I think I'll be able to assure you that Meadowcroft had no more idea of secreting away my ring as a memento than she had of paying off her nephew's nonexistent debts by selling it.

And a few minutes later, when Meadowcroft had gone, leaving little Smithers to perform the important task of replacing the soap, it was no more than a variant of Miss Marple's seemingly trivial question that was needed.

"Oh, Smithers, I have been thinking. You have been with us almost a year now, have you not?"

"Oh, yes, ma'am."

"And you're happy with your work?"

"Oh, ma'am, yes. It's— It's just great, ma'am."

"Great, is it? So you're not thinking of moving on to somewhere perhaps less demanding? Or to where you have more responsible tasks than replacing our soap?"

"No, no, ma'am. I— Well, I'd like to end up being with you as long as Alice—as long as Meadowcroft, that is, ma'am. Truly."

"Well, I hope you will be, Smithers. I hope you will be. Good night then."

"Oh, good night, ma'am. Good night."

But, she thought, that leaves things almost more mysterious than they were before. I'm certain now neither of those two took my ring. But if they didn't, who did? Who on earth did?

And then the answer came to Miss Marple.

"Yes," she murmured to herself. "Yes. Soap. That's the important thing."

* * *

"Soap, Super—I mean, Robin. I'm afraid it came to me later than it should have done. But the soap in my basin is what really told me the truth."

"The soap, ma'am?

Sir Robin Pastonbury-Quirk looked utterly baffled.

"Yes. You see, Robin, when you searched this room and my bedroom and my bathroom just after I'd found the ring was missing, I suggested you should wash your hands because you said you had been doing the crossword, and one always nowadays gets one's hands filthy reading *The Times*."

"Yes. Quite so, ma'am. And I did wash them. I didn't want to get your—er—your, well, sheets all covered in black ink."

"Very thoughtful, Robin. Only your hands weren't dirty. I noticed them when you came in. They looked, as they always somehow do, as if you'd only just scrubbed them with pumice stone."

Sir Robin looked down at the ground.

"Perhaps— Perhaps I—"

"No, Robin."

He brought his gaze slowly up to face hers.

"Ma'am, you're perfectly right, of course. I wasn't doing the crossword. I was . . . I was . . ."

"Robin, it's better that we should have out the whole truth once and for all. You've allowed yourself to fall in love with me, isn't that it? I suppose I've been half-aware of it for a long time, though I hadn't realized it. But your devotion—yes, that's the only word—your devotion to us is so excessive that there's no other explanation. You're in this state, and when you were in here the night before last, as is the equerry's duty, whether it's you or Sir Henry or any of the others, to come in for last-minute changes, you yielded to sudden temptation. Of course, I never took you into account. You were like the postman in the murder stories that nobody ever thinks of as a suspect. But you slipped into the bathroom while I was still watching television and seized on the first—what?—keepsake you saw. And you were gazing at it— Oh, Robin, like a lovesick youth—instead of doing the crossword as you usually do. That is it, isn't it?"

"Oh, ma'am, how could I have—"

"Well, we won't go into that. But perhaps you should just hand it back."

Sir Robin dipped two fingers behind his schoolboyishly askew gray silk tie and drew out a little leather pouch hanging from a fine silver chain round his neck. He pulled it open and turned it over. Onto his outstretched palm there dropped a thin circlet of gold.

The Reckoning

by Graham Joyce

May 13th 1593

"What? Is the Kyd arrested then?"

Poley packed his pipe with the new weed. Before putting a lighted taper to it, he pointed the long stem at Marlowe. "Arrested twenty-four hours since. Which is how long I give him before he starts to dagger others. Like you."

This was not good news. Marlowe pushed his pot of ale aside. It had turned sour in the jar. Poley was right about Thomas Kyd, sure enough; but what disturbed him more was the set of papers he'd loaned to Kyd over a month ago. If Kyd had been arrested, then his chamber would have been searched and the papers would now be in the hands of the Privy Council. Or their torturer's hands.

Poley, a large man with cold eyes and a smiling mouth, was generating an infernal cloud of gray smoke as he warmed to some imagined scene. "Now down at Bridewell I hear they have a grand array of fanciful tools for the loosening of tongues and the correction of heretics. Tom Kyd, you come and inspect these here! And they'll only have to show him, then they better get a dozen clerks to write down what he'll tell. Then—"

"Enough!" Marlowe said sharply.

Poley smirked from within his aromatic cloud. He exuded poison charm. He had been Walsingham's most trusted agent-provocateur, and a recent change of spymaster had harmed his career not a whit.

Marlowe glanced over his shoulder, as though enemies might be gathering in the shadows of the tavern. He had good reason to fear the inquiries of the Privy Council. That month had seen riots and disorders in London, directed against foreigners and strangers; the Privy Council had commissioned an investigation, with a reward of one hundred crowns offered for the author of "mutinous libels." He was regretting his part-authorship of a play documenting the "Evil May Day" anti-Stranger riots of Henry VIII's reign.

And now there were the papers, seized from Kyd's chamber.

Marlowe paid the reckoning and got up to leave. From inside a fug of tobacco smoke Poley waved his pipe stem at the departing figure. "Watch your back, Kit Marlowe!"

May 15th 1593

It was ten o'clock. Marlowe emerged from the bustle of Saddler Gate and affected to gaze into a dazzle of morning sunlight on the Thames. His apprenticeship in the Service had given him a sixth sense about being followed. He turned suddenly.

He was indeed being trailed, and by two men. The first of these turned amateurishly to inspect saddles. Marlowe recognized him as Service from his days in Rheims. *That's clear,* he thought. *But the other one I don't know. And the first is not aware of the second.*

The second man was attired in expensive black doublet and hose. He knew he'd been spotted by Marlowe and made no stupid effort to conceal his interest.

Since Kyd's arrest the playwright had been seeing spies in every quarter. The problem was how to distinguish bugbears and hobgoblins from real persecutors. The Service had equipped him with skills for evading pursuers; it hadn't taught him how to prevent phantoms from multiplying.

Marlowe stepped quickly inside the Blue Boar. Once within the doors of the inn, he sent stools skittling as he charged through the kitchens, ignoring the cries of the landlord. Outside, a long hedge ran down to the river. He darted beside it like a rat coming to the water. There he hailed an oarsman.

"Follow the current. Quick about it!"

The boat carried him swiftly away. He was accustomed to playing this game, but it all seemed pointless. Marlowe knew it was only a matter of time before he would be taken for questioning.

But who was the second man?

He was still looking back at the bank across the heaving shoulders of the oarsman. Bright beads of water caught the sunlight as they ran from the laboring oars. He had too many enemies. When he was younger, he didn't care how many enemies he made. But in those days he had the protection of the Service. Since Walsingham's death, things were less certain. The tall figure in black could possibly have been just another of Heneage's Service men. Marlowe knew that Heneage, the new spymaster-in-chief, often assigned two men to every mission, each unaware of the other. But equally it could have been one of Raleigh's cutthroats. Marlowe had acquired a small tobacco concession that had been more trouble than it was worth. Or maybe it had nothing to do with the tobacco-gangs: Raleigh was a freethinking friend until such time as his own security was imperiled by the rack, and there were men out to get Raleigh who might use Marlowe as their means. Or it could be one of Cholmley's gang of sixty. Or then again . . .

For so it went, the mist of enemies and intrigue filling the air like tobacco smoke. And now these papers from Kyd would cause him more trouble. Had he called on his connections in the Service too many times?

The boat bumped roughly against the landing pontoon. Marlowe got out, clouded in thought, and made to step off the pontoon. "Sir, sir!" the oarsman was saying. "The fee!"

May 17th 1593

Marlowe lay abed that evening when there came a soft knocking on his door. He got up to answer it.

"Poley! I have something to ask ..."

The visitor raised a finger to his lips. Though intended to be intimate, it was not a comforting gesture. "Will you keep me on the threshold?"

"Come through."

Poley stepped inside and took in everything at a single, sweeping glance. Kit had cleared his papers on learning of Kyd's arrest. He was glad he'd moved swiftly, for on the day he'd escaped his watchers upriver, his chamber had been carefully searched. Now something told him that Poley had been doing the searching.

"As I'm your friend, Kit," Poley said, smiling with his large mouth, "I came to tell you something." False bonhomie jangled in him like the currency of a Judas. "Your arrest warrant will be issued tomorrow."

"I thought it likely."

"Some papers of Kyd's ... I see you know it. Well, some advice. You'll be treated well, not as a prisoner. The Service looks after its own. Now, as a friend, what I say to you is: should the questioning from my lord the earl of Essex *rally* to a certain point, you should know the answer. Do you follow?"

So that was it. They *were* going to squeeze him on Raleigh. Essex was Raleigh's deadly enemy, and he'd seen in this an opportunity to collect testimony on Raleigh's freethinking and atheism. They wanted Marlowe to give them Raleigh, just as Kyd had given them him. If he didn't cooperate, he'd be denied his liberty for certain; but if he did, it would invite death. Raleigh had his own information sources back to the Privy Council.

Marlowe sighed. Poley was waiting for an answer. "Is this how I'm to be paid for my Service?"

"You've called on the Service many times to pull you out of the mire, Kit. Now it's the Service that calls to be paid. What shall I say?"

"Tell them I'm ready."

It was not the answer Poley wanted.

May 20th 1593

"What did you mean by saying St. Paul was but a juggler?"

"I never said St. Paul was a juggler."

"Come along Kit Marlowe; Kyd reported it, and anyway it's well known, this blasphemous remark of yours."

"No, I never said it. I said Moses was but a juggler. Moses."

The archbishop held his head in his hands. The Privy Council interview had been going on for over an hour. The lord admiral was an admirer of his plays; Sir Robert Cecil knew him from Cambridge; and Sir Thomas Heneage knew, at least, of his record in the Service. They had treated him as a witness rather than as a prisoner. Only Essex was hostile, and the archbishop exasperated.

"*In what way . . .*" started the archbishop, then began again more calmly. "In what way was Moses a juggler?"

"A conjurer. A necromancer."

"Conjurer? You suppose the prophet performed his feats by means of conjuring?"

"Why, there's one Herriot, necromancer, astrologer, and mathematician under Raleigh's service can accomplish better than Moses. And he'll show you."

Essex suddenly became interested again. Marlowe regretted mentioning Raleigh. "And does this Herriot, and does Raleigh share this view of yours concerning Moses, would you say?"

"I've never discussed it with either."

"Let's forget this nonsense concerning Moses," the archbishop said irritably. "What of these atheistic papers? Kyd says they are yours."

"They are."

"You don't deny it?"

"They are mine. They are a summary of the beliefs

of the Arians, denying the divinity of Christ. I have them because I am writing a tract to refute them. How can I argue against such stuff if I don't have what they say before me? I am a scholar of theology, I remind you."

"Christopher Marlowe," Essex said dryly, "that well-known defender of the faith." Marlowe ignored the remark. "Have you also shared these papers with Raleigh?"

"No, I do not think they would be much interest to him."

"You just visit him to smoke tobacco, no doubt."

"This is tedious," said the lord admiral.

"I'm not satisfied," said the archbishop with finality. "This case will remain *sub judice* until I've learned more. Marlowe, you will stay within the reach of Westminster and give daily attendance on officers of this court until the case of Kyd is decided."

"But your lordships! I must go to Canterbury! I must—"

"The Privy Council," Essex snarled, "is not in the habit of repeating itself."

Marlowe understood perfectly the political issue of the day. It concerned the Puritan or Catholic future of the state, and atheism or wild heresy was used as a pretext for radicalism on both sides. Many mouths had been stopped for less. Only recently a pamphleteer had lost his hand in a public amputation. Marlowe got to his feet and faced the new spymaster, Sir Thomas Heneage. "My lord, I appeal for the intervention of the Service."

Heneage looked back without sympathy. He seemed to speak without moving his lips greatly. "Marlowe, the Service repaid you on the matter of your uncompleted degree from Cambridge. The Service also repaid you when you were tormenting the beadles of Shoreditch. The Service repaid you still when you were caught counterfeiting gold coin in the Netherlands. And again, when you stood accused by Richard Baines of going over to the enemy. Now I'm no word-

smith, like you, sir. But isn't it a case of the pitcher being taken to the well once too often?"

"He'd mint it newer than that," said the lord admiral. "Let's hear the next case."

Before Marlowe reached the gates of Westminster, a
figure stepped out of the shadows, blocking his path.
The man stood a head taller than Marlowe, wearing
doublet and hose of jet black. Marlowe blinked into the
sea-gray eyes, recognizing the man from whom he'd
fled down the river. He took in the gilt pommel of the
sword and the jewelled handle of the stiletto at the
man's belt. Expensive, foreign-crafted arms.

"Come with me," the man whispered, and without
waiting to see if Marlowe kept pace, he hurried along
a path, disappearing through a side door.

Marlowe considered for a moment, and followed.

The stranger led him through unlit corridors. They
encountered no one. Then they passed into an ante-
room where a closed door was guarded by a single hal-
berdier. The guard allowed Marlowe's guide to knock
softly. They went in.

The room was weakly lit by flaming brands in wall
sconces. A dim fire flickered in the grate, from where
a shadowy figure was taking warmth. When the figure
turned around, Marlowe was too stunned to remember
the forms of address. He found himself stammering.

Queen Elizabeth held up a hand. "Just be seated,
Christopher Marlowe."

Marlowe was nudged toward a seat by the man who
had brought him there, who did not sit but who hovered uncomfortably behind him. The Queen's face
was almost entirely in shadow, and she seemed deliberately to want to keep it that way. It was undoubtedly
the Queen, but perhaps she found the light unflatter-
ing.

"We liked your *Doctor Faustus*. Yes. We did." The
Queen had a perceptible hiss to her speech.

"I'm honored."

"Yes. A very Christian play. Not at all an atheist's
play."

"Your Majesty is correct."

"We keep abreast. We do. Your work is in the fashionable talk. So what we want to know is this: could you pen a play for us?"

"Consider it done."

"We don't mean a dedication. We mean could you fashion a play around a given condition? Yes? Here it is. Suppose you were to pen another work of such quality, and it were daggered at the Puritans in our kingdom?"

"But I don't understand. Your Majesty is opposed by the Catholic cause—"

"—Catholic conspiracy."

"Indeed by the Catholic conspiracy, not by the Puritans."

A gloved hand was placed on Marlowe's shoulder from behind. "Her Royal Majesty is not accustomed to detailing her motives."

Marlowe blanched. "I apologize. I merely meant to say—"

"No heed, Mister Skeres," said Elizabeth. "We want Christopher Marlowe to understand my problem. We want our finest playwright to understand all at issue. The Popish conspiracy is over. And now the Puritans bark like dogs, and every kitchen maid in the land thinks herself at liberty to criticize the clergy. We want to restore dignity. We have no desire to see further persecutions, and you, I think, would have no love for the Puritans."

"No, Your Majesty, since they pluck down the theaters."

"Then make it. Make clowns of them. Make them rustics and dullards; you know the way, such is your craft. Can we say it will be done?"

"It will be done."

"And may you call your play *The Reckoning*?"

"May I ask why?"

"Call it a whim." The Queen stepped out of the shadows, but averted her face as she offered a gloved hand for Marlowe to kiss. "Take care of him, Mister Skeres. Christopher Marlowe pleases us." Then she departed through an inner door, leaving Marlowe alone with Skeres.

"Of course," said Skeres, "you were never here. You never saw the Queen. She asked nothing of you. This play you write will show nothing of her patronage, for there will be none."

"Of course. But will it help me in my business with the Privy Council?"

Skeres pretended to look baffled; he succeeded in appearing menacing. "Will *what* help you?"

"I understand," said Marlowe.

May 22nd 1593

"The reckoning!" Marlowe sat up in bed gasping, crying out, lathered in sweat.

It was a night fever. A nightmare.

He pushed a hand through his hair and looked out of the casement window. A sick, waning moon hung low in the sky. In the dream was the youth Babbington. They were dining together when they took him. Babbington knew his time was come around. He got up to say he must call the landlord to settle the reckoning; and leaving his coat and sword went to pay, and then ran, only to be taken by Walsingham's men; and then hung. And as he hung, the scaffold became a stage and Marlowe went to the crowd with a cap to collect their coin like a common stroller. Only the crowd turned brutal chanting *The reckoning! The reckoning!*

But it was only a night fever. Some bad ale he'd drunk. The body pays for its abuses, he thought. He went back to sleep.

May 25th 1593

"This audience with the Queen, Kit. May I not be privy to some of it?"

"I've told you a dozen times, Poley; there was no audience with the Queen. What do you imagine? That she keeps some palace back room with a small light burning for assignations?"

"I know she does."

"Don't be a fool."

"You abuse my friendship, Kit." That slack-jawed smile.

Marlowe was losing patience. "There's an end to it."

Poley came and went like an evil spirit, clouding messages, forging letters, dabbling in ciphers, picking up bribes, muddying communications. It was never easy to find Poley. Poley always found you. This time he'd found Marlowe in conversation with others at the Rose. He'd steered him by the elbow to the proscenium where their conversation could be drowned by the rehearsals taking place on stage. Marlowe was hack-writing *The Contention* with three other playwrights. A stage-builder in a leather apron worked with his back to them, his hammering drowning their voices.

"Don't expect," Poley said, "to find in Heneage the sympathetic ear. Walsingham is dead; your protector is gone. And Heneage takes the view the Service is rotten." Rotten. Wherever Poley went, he exuded an aura of rot and putrefaction. He grinned and pulled at his beard, a stage fight going on over his shoulder. "You could help your situation with the Privy Council if only you'd spread a little intelligence concerning the working of the Queen's mind. Among friends and patriots of course."

"I have to work," said Marlowe.

"Work? This hack business? It seems to me the play is writ."

"The ending is only rough-hewn. Now give way."

After the two men had moved away, the stage builder came forward from the wings of the theater, nails between his teeth and a hammer in his paw. It was Skeres. He took off his leather apron and made his exit from the back of the Rose.

May 26th 1593

Marlowe was roaring drunk. The bawd Janet was too, though she had urged restraint. Kit had taken to the White Hart, a vinegary tavern of sour ale and broken stools, saying he wanted to be among cutpurses and whores, "the only people he could trust." Having failed to initiate an argument, he'd pissed on a dog sleeping in the corner of the tavern; now he was subdued after the landlord had threatened him with a spiked club.

He was drunk on a potent brew of fear as much as ale. His head bobbed toward the table. Then he suddenly looked up. The tavern was thick with the smoke of the new weed.

"Let's have another pot of ale."

"Have you the wherewithal to pay for all this spilled drink?" asked Janet.

"Shut up, you whore. Don't you know I make money?"

"Make it?"

"Yes, make it, trollop. I had a factory in Rheims. I pressed it." He squeezed her breast. "Coins like the aureole of your bosom."

"With the head of Elizabeth?"

"No; I'd make 'em with your head, Janet. You're much the prettier. I've seen her. We have secret meetings, you know. Don't believe me? Well, that's because you're a whore."

"As you are. A writer of plays for favors."

"You know why I love you, Janet?"

"Ha!"

"You're pure. You're a puritan."

"Ha! Still!"

"Yes yes yes, a puritan. These who call themselves Puritans, they are not. Because to them all things are impure. So why are they Puritans, tell me? No. You are pure whore. Pure corruption."

"What's this talk?"

"You dull harlot. Look me in the eye. Am I not a pure man?"

She reached over and squeezed his codpiece. "You're a man, pure."

"You zero. You cipher. You clod. Did you know I have a secret? Eh, Janet? Eh?"

"Come upstairs with me," said Janet. "You can show me your secret."

Marlowe climbed unsteadily on the table. "For all the world to see?"

"Aye, have it out!" another bawd shouted.

"Silence, slut! Listen, you whoresons! Even jades such as you will seem virgins when you hear what I have to tell! *Silence!* "

The dog he'd abused earlier started barking. Someone tossed half a pot of ale at him. "The Queen is . . . *ugly!* "

"Take him upstairs, Janet, and spare us," someone shouted. There were more crude comments and raucous laughter. The other drinkers turned back to their own tables. He swayed unsteadily. He'd stopped shouting and was mumbling now, almost incoherent.

"Come down, Kit," said Janet gently.

He got down, befuddled. Janet helped him to the door, but Marlowe seized her by the collar. "I don't fear the Archbishop of Canterbury and his gallows. Nor Heneage and his army of spies, nor Poley. Nor Raleigh and his tobacco gangs. But I fear the Queen. Because she would make a pure whore of me. And then I'm undone."

"Go home, Kit."

Marlowe staggered out of the tavern. Janet merely shrugged at the lost trade.

May 28th 1593

"They know Marlowe. They will want to sweat him. And they will never believe you commissioned him merely to write a play."

Skeres was able to see the Queen's smile even within the dim candle light. "You are certain Essex will make his move?"

"His hatred of Raleigh will spur him. He will see in

this commission some advance for Raleigh and will want to know of it. Essex will have Heneage put out his spies to sweat Marlowe, and Marlowe will want to use what he knows to save his neck with the Privy Council. More importantly, Your Majesty will have collected another offense from Essex."

"Which we'll need when it comes to cutting him down. Every day he grows more powerful. He makes himself the Puritans' champion and the hero of the people. Though we may love him now . . ."

". . . Nothing is more certain than his future treachery. There is not a more ambitious man in all of Christendom. Give him this Marlowe to begin with. Give him yards of rope. Essex is his own gallows."

The Queen approached Skeres and patted his face lightly with her gloved hand, allowing herself to be seen fully in the light. "And so I shall have my reckoning with Essex. Where would I be without my Skeres? And what of this noisy playwright?"

"Should he come to harm, you are rid of another blasphemous atheist. Just another evil scribbler. And Your Majesty's kingdom is full of playwrights. The tanner from York, the glover from Stratford . . ."

May 30th 1593

Marlowe arrived at Mistress Bull's house in Deptford just after ten o'clock, as instructed. Poley's note had been delivered while he slept. He would have felt safer in a public tavern rather than in a private house adopted by the Service, but he understood the need for secrecy if the secretary of state, Heneage, were to be present.

The house was by all means respectable. Mistress Bull obviously had some connection with court, and that made Marlowe feel a little more secure as the widow showed him to an upstairs room. What astonished him was to discover Poley and Ingram Friser in the presence of Skeres.

Ingram Friser he detested. Friser was a Service man and an old rival. The animosity was a festering one:

Marlowe's loss of favor with Heneage he attributed to Friser. Meanwhile Skeres was obviously here to ensure Marlowe kept his mouth shut.

"Kit! Here you are!" Poley greeted him warmly, his lips red and moist. "Ingram Friser you know. And let me introduce you to Skeres."

Skeres, leaning against a window, nodded briefly.

Friser was setting up a board of backgammon. "Come on, Kit. Let's have a round of tables. I owe you a beating."

"Where's Heneage?"

"If he comes, he comes," said Poley. "We're set up to wait for him, Kit. Here's ale, and Mistress Bull to attend on us with food. Be easy. We're all Service here."

Marlowe looked at Skeres doubtfully. "Is Heneage coming?"

"I hope so, Kit. I hope so. Duties of Privy Council detain him. Now, I'm wagering a crown to double on a round of tables." Poley's simulated *bonhomie* was like a breath of poison.

"Perhaps Kit fears the reckoning on that," said Skeres. Marlowe stiffened at the word. Was there some malice behind it? Skeres looked puzzled. "Did I offend?"

"Offend?" said Poley. "Kit has gambled ten times that on a game of tables before now ... wait! I see what it is. Some old enmity between Friser and yourself, Kit. You nurse a grudge too long. Isn't it in the past?"

"For me it is," said Friser, laying out the blots on the board.

Mistress Bull brought a tray of victuals around about midday, and Marlowe realized Heneage would not be coming. It was all a lie to lure him there. Friser was drinking steadily, but he noticed Poley, while making a great show of raising his glass, was actually imbibing little. Skeres hardly drank at all.

So that was to be the pattern. The cold sweat.

Marlowe knew it was pointless to mention Heneage
again; Poley meant to have his information however
long it took. At one point Marlowe excused himself.

"I'll go to the jakes," he said.

"I'll escort you," Poley had said with a wink. "In
case you've forgotten how."

Skeres cleaned his fingernails with his stiletto.

Later in the afternoon he and Poley took a turn
around the garden while Skeres and Friser stayed at
backgammon. Marlowe understood well why widow
Bull's house had been chosen. The garden was surrounded by an eight-foot brick wall. There was no
chance of making a run for it. A gate at the bottom of
the garden was heavily barred. There was only one
way out, and that was through the front door.

He assumed Mistress Bull was being paid to play
her part in this. If he couldn't leave, he was determined
to sit the day out.

In the afternoon Marlowe played Skeres at tables.
Skeres played in silence, and Marlowe, playing a reck-
less back game to his opponent's running game, lost a
lot of money. The ale was making him irritable, and he
jibed at Skeres's cautious play.

"I said you were afraid of *the reckoning*."

He looked at Skeres with venom. The man knew
that phrase would ring in Marlowe's ears like a
cracked bell. Skeres smiled and scooped his winnings.

When Poley rang for widow Bull to bring supper,
Marlowe protested he had nothing left to take care of
his share of the bill. Friser, feeling a grudging sympathy for Marlowe's plight, said innocently, "I'll take the
reckoning." But Marlowe stiffened so visibly, a silence
descended on the company.

Marlowe looked from Skeres to Friser. "You'll not
take my reckoning."

"Please yourself," said Friser, already regretting his
generosity, "but someone will."

Mistress Bull came into the room and set down
supper without a word, closing the door behind
her.

"There it lies," said Skeres, "and somebody must take the reckoning." He made his jaw clamp on the word.

How could they goad him so easily with a single word? Marlowe's dream of Babbington came back to him; sweat blistered on his forehead.

"Here's a solution," said Skeres. "A chance for Kit to make back his losses on the tables. Or take the reckoning."

So they played a four-way game. Marlowe began throwing back ale, along with Friser, skittering dice across the board. It came down to him and Skeres. He played his usual back game, and it was going badly. The two men sat across the table, playing at speed, and with his free hand, Skeres jingled his pile of won coin, knowing how each rattle of the coins parodied the hated word.

Poley, becoming interested in the growing tension, sat on the bench to Marlowe's right. Friser, watching the climax of the game from behind, joined them on the bench at his left. Marlowe felt the force of their thighs at either side of him. He was trapped, pinned between the two.

"The reckoning," whispered Skeres.

"The reckoning," said Friser.

"Aye, the reckoning!" screamed Marlowe. Unable to break free, he lunged for his dagger and lashed out against Friser's head, but with the pommel handle and with the blade held back. Poley leaped off the bench in astonishment at this sudden turn; Friser meanwhile smashed his arm upward and across Marlowe's face. Skeres saw his opportunity. He reached forward, twisting back the wrist wielding the dagger. He spun Marlowe around so as to obstruct Poley's view; and, his body shielding the action, with a sudden impulsion he forced the dagger into Marlowe's eye.

It was an expert aim. The dagger point slid over the eyeball and entered the skull through the orbital fissure where the eye nerves pass through to the brain, meeting the blood vessel that drains into the jugular and thence into the heart. It was the personal signature of the provocateur-assassin, and to an untrained observer a fluke thrust.

There was a seeping tide of rich, wine-dark blood.

"What have you done?" Poley had drawn his own blade.

Skeres too had his sword drawn. "It was Friser's blow. The blade turned on himself. I was trying to intervene."

The drunken Friser, still reeling from his blows, could only protest innocence.

"But he was about to speak!" said Poley. His mission was bungled.

"He'll not now," said Friser.

Skeres shook his head "This was done badly. Were you not aware he was a favorite of the Queen?"

Marlowe was dead on the floor, and the flow of blood did not abate. Poley eyed Skeres with suspicion. The two men, weapons drawn, were at standoff. Poley was first to put away his sword. He was thinking of Essex. "I'll call for a surgeon."

"What shall we say?" said Friser.

June 1st 1593

The Service could rely on the Queen's coroner giving them the benefit of the doubt. Marlowe was found to be the victim of his own attack on Friser. Poley had failed in his mission to discover the Queen's mind, and was more concerned about facing the combined wrath of Sir Thomas Heneage and the Earl of Essex. Privately, Essex in particular emerged as the author of the slaying. Publicly however, and in view of Friser's injuries, the jury accepted a plea of self-defense in an argument over the payment of Mistress Bull's reckoning. The seals of the coroner and the jurors were set.

Because of the plague Marlowe's body was buried immediately after the inquest. His body was carried to St. Nicholas churchyard in Deptford Green and there buried in an unmarked grave.

Essex, still protesting his loyalty after a catalogue of offenses against the queen, was some years later condemned to death.

Victoria

by Mark Timlin

I was standing, looking out at my office window when he arrived. He was in the back of a gun-metal gray Daimler with military plates. The chauffeuse, all neat in black stockings, jumped out of the front and opened the curbside rear door. He unfolded himself from inside, then leant back in and collected his brolly. Don't ask me why, as it hadn't rained for weeks. Maybe he felt undressed without it. Maybe he took it to bed with him. I wouldn't like to say.

Of course, then, I didn't know he was coming to see me. And even a few seconds later when he pushed open my office door, I wasn't certain. "Mr. Nicholas Sharman?" he said, with a question mark attached. Then I knew.

"That's me," I said, walking around behind my desk in case his accent was infectious. It could have cut glass. At forty feet. You don't get much of that in Tulse Hill. But then you don't get too many like him at all. He was six foot eight if he was an inch. And wafer thin with it. And the fact that he stood as straight as a metal rule made him look even taller if that were possible. I would have put him about sixty, but the skin on his face was pink and smooth and unlined, and shaved to a millimeter of its life, except for the silver bristle of mustache on his top lip. On his head he sported a silk bowler that he wore down over his eyes, guards' fashion. His neck was throttled by a stiff white collar attached to a raspberry-colored shirt by a gold stud. Above the stud, knotted tightly, was what looked suspiciously like an old Etonian tie. Even on that warm day he wore a double-breasted overcoat of a navy material that by its sheen I took to be cashmere. Under the overcoat were visible a pair of stepped-bottom trousers, creased sharper than a landlady's tongue, that broke over elastic-sided boots with a shine that would shame a mirror. The umbrella he carried had an antique wooden handle and was furled so neatly and tightly I doubted that it had ever got damp. "I wonder if I could have a word?" he asked.

"Of course," I said. I was beginning to get intrigued. And polite. Too polite. I'd have to watch that.

He pulled up the hard wooden chair I keep for the customers, removed the bowler to expose a full head of hair that matched the color of his mustache cut close to his scalp, hooked his brolly over the chairback, opened his overcoat to expose a double-breasted suit jacket, sat down, hiking up the strides as he did so, and crossed his legs. "May I smoke?" he asked.

"Of course," I said again.

He extracted a silver cigarette case from the inside pocket of his jacket, opened it, and offered the case to me. I was trying for the four hundred and fourteenth time to give up. Unsuccessfully as it turned out, but even so I refused. He shrugged and placed an untipped cigarette between his lips. From his outside jacket pocket, right-hand side, he took out a matching lighter, flicked the wheel, and touched the flame to the tip of the cigarette and inhaled. "Disgusting habit," he said by way of apology, though he needn't have bothered. "But I've been doing it for forty years, and I don't think I'll ever stop." He coughed discreetly. "Until they cart me away, that is."

I nodded in agreement. I couldn't think of anything else to do.

"Mr. Sharman," he said. "Do you remember signing the Official Secrets Act?"

I must have looked surprised at the question.

"When you joined the police," he explained.

I nodded again.

"It still applies." He looked round the room. "Do you have an ashtray?"

"It's a secret," I said.

It was his turn to look surprised. Then he laughed. A ferocious bark. He sounded like a walrus demanding to be fed. "Your famous sense of humor," he said. "I've been told about it. Now, an ashtray if you don't mind. There's a good fellow." I got one from on top of the filing cabinet and put it on the edge of the desk in front of him.

"Are you a secret, too?" I asked.

"I'm sorry," he said.

"Your name."

"My dear chap, I do apologize." He stood up and stuck his hand over the top of the desk. "Cave-Browne-Cave," he said. "Browne with an 'e.'"

I shook the proffered mitten. "It sounds like a firm of solicitors," I said.

He barked another laugh. "Rich. Very rich," he said. "I must remember that. But it is my name nevertheless. Peter Piers to be precise. Major. Ex-Blues and Royals, presently seconded to Buck House."

"Really?" I asked. If it hadn't been for the car and the chauffeur, I would have put him down as an absconder from the Maudsley Psychiatric Hospital up the road, given him half a quid, and told him where the bus stop back was.

He let go of my hand and pulled a black leather folder from his overcoat pocket. He flipped it open and held it six inches from my face. Inside were his credentials, complete with a very flattering photograph. Professionally posed I guessed. I'd only seen similar credentials once before. When I was in the job. They were carried by the man who carried the briefcase which contained the codes that triggered Great Britain's nuclear strike force. He accompanied the prime minister when he or she went walkabout. Never more than a few yards away. They were the kind of credentials that opened any door in the land. Believe me, they don't come inside cornflake packets. I was impressed. More than impressed in fact. "Really," he said and returned to his chair. "Security to HM personally. And I'd like to remind you that breaches of the OSA bear rather serious penalties." He looked round the room again. "I'm sure that even this place is preferable to a cell in Wormwood Scrubs."

"If you're threatening me, Major," I said, "perhaps you could tell me why."

"Threatening you? No, no, no. Just a thought, that's all."

I wondered if he'd ever come to the point. He must have picked up my thought. "At present you are engaged in the activity of a self-employed private detective, are you not?" he asked.

Through all the verbiage I picked out the nub of the question. "That's right," I replied.

He looked round the room for the third time. "Has this place been swept recently?" he asked.

"I give it a dust now and then and run the Hoover round on a Saturday morning," I said.

Again the laugh. "No. Swept for bugs. Listening devices."

"Here?" I said. "Who would bother to bug this place?"

"You'd be surprised. I think we'd better continue our conversation in the car. You have no objections, I trust."

"Whatever," I said. Anything to get to the point of his visit. He collected his brolly, and we went out to the Daimler. I locked the office door behind us. The chauffeuse opened the car door for us. I smiled at her. She didn't smile back. Once inside the opulent leather interior of the motor, he instructed the driver to take a slow poodle, as he put it, and closed the glass partition between us and her. When the car was safely on the South Circular heading away from town, I asked him, "Do you need a private detective for something?"

"No."

"Then why—?"

"I need you," he interrupted. "You in particular."

"Why?"

"Because you know every sleazy little crook in the area," he said.

"Do I?"

"Oh, yes. I've done my research, asked around. And the consensus of opinion is that, if I need to find one, then you're the man."

"And *you* need to find one?" I said, allowing a little note of disbelief to enter my voice.

"Exactly. To be precise a second story man. I believe that's what you call them."

"Not me," I said. "George Raft maybe, but not me."

"What then?"

"Burglar'll do," I said.

"Yes, you're right," he agreed. "A burglar *will* do. One that can crack the combination on a safe."

"A peterman," I said. "Curiouser and curiouser. But why do you need a burglar and a peterman?"

He reminded me about the Official Secrets Act again. Then he told me: "A certain member of the Royal Family," he began. "A female member. A married female member, whose marriage is not all it could be. Should be. Recently had an unfortunate dalliance with a young man. A young man she met at an embassy dinner in a foreign country. A foreign country, with which on the surface we appear to have good relations. But in fact we don't. The young man took advantage of her and the situation, or she of him. It doesn't really matter. Unfortunately, he was not an honorable young man, I'm afraid. The dalliance was short, but the repercussions could be long-lasting. The young man stole something from her. A ring. A very valuable and singular item. The singularity is the problem, not the value. It is easily recognizable as part of the crown jewels of our sovereign lady." He stopped and looked out of the window at the passing traffic.

"The ring is now in the hands of another lady." The way he said "lady" told me that she was not his idea of one, but he was too polite to mention it. "She is the wife of the ambassador of that country to the Court of St. James. Next week the lady in question intends to wear the ring to a state banquet at Buckingham Palace.

It will cause a scandal, and embarrassment to all concerned." He looked at me. "I imagine you think that is foolish. But believe me, in the circles we are discussing it is of paramount importance."

"And?" I said.

"We have a mole in the embassy. The mole has the ear of the ambassador's wife. That is how we know she intends to wear the ring to the banquet."

"How did the ambassador's wife get the ring?" I asked.

"From the young man who stole it. He had an affair with her also." His mouth twisted in distaste.

"Couldn't he get it back for you? Couldn't you put pressure on him?"

"Unfortunately not. He died a few months ago. A skiing accident at Klosters. His neck was broken." He said the last with relish.

"An accident?" I asked.

"That was the verdict of the coroner. Would you question the verdict of a Swiss coroner, Mr. Sharman?"

"Illicit sex can be fatal," I said.

"AIDS?" he asked innocently.

"Or a broken neck," I said.

He barked his laugh again. "No comment," he said. But I knew. I was beginning to think the major was more dangerous an individual than he looked.

"So you want me to arrange a burglary for you?"

He nodded.

"But you have the full resources of the army and the police, not to mention MI5 and 6 to call on. I'm sure there's a few burglars on their strength. In fact, I know there are. Why come to me?"

"This isn't an embassy siege we're talking about. I can't send in the SAS with stun grenades to get the ring back, although God knows I'd like to. If I send someone in and they get caught, the scandal will be twofold. Can you imagine it? It will be a cause célèbre. And if the newspapers got hold of it . . ." He shuddered at the thought. "And I'm sure that the government of that particular country would make sure they did. If not here, then abroad."

"And if someone I send in gets caught?"

"Then that's his problem. But if you send the right man, he won't, will he? Besides, you're not going to tell him why he's stealing the ring, are you? That's just between the two of us."

"But if he does get caught?"

"He'll probably be terminated with extreme prejudice."

"A nice thought," I said.

"I don't believe in pulling punches. Or sending in troops without all the intelligence I can muster."

Troops, is it now? I thought. "And if he does and I go to the newspapers?"

"Official Secrets Act, Mr. Sharman. Remember that."

"But if I did," I persisted. "Would I be terminated with extreme prejudice, too?"

"Quite frankly, Mr. Sharman, I don't think we'd have to bother. You see, even if you did, who's going to believe you?"

"What? Take the word of a sleazy little south London private detective like me, against a big soldier like you?"

"Exactly."

"It's nice to know that your informants have such a good opinion of me. So what's in it for the sleazy team?"

"I thought you'd never ask," he said and reached into the inside pocket of his jacket and took out a thick brown envelope and gave it to me. I opened it. Inside were five plastic packets of bank notes. "There's a thousand in each packet," he said. "Five thousand now. Five thousand more when I receive the ring. You can divvy it up with your man as you see fit. I'm sure you will anyway. Just one other thing. Leave anything else that is in the safe as it is."

"Why?"

"Because then the ambassador and his wife will know exactly what was wanted and exactly who took it. So get someone you can trust to do the job."

"Trust," I said. "That's a big word round here."

"It's a big word everywhere. So you'll arrange it?"

"With a pay packet like this, and the charming way you asked, how could I refuse? But I'll need more details."

"I have the plans of the building in my case," he said. "But I doubt you'll need them. We've made things easy for you. Or at least our mole has. There has been unfortunate structural damage to the embassy. Nothing serious. A section of the roof above the ambassador's quarters has sprung a leak. It is going to be repaired on Friday morning. Three days hence. The scaffolding goes up on Thursday afternoon. That night there is to be a reception at the embassy, so the ambassador and his lady wife will be busy between 8 P.M. and 2 A.M. Their apartment will be empty between those hours. Between midnight and 12:30 A.M. the bulb in the light above the balcony doors and the alarm system on those doors will disfunction." He smiled to himself with satisfaction.

"How come your inside man can do all that, but can't get the ring himself?" I asked.

"The ring is in a safe. A very sophisticated one. He doesn't know the combination, and his talents don't run in the direction of safecracking. So now do you see?"

I nodded. "They'll know it's an inside job."

"By that time it won't matter. Now the safe is behind a Constable."

"A policeman?" I interrupted.

"A picture," he said dryly. I must confess it wasn't one of my best. "The picture is in the bedroom. The subject is a picnic at harvest time. You can't miss it. Is that clear so far?"

"As crystal," I said. "What do I do with the ring when I get it?"

"You'll be contacted."

"C.O.D.?" I asked.

"Of course. Don't worry, there's plenty of money in the public purse. Taxpayer's money. You *do* remember taxes, don't you, Mr. Sharman?"

I didn't answer.

"Don't worry," he said. "I won't tell."

I smiled a thin smile at the implied threat. The old bugger *had* been doing his homework.

"So let's get down to cases," he said and pulled his briefcase onto his lap and opened it. Inside was a sheaf of papers. He took them out and unfolded the bundle. "First," he said. "The way in." The top paper was a plan of the embassy and the surrounding streets, complete with a number of photographs of the building. It was located near The Temple, between Fleet Street and Victoria Embankment in the maze of small streets that ran down to the river. It didn't look like much. A modest Georgian house, painted white, set in a tree-filled garden. Mind you, in that part of town, even modesty cost over a million quid an acre. Once again he sensed my thoughts. "Don't be misled by the photos," he said. "The grounds are quite extensive. And pretty wild. And patrolled on a regular basis, night and day. The building is surrounded by a fifteen-foot-high wall with an electric charge going through the razor wire that runs around the top. This serves two purposes. One, to give anyone trying to get in a nasty shock, and two, to trigger the alarm system." He pulled out photographs of two sets of gates. "Front." He tapped one. "Back." The other. "Guarded twenty-four hours a day by armed men. Don't mess with them. They're armed with Heckler and Koch's, as are the guards who patrol the grounds."

"A piece of piss," I said. "Can we borrow a helicopter from the queen's flight to land on the lawn?"

He laughed again and found another photo stapled to an envelope. "This," he said, "is your access point. It's a small wooden door in the east wall. It hasn't been used for years. It's on the guards' route, but they never check it. It's overgrown with bushes on the inside, and it's more or less been forgotten. Our man has got a copy of the key, and he's even gone so far as to oil the locks and hinges." He opened the envelope and took out an old-fashioned silver key and gave it to me.

"I hope he hasn't done too good a job," I said. "I'd

hate for somebody with an automatic weapon to be waiting on the other side when my man goes in."

The major shook his head. "No," he said. "He's very discreet."

"Isn't it wired into the alarm system?" I asked.

"Don't worry. It's all taken care of," he replied.

I hope so, I thought.

He pulled out another photo. "This is what you're after," he said. It was a color shot of a gold and diamond ring on a blue velvet mount. He touched the photo. "As you can see, the setting is very distinctive. Get your man to study it closely. I want no mistakes."

I nodded.

Finally, he turned to a smaller sheet of paper. "This is the make, model, year of manufacture, and serial number of the safe. It might come in handy. Forewarned is forearmed. Give that to your man, too. And when you've finished, make sure the whole lot is destroyed. I don't want any evidence left hanging around. Understood?"

"Understood," I said.

"Good. Now I'm counting on you, Sharman. Don't let me down. Next Friday, 12:30 ack emma. It's all arranged. Be there. It'll be easy."

Too easy, I thought. "Yes, Major," I said.

He tapped on the glass between us and the driver, and she turned off at the first opportunity and headed back in the direction of my office. When we pulled up outside, the major said, "Until we meet again, Mr. Sharman."

"I can't wait," I replied and got out and watched as the car did a three-point turn, rolled down to the main road, joined the stream of traffic, and disappeared.

Even though Major Cave-Browne-Cave thought I knew every sleazebag and petty crook on the ground, I didn't. But I knew a few and had one in particular pegged for the job. So I went looking. I found "Monkey" Mann in Edward G's. Edward G's is a theme bar tagged onto the Slug and Lettuce public house just outside Beckenham. I don't think it had been a great success. Maybe Beckenham just wasn't ready for the concept of a prohibition bar. Maybe it never would be. I know I wasn't. But needs must. And it fitted perfectly with the major's prewar, Warner Brothers' gangster movie image of villainy in the suburbs.

It was a great barn of a place that had once been the billiards room. It was overheated and underlit. The blowups of Edward G. Robinson that decorated the walls were crooked and dirty. The plastic seating was pockmarked with cigarette burns and ripped and cut so that the foam padding inside burst out like some kind of exotic fungus. In some places it had been repaired with tape, but mostly not. The carpet was spotted with ground-in chewing gum. The sticky cocktails had been replaced with bitter at under a pound a pint during happy hour, which as far as I could make out lasted from opening to closing time, and the juke box had been loaded up with a collection of scratchy Irish favorites. Monkey was sitting next to the pool table. "Hello, Mr. Sharman," he said, without a trace of surprise in his voice. "What brings you here?"

"You, Monkey," I replied. "Want a drink?"

"I'll have a Blackbushe," he said. "Large."

"Fine," I replied and went to the bar. The guv'nor was wearing a silver mohair suit, so stiff that he could hardly bend his arms, and white high-heeled winklepickers that laced up the sides. I'd've bet he got them on his last sabbatical in Marbella. "Large Blackbushe," I said. "And a pint of lager." As the guv'nor was getting the drinks, I peered through the gloom. There were just a few customers in the place, mostly men sitting in the booths that lined the walls. They were mostly alone. It was that kind of boozer.

I collected the drinks, paid, and took them back to Monkey.

Monkey got his name by being able to climb anything, anytime. Just what the major ordered. A second-story man and a safecracker to boot. At fifty odd, with thinning hair and a love of Irish whiskey, a bit past his prime, maybe. But a real pro.

I put the drinks down and sat opposite him. "What can I do for you, Mr. Sharman?" he asked.

So I told him. Just the bare bones like the major wanted. I showed him the photos and the details of the safe.

When I'd finished, he said, "How much?"

"Three grand now. Three grand when the job's finished." I thought that was fair. The rest was a finder's fee. Things hadn't been going too well for me lately.

"Let's see the dough," he said.

I passed him an envelope I'd prepared earlier. He thumbed the notes. "All right," he said, seemingly satisfied. "When?"

"Thursday night," I said. "But there is one thing, Monkey."

"What?"

"You just take the ring. Nothing else."

"What else is there?"

I shrugged. "Don't ask me."

"How would anyone know?"

"They'd know, believe me. And the people who want this job done. They *never* forget. I doubt if you'd have time to enjoy it. The money's good. Be satisfied."

"Okay, Mr. Sharman, whatever you say."

I believed him; thousands wouldn't. "I'll take you there," I said. "Get you into the grounds and wait. Watch your back. Is that okay?"

"Fine. I prefer to work alone."

"Right. I'll pick you up here Thursday at about eleven. Don't let me down."

"I won't."

"And lay off that stuff." I pointed at his glass.

He seemed offended. "I never drink when I'm working," he said.

"That's what I like to hear. Till Thursday then," I said, finished my pint, and left.

Monkey was waiting right on time on Thursday night in the car park of the pub. He materialized out of the shadows like a phantom, wearing dark clothes and carrying a small bag. I was wearing black Levi's, black soft-soled shoes, a black roll-neck sweater, and a dark leather jacket. Just in case, under the jacket, in a shoulder holster I carried a Colt Commander Light Weight, seven-shot .45 semi-automatic pistol. If the job was going to be as easy as the major had said, fine. If not. Well, it pays to be prepared.

We were in town by twelve, and I parked up in the next street to the embassy. Monkey and I padded through the shadows to the embassy wall. I'd made one reconnaissance trip the previous night. I'd found the small door, tried the key, and opened the door. I'd waited ten minutes and no security men had shown up. The major's mole had been right about that at least. A man of many talents obviously. I hoped he was going to be equally right about the rest.

When we got to the door, I checked for passing cars and pedestrians, but the street was empty, and I was just about to insert the key into the keyhole when Monkey said, "Mr. Sharman."

"What?"

"There's a slight problem."

"What?" I said again.

"I don't know how to tell you."

"Tell me Monkey," I said and noticed that his face was slick with sweat.

"You see . . ." he said and hesitated.

"Just tell me, Monkey," I said. "Before someone wonders what the hell we're doing standing here like a pair of prats."

"It's the climb."

"What about it?"

"I can't do it."

"What you? Monkey Mann, the human fly."

"I'm sorry, Mr. Sharman, but me bottle's gone."

"Oh no, Monkey," I said. "Tell me that I'm dreaming."

"Sorry, Mr. S. It's the truth."

"But Monkey, there's a scaffold up. It'll be like climbing a ladder."

"It was a ladder what done me. I fell off painting me

sister's ceiling. I can't stand heights since I done it. I can't even go upstairs on a bus."

"So why did you say you'd do the job?"

"The dough. I'm skint. I can hardly claim redundancy money, can I?"

"Why did you show up tonight then?"

"I'm a pro, Mr. S. I thought it'd be all right once we got started."

"But it's not?"

"Sorry," he said again. And I think he really was. He had a code, and he hated to break it. But that didn't help the situation.

"Bloody hell, Monkey," I said. "What are we going to do?"

He shrugged.

"You've dropped me right in it, you know that? I suppose you've spent the money."

"I had some pressing debts."

"I just bet you did," I said and made a decision. "Right, Monkey. I'm coming with you. You're going up to that balcony if I have to carry you. And me with a bad foot."

"Mr. S., please," he said pathetically.

"Just shut up, Monkey," I said and checked the street again. No change. I did the business with the key, opened the door, and I pushed him through the gap. I closed the door behind us, but didn't lock it. The overgrown shrubbery inside sheltered us from the house. The scaffolding was straight ahead. "Get going," I hissed. "You first." We pushed through the undergrowth, snaked between a couple of stunted trees, across a lawn, and there, exactly as promised, was the scaffold attached to the side of the building. I dragged Monkey into its shadow. "Up you go," I ordered.

"Mr. S.," he said so plaintively I was almost sorry for him. Almost.

"Monkey, believe me," I said. "If you think this climb's frightening, you haven't seen me mad. And the people who supplied that three grand make me look like a sweet little pussycat. Understand?"

"All right, Mr. S.," said Monkey. "I'm going."

And he did. Slowly and reluctantly, but he went. Hand over hand, not looking down. It was all so pathetic I almost felt sorry for him again. But not quite.

I followed him up. It was an easy climb. Just as I'd said it would be. Like a ladder. We got to the balcony, which was in darkness, and climbed over the stone balustrade and onto solid concrete. Monkey breathed a sigh of relief, and so did I to be honest. I've never been mad about heights myself, but I wasn't going to let him know that. I tried the French doors gingerly. They opened without a sound. I pushed through the thick curtains into the apartments, and Monkey followed me. Once inside, I drew them tightly behind us. The room was softly lit by wall-mounted lights, and as I looked round, I realized I was in the presence of sheer luxury. Maybe a bit Imelda Marcos in style, but sheer luxury nevertheless. There were silk drapes and tapestries on the walls. Porcelain statues and vases on every surface. A couple of discreetly placed concealed spotlights picked out paintings that would have made an art expert drool. The furniture was leather or what looked suspiciously like real leopard skin. From somewhere below us I could faintly hear music. The reception, I guessed.

"Nice," whispered Monkey. It was the way he'd have had his council flat furnished if he could have afforded it.

"Bedroom," I said and gave him a push.

According to the plan the major had given me, there was a connecting door between the main salon as it had been described on the blueprint, and the master bedroom, ditto. The plan had been correct. Inside the door was more softly lit luxury. At least we weren't going to need torches. A small mercy. On the wall opposite the super king-size waterbed was a four-foot-by-three framed oil painting of a rural picnic, signed "Constable." Monkey, who appeared much more like his old self, took over from there. The frame of the painting was attached to the wall by hinges, and he opened it like a cupboard door to reveal the face of a safe set into the wall behind it. He put down his tool bag and opened it. From inside he took out what looked like a digital egg timer.

"What the hell's that?" I whispered.

"You watch," he said. "Beats the old stethoscope hands down."

He touched a switch on the machine, and six zeros popped up on the liquid crystal display on the front. He held it against the door of the safe close to the combination dial, and as he turned the dial gently, he moved the little box across the face of the safe until the display went crazy. "Gotcha," he said, reset it, and placed it back on the face of the safe in the same position. Then the hard work started. As he manipulated the dial, the display changed again, but more slowly. "This could take a while Mr. S. Why don't you sit down and relax," he said.

I tried, but I found it very hard. I was on hot bricks. Each move of the dial seemed to take hours, and I couldn't even smoke. After about fifteen minutes Monkey said, "Won't be long now."

"Thank God," I said. "I've got to take a leak. I'm bursting." I went into the en-suite bathroom and admired the solid gold fittings as I did just that. As I was finishing, I heard voices from the bedroom. I froze, then went and listened at the door. Definitely voices. Male. One was Monkey's.

Oh shit, I thought and took the pistol from under my arm, let off the safety, and cocked it. I opened the door slowly and silently. Monkey was standing by the safe, which was open. Facing him, with his back to me was another party—average height, black, slicked back hair, and a dinner suit. He must have been a refugee from the reception. He was holding a revolver in his right hand pointed at Monkey's midsection. In his left hand was a large briefcase he tossed to Monkey. "Fill it up," he said in a voice that only had a trace of a foreign accent. Monkey must have seen me, but being the pro he was didn't bat an eyelash. He caught the case and stood holding it. I crept over the thick carpet toward the man. "Come on, quickly," he said.

I touched the back of his neck between his hairline

and his stiff white collar with the barrel of the .45. He stiffened, and I saw his finger tighten on the trigger of the revolver. "Don't even think about it," I said. "Yours is double action. Mine's cocked. You'll be dead before you can shoot."

He took my word for it. Wise man. And I saw his finger relax. "Good boy," I said and reached over and took the gun out of his hand. "Now turn round."

He did as I ordered. He was a stranger to me. "Mr. Mole, I presume," I said.

"Have you seen what's in here?" said Monkey.

I stepped back slightly out of the mole's reach and looked. The safe was packed with bank notes and jewel boxes.

"There must be a quarter of a million quid here at least," said Monkey. "In cash. And a load of tom. He wanted the lot." He sounded quite offended.

"So that was why we were supposed to leave everything but the ring," I said to the mole. "Your payoff."

The man said nothing, just shrugged his shoulders an inch, and twisted his mouth in a grimace.

"But you wanted the ring too, didn't you?"

Another shrug, another grimace. Almost a smile that time.

"That would have been a nice little pension for you, wouldn't it? No wonder you made it so easy for us to get inside. But you weren't expecting two of us, were you?"

He opened his arms in gesture of surrender.

"Is the ring there?" I said to Monkey.

He fiddled about inside the safe and opened a couple of ring boxes, then said, "Here it is."

"Right. Give it to me, and let's go."

"What about the rest?"

"We leave it. That was the deal."

"Mr. S."

"That was the deal. Now do you want a foreign government and our own after us for the rest of our lives? I told you these people never forget. Leave it. Give me the ring and let's get out of here."

"If you say so."

"I do."

Monkey walked round to me, being careful not to cross my line of fire, and gave me the ring. It was beautiful and reflected the light like a miniature sun. "What about him?" asked Monkey.

"I'll lock him in the bathroom," I said. "Come on you." I pushed the mole into the room I'd recently vacated, shut the door, and locked it on the outside. I emptied his gun and dropped it and the bullets on the floor, then I holstered mine and we left.

Monkey looked terrified again when we got out on the balcony. "Go," I said.

He hung his bag over his shoulder and started down. I followed. Halfway down he froze. Solid. His hands clenched on the scaffolding rails. "I can't Mr. S.," he said. "I can't."

I banged on his hands with my clenched fists. "Go Monkey," I said. "You've got to move."

"No." As he said the word, I heard shouting from above us and the sound of breaking glass, and the mole stuck his head through a window and started shouting in a guttural language I couldn't understand. It looked like he'd gone double on us and was trying to save his own skin. I knew I should have knocked him out. From the front of the house I heard answering shouts. I leaned right over to loosen Monkey's grip, and the Colt .45 slid out of the holster under my arm and fell to the ground. I made a despairing grab for it, but missed. As it hit the ground it went off, and a bullet spanged against one of the scaffolding supports. The noise of the gunshot and the whine of the bullet as it ricocheted by us galvanized Monkey into action. He let go of the pole he was holding and scuttled down the scaffold like greased lightning. I wasn't far behind him. We dropped the last few feet. There was no sign of the gun, and I didn't have time to stop and look for it because as we hit the ground two men came round the side of the house just a few yards away from us. Both men were carrying machine pistols. I gave Monkey a shove, and we ran toward the gate we'd come in by. We crashed through the under-growth, the men in pursuit. I pulled open the door, dragged Monkey through after me, slammed it again, and locked it.

He was trembling and pale in the light from the street lamps and breathing hard. We turned in the direction of my car, when another two armed men turned the corner from the direction of the front gate and cut us off. "This way," I shouted, grabbed Monkey's arm and headed downhill in the direction of the river.

From behind us I heard the sound of gunfire. Our original two pursuers were shooting the lock off the gate. The odds were getting worse. I touched the ring that nestled in the pocket of my jacket and urged Monkey to go faster. We got to Victoria Embankment, dodged through the traffic heading east, jumped the central reservation and across the other carriageway. Monkey was breathing like an engine. "I can't, Mr. S.," he gasped. "Leave me, I'm done for."

"No," I said. "We're together whatever happens." We reached the pavement by the river, and Monkey fell against the embankment wall. I could see that he was finished. The guards had reached the other side of the road and crossed through a break in the traffic. I looked around for help, but the road was empty except for the cars that rushed past. It was all over for us. I pulled Monkey up to his feet, and we stood watching as our pursuers moved in for the kill. The first one to reach our side of the road pointed his machine gun at us. No one said anything. As the rest arrived, we were covered by half a dozen weapons. Then the mole came running down the hill, crossed the road, and catching his breath, said, "You have something that belongs to us."

"No," I said. "I have something that belongs to the Queen of England." Pompous, maybe, but the best I could come up with at short notice.

The mole held out his hand. "Don't be foolish," he said. "Give it to me."

"And if I don't?"

"Then we kill you and take it anyway."

I put my hand in my pocket and took out the ring. It shone like ice and fire and picked up the colors from the lights along the embankment and in the houses and offices opposite us. "No," I said. "You can't have it."

One of the armed guards moved toward me, and I turned and hurled the ring as far as I could across the black water behind me. I didn't even hear a splash. "Go on then," I said to the mole. "Fetch it, boy."

He stepped over and slapped me hard across the face. One of the other guards made ready to fire. They were so busy that they didn't hear the sound of the three dark-colored Ford Granadas pull up at the curbside a few feet from where we were standing. They didn't hear the doors opening, or the eight khaki-clad men step out. But they did hear the sound of eight automatic weapons being cocked ready to fire. The guards froze, and as the soldiers' weapons were also pointing at Monkey and me, I moved my accomplice out of the line of fire. I was prepared to do a lot for my queen and country, but dying at the hands of our own security forces was not one of them.

"All of you, weapons on the ground, move away, and lie facedown. Now," said one of the soldiers. Then he spoke in that guttural language the mole had used. I imagine he was repeating the order for anyone who didn't speak English. The guards seemed to get the message. One by one they put their guns on the pavement, moved away, and lay facedown, arms and legs outstretched. "Now you two," said the soldier to me and Monkey. "The same."

"Give us a break," I said. "We're on your side."

From one of the cars stepped the major. He was as immaculate as ever. "Leave them, Jones," he said. "I'll deal with them."

"Sah," barked the soldier and lowered his gun and went to help his mates deal with the guards.

"Bit of a cock-up," said the Major to me.

"Not our cock-up," I said. "Your man tried to double-cross us."

"Did you get the ring?"

"'Course we did," said Monkey. "A piece of cake."

The major smiled thinly. "So where is it?"

I looked at Monkey, then the major. "I wish you'd got here a couple of minutes earlier."

"Why?"

"I thought they had us."

"And?"

"And I wasn't going to give them the ring back."

"So?"

"So I threw it in the river," I said. I pointed behind me. "In that direction. I don't know exactly how far. Sorry."

"Sorry," repeated the Major. "Is that all you can say?"

Needless to say we didn't get *all* the rest of the money promised. But I convinced the major to give Monkey his three grand as arranged. After all, although the ring was lost forever in the silt of the Thames, at least we'd saved Her Majesty the embarrassment of it being worn to the palace by a foreign diplomat's wife. Also, as I explained, people like Monkey don't understand the subtle nuances of the Official Secrets Act. They just understand cash. I even slung him my original deuce to sweeten the pot. I didn't think that Monkey was going to be shinning up too many drainpipes in future, and it's hell getting on a government retraining scheme at his age. And he had turned up, scared as he was. That had taken a lot of guts, and I admired him for it. So in the end I came out with nixes. But that's the breaks.

I didn't hear from the major for over two months. Autumn had come, and the nights were drawing in. I was in my office again one Friday morning when the phone rang. "Sharman," I said.

"Good morning."

I recognized the glass-cutting tones at once. "Major."

"She wants to see you."

"Who?"

"Who do you think?"

"You mean ..."

"This is an open line, Sharman," he interrupted. "No names, please."

"Of course. When?"

"Tonight."

"Where?"

"She's attending a civic function in Croydon." He said "Croydon" as if it were a disease. Which I suppose in a way it is.

"What time?"

"I'll pick you up at seven at your office. You do know how to behave, I trust."

"I was a policeman, remember. It's one of the first things you learn."

"Capital. Seven o'clock then."

"I'll be here." And we both hung up.

He was right on time. So was I. I wore a navy blue suit, white shirt, subdued tie, and shiny black shoes. I'd shaved twice and had a hair cut. He looked me over when I got in the back of the Daimler. "You'll do," he said. I took that as a compliment.

We were in Croydon by 7:30, and the chauffeuse steered the car into an underground car park near the town hall. It was huge and empty except for a Rolls-Royce at the far end. "Go on then," he said. "Don't keep her waiting."

"Aren't you ... ?"

"You're on your own. It's not me she wants to see."

I stepped out of the Daimler and walked across the car park, my heels clicking on the concrete. As I got closer to the big car, I saw the royal pendant on a tiny gold pole on top of the radiator where the flying lady normally was. As I got closer still, a uniformed chauffeur leapt out of the front and ran round and opened the passenger door closest to me. I walked up to the open door and peered inside. "Do get in, Mr. Sharman," said a woman's voice—one I recognized from countless radio sound bites and TV news segments. "It's freezing in here."

I did as I was told and perched on the edge of the

wide leather seat. The chauffeur closed the door after me and stood a few feet away from the car, hands clasped behind his back. I felt I should stand to attention and bow, but it's difficult in the back of a car, even one as large as the Rolls. As my eyes became accustomed to the darkness in the car, I saw her sitting in the far corner. The heater was on and the car smelled of expensive perfume, and was so quiet I heard the rustle of her nylon-clad legs as she moved. "You wanted to see me, ma'am," I said. "Ma'am." How bad's that?

"I wanted to thank you."

"It was nothing."

"I'm sure it was."

I didn't reply. Modesty forbade it.

"I don't have to tell you the favor you did me," she continued.

"Anyone could have done it."

"I doubt that. Unfortunately, there can never be any official recognition of what you did."

"I didn't expect any," I said. "Besides, we were well paid."

"No, you weren't. You gave yours to your friend. I know all about it. I think that was very honorable of you."

Honorable, that was a first, but I loved it.

"Anyway money isn't everything," she went on. "I know that better than most, believe me. So I wanted to give you this." She extended her hand, which held a small, battered leather box.

"It's not necessary," I said.

"It is. This belonged to my great-grandfather. He won it in the First World War. It's one of the few things I actually own myself. So it's very precious to me. That's why I want you to have it."

"You're very kind."

"I'm famous for it. Take it, please."

I reached over and took the box. As I did so, the light from outside caught the stone she was wearing on her finger. I recognized it right away. "Is that the ring?" I asked.

"Yes," she said.

"But I threw it in the river. Did someone dive for it?"

"No. It was discussed, but the mud there is three feet deep at least. It would have been impossible."

"So how come?"

"The one you recovered from the embassy was a copy. A very good copy. There are copies made of all the crown jewels."

I felt confused. "So why bother getting us to steal it back?" I asked.

"Because real or not, the very fact that that damned woman was going to wear it to the palace would have caused no end of fuss."

"So we risked our lives for a piece of paste?"

"No, Mr. Sharman, you risked your life for me. Would you have done that if you'd known?"

I looked at her shadowy figure. "Of course," I said. And do you know, I would have, too.

"Then open the box."

I did as I was told and turned it into the light to see what was inside. It was a medal—a very old medal with a faded purple ribbon. "Ypres," she said.

"I really can't accept this," I said.

"I insist. It's an order, Mr. Sharman. A royal command if you like. You can't refuse. I could have your head cut off if you tried."

"Then I'm very proud."

We sat there for a moment in silence. Then she said, "I'm afraid I must go. Duty calls. It's a bore. I'd rather sit here with you and talk some more."

"I'm flattered," I said. And I was. But I knew when it was time to go. I reached round and opened the door and backed out. "Good night," I said.

"Good night."

I closed the door behind me. The chauffeur ran back to his seat, and the car pulled off. As it went, I saw her pale face looking out of the back window at me. I went back and joined the major. "What happened?" he asked.

"She gave me this," I said and showed him the box

and its contents. He took out the medal and looked at it.

He was silent for a moment, then said, "For valor. Stuff and nonsense."

Then he got his chauffeuse to drive me home.

The Lemon Juice Plot

by Molly Brown

A crowd armed with staves gathered in front of St. Mary's Church, Oxford. Men wearing hats strung with green ribbon handed out leaflets depicting the Catholic Duke of York with horns and a tail, setting fire to London. One of their number ascended the steps to address the crowd: "Shall England be subject to the whim of Louis? Shall proud English men be slaves to the will of France and the Devil that sits in Rome?"

"No!" the crowd replied.

"No slavery! No popery!" the men distributing the leaflets prompted the crowd. Immediately they took up the chant, "No slavery! No popery!"

"Look!" said the man at the top of the stairs, pointing. An ornate coach came into view, heading toward Christchurch, where the court was in residence while Parliament met in the university city. The sole occupant of the coach was a woman. Chestnut ringlets framed the heart-shaped face beneath her large round-brimmed bonnet, a copy of the latest style from France. Her dress was copied from the French court's style as well: wine-red satin with a white lace collar, cut low. Around her neck she wore a chain of pearls set in gold. At the sight of her, the crowd went berserk. "It's Madam Carwell herself! The Catholic whore who poisons the mind of the king!"

Someone shouted, "Death to the Catholic whore!" The mob surged toward the coach, repeating "Death to the Catholic whore!"

The coach was quickly surrounded; the crowd rocked it back and forth, baying for the blood of the Catholic whore. The woman inside it took a deep breath and opened the window. "I pray you good people, be civil," she said. "I am the *Protestant* whore."

The man closest to the window shouted to those around him, "Stop it, you fools, it's Nell Gwyn!" He turned back to the woman in the carriage. "Please forgive us, Mistress Gwyn. We thought you were the Duchess of Portsmouth."

The crowd stepped aside and allowed the carriage to continue on its way.

It was the 28th of March, 1681.

Nell walked into the hall at Christchurch, made her way up the stairs, and paused outside the king's private chamber. She knocked on the door, ruffled her hair, and struck a dramatic pose, gasping for breath and clinging to the wall.

The door was opened by Louise Renée de Keroualle, the Duchess of Portsmouth, dubbed Madam Carwell by the common people who could not pronounce her name. "*Mon dieu,* Nellie," she said, "you do look a mess. Have you been back at your old profession?" She turned to the king, who was lying asleep on a sofa on the other side of the room, dressed in red knee-length velvet breeches and nothing else. A long black wig hung from a hook on the wall; the king's head was bare, revealing the close crop of his own hair, which was now more gray than black. "Charles, the ageing orange-girl is here to see you."

The king opened his eyes; he leapt up and rushed to the door. "Odd's fish," he said, placing one arm around Nell. He led her over to the sofa and had her sit down beside him. "Nellie, what happened?"

"I was nearly murdered by a mob, sir."

"What?"

"It's true, sir. They wanted to tear me limb from limb."

Charles pressed her face into his bare shoulder and gently patted her head. "There, there, my poor darling. It must have been dreadful for you."

Across the room the Duchess of Portsmouth drew

her mouth into a thin line and crossed her arms. She cleared her throat loudly.

Nell raised her head and looked straight into Charles's eyes, her own open wide and sparkling with mischief. "No sir, indeed I thought it quite wonderful, really." She indicated the duchess of Portsmouth with a tilt of her head. "They thought I was *her.*"

"Nellie, for shame," the king said, stifling a laugh. Louise de Keroualle ran from the room, slamming the door behind her.

"Now that's done it," Charles said. "There'll be no peace in court for a week."

When Nell returned to her own room, her maid presented her with a sealed envelope, addressed to Mistress Eleanor Gwyn. Though the message was brief, Nell spent several minutes staring at its contents, frowning in deep concentration. Completely illiterate when she first came to court, she still found reading a slow and difficult business. Finally, she threw the letter on the fire and instructed her maid to pack her belongings immediately, she was returning to London.

It was a moonless night. Two men carried a sedan chair through the twisted streets and alleys off Drury Lane, preceded by a link-man with a lantern. Young boys carrying long hooked rods scattered, exposed by the light. Passing beneath an open window, the chair was splattered with the contents of a chamber pot.

When the chair turned into Lewkenor's Lane, the lantern became the cause of much consternation and cursing from the shadows—more than one couple hastily rearranged their clothing at the approach of the chair. The chair came to a stop, and Nell Gwyn stepped out, her face hidden by a mask. "Wait for me," she said.

She approached one of the houses and knocked. The woman who answered the door reeked of strong ale and old perspiration. "Lost your way, dearie?"

"I wish to speak to Madam Ross."

"Looking for a job, dearie? We'll have to see what's

underneath that mask first, won't we? Your figure
looks well, but your face may be scarred by the pox for
all we know."

A short, thick-necked woman came to the door and
pushed the other aside. "Come in," she said, "we can
talk upstairs." The thick-necked woman's hair was
gray and so thin her scalp showed through it; in length
it barely reached her shoulders. Her nose was large,
threaded with blue and red veins, her eyes were blood-
shot, and she had no teeth. Nell followed her through
a noisy front room, crowded as any tavern. The air was
heavy with a mix of cheap perfume, smoke, and the
smell of raw sewage. Raising a small lace handkerchief
to her nose, she struggled to hold her breath.

As she passed, one man, who already had a woman
sitting on one knee, called out that he had another knee
ready and waiting at her service, and knees weren't all
he had to offer. "Your loss," he muttered as she kept
walking.

"Why the mask, Nellie?" the thick-necked woman
asked when they were alone in an upstairs room, furnished with nothing but a bed and two chairs. "You
were raised in a house much like this one. Are you too
grand to be seen with the likes of us now?"

Nell removed the mask and flopped into one of the
chairs. "Too grand?" She shook her head. "No, not I.
But there are those who would use my visit here
against me if they were to learn of it. I should have
traveled to Windsor with the court now Parliament is
dissolved, but I begged His Majesty to allow me to return to London as a dear friend was ill. So please,
Madam Ross, tell me what matter of life and death is
so urgent that I must lie to the king and jeopardize my
position at court."

"Just a minute. I must fetch someone first." She left
the room and returned a few moments later, accompanied by an old man. His knee-length frock coat and
breeches were made of coarse, dark brown cloth; his
stockings and his shoes were caked with mud. The fingers of his right-hand glove were nearly worn through.
The man's gray hair was lank and greasy, hanging well

below his shoulders, but his posture was straight and his eyes were alert and intelligent.

He smiled broadly, revealing a full mouth of tobacco-stained teeth. "If it isn't little Nellie! My, what a fine lady you've become."

Nell stared at him blankly.

"You haven't forgotten me, have you? Thomas Shaw? I knew your mother when you were a child."

"Thomas? Of course I remember! I must have been five or six years old, and my father was in prison and my mother had no money, and my sister and I might have died of the cold had you not brought us coal for the fire and socks for our feet. How could I ever forget such kindness?"

"Madam Ross said you would not forget an old friend and she was right."

"What can I do for you, Thomas?"

"I would never ask you for money, though a few shillings from one in your position—who surely must have pounds to spare—would not be unappreciated. No, there is another reason for requiring your presence so urgently. I have something to tell you of great importance: Madam Ross and I believe we have uncovered a plot."

Nell rolled her eyes and threw up her hands. "God's flesh, not another plot! His Majesty is sick to death of plots. I am sick to death of plots. Everyone is sick to death of plots! Thanks to Lord Shaftesbury and his informer, Mr. Titus Oates, we've heard of nothing but plots and conspiracies for three years now! What, pray tell, are the pope and the Duke of York up to this time? Thanks to good Mr. Oates, we now know the papists set fire to London, and we know they were responsible for the plague. So what will their next trick be? Are the Jesuits secretly draining the Thames dry? Or perhaps the French plan to invade by digging a tunnel beneath the Channel! Surely that's no more ridiculous than anything the Whigs would have the people believe."

"Hush, Nellie, and listen," said Madam Ross. "Thomas has found something in a book."

"A book? Is Thomas a man to read books?"

"I have it here," said Thomas. He reached into a coat pocket and handed a small leather-bound book to her. The cover was charred black, and the pages within were singed at the edges. "I'm afraid it's slightly burnt."

"Why? What happened to it?"

Thomas cleared his throat. "When I first came upon it, the pages within were blank. I thought it worthless and tossed it on the fire. The book fell open and in the heat I saw writing appear on the pages as if by magic, so I fetched it out again."

Nell raised one eyebrow. "Magic? The traitor Coleman used lemon juice."

The old man shrugged. "Just look, and you will see why the writing was hidden."

Nell slowly made her way through several pages, moving her lips and pointing to each word with one finger.

On the first page were inscribed the words: *To my most kind patron, a record of my experiments.* The rest was in the form of a diary, with scribbled entries beneath each day's date. Much of it was incomprehensible; it appeared to be written in a foreign language. Other pages were covered with nothing but rows of numbers and strange symbols. But then she came upon a roughly sketched map of Whitehall and the words: *Have made contact with one in her service. Price £200. Obtain from L.S.?* There were two X's, a short distance apart on the map; Nell recognized the locations they marked. An entry dated 18th March read: *Parliament to Ox. C. remains London. Meet C. tonight.* Under 20th March were the words: *C. instructed in knife. Before king and others? Best way to avoid suspicion. Must wait for return of court.* The final entry was for 26th March, the previous Saturday: *To my sister in Essex. Back Friday to meet C.*

Nell looked up, her lips pursed in thought.

"Don't you see, Nellie?" said Thomas. "They plan to kill the king. With a knife, in the very heart of Whitehall Palace! See how they've marked his quarters with an X?"

"Surely such intelligence is worth something," said Madam Ross, "and there's the proof in writing. Is not the king generous to friends who would save his life?"

"If this is what you think, then why summon me? Why not take this to a magistrate?" Nell asked, removing several coins from her purse.

"A magistrate would ask me where I got it."

She held the coins just beyond the old man's reach. "And do you really believe I will not ask the same question myself, Thomas?"

The next morning, Nell took a coach to the home of the playwright Aphra Behn. Nell sank into a thickly padded sofa while Aphra studied the charred diary at a desk beside the window. At the age of forty, the playwright's light brown hair was already streaked with gray, and her once-round face had begun to sag, forming deep creases on either side of her mouth.

Nell closed her eyes and found her thoughts wandering back to the days when she was the seventeen-year-old toast of the Drury Lane stage whose face and wit had captured the heart of a king. She was thirty-one now, and suddenly she felt very tired. Her eyes fluttered open at the sound of Aphra's voice. "I use blank books such as this to do my own writing. But the contents of this journal are most strange. Wherever did you come across this curious volume?"

"I was given it by an angler who sent me a message through Madam Ross, begging me to return to London at once."

"An angler? One of those rogues who push hooked rods through open windows? Let me understand this. A common thief summons you to London and you abandon the king of England to keep the appointment?"

"He believes the book refers to a plot—"

"A plot! That's original," Aphra interrupted dryly.

"—against the life of the king," Nell continued, ignoring her, "and Madam Ross agrees with him."

Aphra threw her hands up. "If a thief and a brothel-keeper believe it, then it must be true."

"But the layout of the map concerns me," Nell car-

ried on, again ignoring the interruption. "Those X's on
the map don't mark the king's apartments."

"Whose apartments do they mark then?"

Nell curled her upper lip. "Squintabella."

"Who?"

"Louise, the Duchess of Portsmouth."

Frowning, Aphra opened the book to the page with
the map and carried it over to Nell. "If this X is her
apartment, what is this X over here?"

"That's her kitchen—all the kitchens in Whitehall
are separate from the residences. The king is building
her a house, over here"—she pointed at another part of
the map—"because she says the twenty-four rooms she
has now aren't good enough and if the king doesn't
build her house exactly the way she wants it, she'll sob
and she'll weep, and she'll make him pull it down and
start all over again. That's what she did the last time.

"The king's rooms are over here, by the river. And
this passage leads directly from His Majesty's bedchamber to those of the Maids of Honor. The
Queen"—she dragged her finger dramatically across
the page—"lives at some distance, over here." She
looked up expectantly. "What should I do, Aphra?
Should I take this to the king?"

"This is all very thin, Nell; there's not much here at
all. Page after page of gibberish, then a map and a few
scribbled notes. We've already had the Popish Plot and
the Meal Tub Plot; would you go to the king with a
Lemon Juice Plot?"

"But it does mention a knife."

"So? We all own knives; my kitchen is full of them.
Perhaps this is nothing but innocent scribbling, though
there are other possibilities you might consider. Perhaps your supposed friends are not your friends at all.
Perhaps they mean you harm and this is a hoax meant
to discredit you, or even to incriminate you. If this
book was truly obtained in the way you describe, are
you not in possession of stolen property?"

"I do not believe Thomas and Madam Ross would
treat me so ill. They both knew me from a child."

"Perhaps they are but unknowing pawns to another

who plots against you. Are there none who resent your influence over the king? None who would be glad to see you banished from court?"

"There is one name that springs to mind. But though the weeping willow may have the desire, she has not the wit."

"But we must not forget one final possibility. Perhaps your friends are right, and the king is in danger."

"It makes me dizzy to consider so many possibilities."

"Then you must reduce them to only one: the truth."

"That I would do gladly. But how do I discover the truth? I have not the slightest idea how to gather intelligence. I have no experience of investigation." She paused for effect, watching Aphra's reaction. "But you do."

Aphra shook her head violently. "No," she said. "I cannot help you."

"But you were a spy in the war against Holland."

"And what did it benefit me? Nothing! My intelligence was ignored, and I was never paid. I have sworn I would never be so used again."

"I'll do everything myself," Nell pleaded. "Just tell me where to begin."

"No," said Aphra. "Instead I will tell you where to stop. Here. And now. Suppose there is a plot? No one will believe you. And no one will thank you."

"They will believe me when I present them with proof!"

"That's what I thought, once. To be a spy is a thankless task, Nellie. I know this from cruel, hard experience."

"I care not what thanks I may receive. And I care not whether experience be cruel or hard. I care for the king, do you understand? Charles is surrounded by those who care only for what he can give them; be it position, power, money. I care only for the man. I love him, Aphra."

Aphra sighed and shook her head. "Let's get started, then, shall we?"

* * *

"Is that the house?" Aphra asked as their coach pulled to a stop in front of a small house only two floors high and extremely narrow.

Nell opened the window and stuck her head through. "I believe so," she said, turning back to Aphra. "This is the address Thomas gave me. He said he was here with his rod late Saturday night."

"I see a small window still open . . . up near the top," Aphra said. "Your friend Thomas's rod must be a long one."

"I assure you I've never seen it," Nell answered quickly.

"According to the diary, whoever lives here went to Essex on Saturday last and does not return until tomorrow. Let us see if this is true."

The two women disembarked from the coach and walked up to the door. Aphra knocked, and getting no reply, examined the downstairs front window. "No fear of running into servants. The shutter is filthy."

They walked through a narrow passage alongside the house. It led to a tiny back garden, planted with rows of herbs, surrounded by a high fence. The gate swung open at Aphra's touch, and she walked down a path to the house's back door. She ran one gloved finger along the frame. "Perfect," she said.

"Aphra!" Nell said, horrified. "I pray you're not thinking what I fear you're thinking?"

"In broad daylight, with the whole street having seen us and a coachman waiting out front? I wouldn't dream of anything so foolish," Aphra assured her. "We'll come back tonight."

At midnight they shared a jug of wine for courage and at half past the hour they left Aphra's house, dressed in clothing borrowed from the wardrobe of Aphra's late husband. Passing as men, with their breeches and long jackets and wide-brimmed hats, they traveled the dark streets on foot, unnoticed— something they never could have done in women's clothing. They walked the long way around, avoiding Covent Garden, which they knew would be full of brawling drunks, and eventually came to Holborn and the lane where the little house stood. The only light anywhere came from the upstairs window of a tavern a short way down and across the road.

Moving stealthily in near total darkness, they crept unseen into the passage and entered the high-walled garden. "There's still time to change your mind," Aphra whispered. Nell shook her head. Aphra reached into her pocket and took out a long, thin piece of metal that she slid between the door and its frame.

They entered through the kitchen, wrinkling their noses at the smell. Some vegetables lay rotting in a basket on the floor; a joint of meat sat on a table, covered in green mold, but the overpowering odor was not one of decaying food. Carrying lit candles, they walked past a rusting metal bath tub and into the tiny front room.

The only furnishings were two wooden chairs and a sofa that had one corner propped up with bricks where there should have been a leg. They entered the hallway behind the front door and walked up creaking steps to the upper floor, the bad smell that permeated the house getting stronger.

In the rear they found a small bedroom; in the front they found a laboratory. The walls were lined with shelves, some piled high with thick leather-bound volumes, others displaying rows of glass bottles and jars, at least three deep. There was a table in the center of the room, crowded with more bottles and jars and various arrangements of glass tubing. Nell held her candle up to one of the jars on the table and grimaced in disgust. It held a dead toad suspended in liquid. A label on the jar read: *venin de crapaud.* Other smaller jars were labeled: Arsenic, Monkshood, Foxglove, Vitriol, Antimony, Prussic Acid.

By the window there was a desk cluttered with notebooks and more bottles. Here they found the source of the smell: the bottle nearest the window had tipped over and shattered, spilling its contents over the desktop. The spillage had since dried, but it still gave off an acrid odor that burned the women's lungs.

"That's thanks to your friend Thomas and his hook," said Aphra, indicating the broken bottle. "So our friend the plotter is a chemist. That explains the pages of seeming gibberish—they were chemical formulations."

"I have seen a chemist's laboratory before; the king has one at Whitehall. But it is nothing like this! How can someone work in such a place as this?"

"I've seen worse," Aphra said glumly, examining the papers on the desk before putting them to one side and opening the top drawer. Inside, she found a collection of anti-papist leaflets and satirical cartoons—and several letters addressed to Jeremiah Hopkin. The letters were unsigned and partly written in a crude form of numerical code, but their meaning was clear: the Duchess of Portsmouth was the plotters' target, not the king.

"Squintabella!" Nell exclaimed. "Who'd want to kill the weeping willow?" She slapped her forehead. "Stupid question! Who *wouldn't* want to?"

"Quiet! Would you have us go to prison? I have been there Nellie, and I can tell you there is no place worse."

"Sorry," Nell whispered.

"So what would you do now?" Aphra said. "The plot appears not to be against your beloved king, but against your worst enemy. You've always said you'd give anything to be rid of her, and now someone seems prepared to do your bidding. This seems a plot to your advantage. Would you still wish to snare the plotters?"

Nell threw both hands up to her face. "I don't know."

"If you wish to pursue this no further, only say the word. We will return to our separate homes and forget the entire matter. My silence may be relied upon."

"Oh no, Aphra! Loathsome she may be, but I cannot stand by and let her be murdered. Let us snare these plotters, if we can."

Aphra shrugged. "I was afraid you'd say that." She reached into her coat, producing a small volume identical to the one nearly destroyed by the angler—except that this one was blank and showed no sign of having been thrown on a fire. She bent back the spine and ruffled the pages to make it look used, then she placed it on the desk, next to the window. "Nothing must be missing, nothing must appear to have been disturbed. Jeremiah Hopkin must suspect nothing, or he will cover his traces, and there is much more we need to know if we would trap him. Now let us risk no more time here. Our purpose for tonight has been accomplished."

They returned to Holborn the next morning, again disguised as men. "We can watch just as well from the tavern over there," Aphra said. "The view should be clear."

They entered the tavern slapping their thighs, winking at the barmaid, and completely overdoing their portrayal of two men in search of a hearty breakfast. The two "men" sat at a table by the window.

A short while later, Aphra stood up. "Look," she said, pointing across the street.

A tall, bespectacled man was getting out of a hackney carriage. He was extremely thin and dressed entirely in black: black hat, black coat, black breeches, and black stockings. He wore no wig and seemed to have little if any hair. He walked up to the narrow house across the way, carrying several bags that he placed on the pavement while he searched for something in his pockets. Then he took out a key and went inside.

Aphra turned to Nell and smiled. "The prodigal son returns."

According to the diary, Jeremiah Hopkin was to meet his co-conspirator, "C," upon his return on Friday. So they waited—sometimes inside the tavern, sometimes leaning against the wall outside—and watched. It was nearly dark when a ginger-haired young man knocked on Jeremiah Hopkin's door and was admitted.

He left half an hour later, followed by Aphra. Nell stayed behind to watch the house. Fifteen minutes

later, the bespectacled chemist walked out into
Holborn, heading east.

Nell could hardly believe it when she saw the house
Hopkin had entered; it was the residence of Lord
Shaftesbury, leader of the Whigs. She waited outside a
while longer and saw a man whose small eyes and
large chin she recognized at once—the man whose testimony had begun the anti-papist hysteria, Mr. Titus
Oates.

When Nell arrived home, Aphra was waiting with
the news that she had followed the ginger-haired man
back to Whitehall Palace and discovered he was a servant in the Duchess of Portsmouth's kitchen. "What
will you do now?" she asked. "Inform the king?"

"I will," Nell assured her. "I will. When the time is
right."

She came upon Charles in the woods outside Windsor, a hooded falcon at rest upon his arm.

"Nellie!" The king's face lit up when he saw her. "Is
your friend recovered from her illness?"

"Yes, sir." She scanned the faces of the courtiers
surrounding the king. "Is Louise not here, sir?"

"I believe she's in her chamber; you know she cares
not for sport. And what will you do, Nell? There are
many diversions here for you to choose from."

"If Your Majesty has no objection, I'm most anxious
to visit dear Louise. I've missed her so."

Nell found it hard not to laugh when she saw the
shocked faces and raised eyebrows that surrounded her
on all sides.

"If you wish," said the king, a puzzled expression on
his face.

Two days after the court returned to Whitehall, Nell
accompanied Louise to the afternoon performance at
the King's Theatre. They took their seats in the middle
gallery during the interval between the second and
third acts. A row of girls stood below them in the pit,

holding baskets of fruit on their arms and calling, "Oranges, will you have any oranges?"

"Wouldn't you be more comfortable down there, Nellie?" Louise asked, tilting her head toward the orange girls with a mirthless little smile. "I'm sure you could use the money. The king gives you so little, and it does show." She shook her head in mock sympathy. *"Mon dieu,* that dress!"

Nell turned to her and smiled, shaking her own head. *"Mon dieu,"* she said, imitating Louise perfectly, "that face!"

In the pit below a dark-haired man approached one of the orange girls. From where she was sitting, Nell couldn't see exactly what happened, but she heard the girl squeal as though she'd been pinched. The man swaggered away carrying several oranges, a smug expression on his face. He was heading toward the middle gallery. "Hide yourself, Louise," Nell whispered, raising a hand to cover her face, "it's that horrid Samuel Pepys."

"Oh no," Louise groaned, raising a hand to her forehead and resolutely staring into her lap. "First you, now him! How can this day get any worse?"

"All the actresses laugh at him and his airs. But he's still one to watch; his hands wander as much as his eyes. Do you know when I was an actress, he used to come backstage into the tiring room to watch me dress!"

"The poor man must have been desperate!"

Without a word or sign of warning, Louise stood up and headed for the exit halfway through the third act. Nell leapt from her seat and followed her up the aisle.

"No need for you to come," Louise hissed.

Nell ignored her, walking close behind and scanning the crowd for any sign of suspicious movement.

They walked out the door and into Drury Lane, where Louise's coach was waiting. "Why must you follow me everywhere I go?" Louise asked as Nell climbed into the coach and sat down beside her. "Why

constantly plague me with your presence? Why won't
you leave me alone?"

"I merely wished to see the play, Louise."

"Then why leave before the finish?"

"It wasn't very good."

"You're planning something," Louise said, her voice
rising to a hysterical pitch. "You think I don't know
you're plotting against me? My maid saw you in the
hall outside my quarters at three this morning. Why?"

"Perhaps I find it hard to sleep," Nell said.

That evening, the guests around Louise's supper table included the king, three members of the Privy
Council, and Nell.

Nell was the only one who hadn't been invited.

"Dear Nellie," Louise had said with a forced smile
as the others arrived, "I'm sure you have important
business elsewhere, and I wouldn't dream of keeping
you from it. If you wish to take your leave, I assure
you no one here will take offense."

Nell had refused to take the hint.

She was enjoying Louise's little party, and she was
particularly enjoying the fact that every word she
spoke caused another little line of tension to form on
the other woman's face. Louise was so obviously un-
comfortable, squirming and seething and struggling to
hold her temper in front of the others, that Nell began
to wonder why she'd never thought of tormenting the
woman this way before. "A toast to my dearest
friend," she said, raising her glass and barely sup-
pressing a giggle.

A young man entered the room, carrying a large silver platter. The king slapped the table. "Ah, at last
here's the meat!"

Nell narrowed her eyes and took a deep breath. She
recognized the man with the platter. She watched intently as he placed the platter on a sideboard and with
a large knife, began to carve the meat and serve it to
the guests.

Everyone had been served except the Duchess of
Portsmouth; the ginger-haired servant paused to wipe

the blade with a cloth. Then he prepared a final slice, put it on a plate, and served it to the duchess.

For a few brief seconds, as he placed the plate in front of her, he was only inches away from her rival. Nell tensed, ready to jump into action. But nothing happened. He put the plate down and moved away. He'd left the knife on the sideboard.

Of course Nell knew it would be madness to stab Louise in front of all these witnesses, but the diary had specifically mentioned a knife—and that he'd been instructed in its use. Then she remembered the part that read: *Before king and others? Best way to avoid suspicion.* Whatever he was supposed to do was *meant* to be done in front of the king and other people—something they would all witness yet never suspect. But what?

She thought again about the knife—he'd cut several slices of meat, wiped the blade with a cloth, and *then* he'd cut Louise's slice. She thought back to the toad suspended in liquid, the labels on the jars she'd seen in Holborn: Arsenic, Monkshood, Foxglove, Vitriol, Antimony, Prussic Acid. All poisons!

Louise speared a piece of meat on a three-pronged silver fork and raised it to her mouth. "Stop!" Nell shouted, leaping from her seat and knocking the fork from Louise's hand.

"*Mon dieu!* Have you gone mad?"

Nell pointed after the young man, who had already bolted from the room. "Seize him!"

"Calm down, Nellie," the king said, embarrassed.

"Seize him! The meat is poisoned!"

The privy councillors gagged and dropped their forks.

"Not yours, hers!"

The councillors ran from the table and sounded the alarm. Guards and servants rushed in all directions.

"The poison was on the cloth," Nell told Louise. "He wiped the blade with it before slicing your portion."

Outside, there were running feet, shouting voices, and blowing horns. Inside, there was Louise, sobbing.

"Oh, Charles, I've never been so frightened. Someone tried to kill me."

The king took her in his arms, cooing and patting her on the head. "There, there, my little Fubs. Charlie's here and he won't let anything happen to you."

Nell rolled her eyes. "Fubs." She hated it when the king called Louise "Fubs." "Excuse me, Louise, but did you perchance notice I just saved your life?"

"Charles, I think I'm going to faint."

Charles, keeping both his arms around Louise, began to lead her toward another room. "Poor darling, let's get you tucked into your bed."

"Wouldn't Your Majesty like to hear how I single-handedly uncovered a dastardly plot to murder one of your court?"

"Later, Nell," said the king, closing the door behind him.

The next morning, Nell took a hackney coach to Aphra's house. She found her in the front room, writing in one of her little blank books.

"Well?" said Aphra, looking up.

"You were right. It was a thankless task."

The Searcher

by *Gwendoline Butler*

(In the late eighteenth century and the early decades of
the nineteenth there was no regular method of record-
ing deaths. Two old ladies in every parish were em-
ployed to view and record all dead bodies. They were
called Searchers. This system was open to confusion
and corruption, especially in the two great cholera ep-
idemics of the period. An act of Parliament was passed
requiring a death certificate witnessed by a registered
medical practitioner.)

I am a Searcher, sir, you may not know that name,
but it is what I am. We go out in twos in each parish
to view the new corpses dead and record the numbers.
They go down in a Bill of Mortality.

I am Betsy Trotter. Trotter, sir, Trotter, and this is
my friend, Martha Cant. We are both widows, sir. No,
I am not sure of my age, sir, but I remember the wedding of King George and Princess Charlotte. I can't
say about Martha, sir, but she is older nor me. That is
a wig she wears.

(I tell this to a sharp-eyed young gentleman in a
bright-colored weskit with lots of black curls. I do not
tell him my age, but I am sixty-seven come Michael-
mas because he is writing down what I say and might
be a government informer. He writes very fast, not in
ordinary writing but full of dots and dashes. Nor do I
tell him that Martha Cant took the wig off a dead duchess and that it had the lice in it.)

Are you sure you are not ill, sir? I see you are crying. There is a great deal of sickness about.

He says no, but he feels emotion easily and ours is

a sad trade. Underneath the wig, Martha is bald, perhaps he guesses. I have to stand on a chair to talk to
him. I am strong in the shoulders and arms but poorly
in the legs. Skimped as to legs, sir, not my fair share.

What shall I tell him? There is much to tell about
death, but not a lot of variety, it is always the same in
the end when I see them. There was the year when the
cholera was on the streets and much panic.

Martha and I see we have a shedful of bodies without a home.

Paupers, beggars, travelers with no name, found
dead in the gutter, in the market or fallen off a stage-
coach.

We go round checking, finding a name if we can.
Not many have a name on them, fewer still an address
or the wherewithal to get buried. A mass grave for
them.

Twelve we have here today.

We work from different sides of the room and meet
in the middle.

"Here's one that's not dead," I say to Martha.

"Leave him be," says Martha. "He soon will be."

We moved round the room.

"Has he got a watch on him, or other waluabbles?"

I put my hand on his chest. No watch, but I feel his
heart beat. His eyes open. I have strong nerves or I
would scream because those eyes have seen death. He
has come back, but he has been there. Persons who
die and whose eyes are not closed have that look on
them.

I got a wet rag and wiped his mouth and squeezed a
few drops of water through his lips.

"Leave him be," called Martha, "he might as well be
dead as not, and he's more profit to us dead."

We are paid by the body count.

I was moving away when his eyes opened and his
lips moved. "Brandy," he muttered.

"You'll be lucky, my fine gentleman," I thought.
"Brandy indeed." But Betsy Trotter has a kinder heart
than for her own good. I chanced to have, it being a

cold day and gin a protection against the sickness as we well know, a bottle of gin and water in my pocket.

I held up his head and let a drop pour through his mouth. "You'll do, my dear," I thought. "But we shall have to come to terms. Gin comes dear where I live." Although he had lost his hat, the quality of which you can always tell a togger by, he was wearing a thick top coat which, stained with mud and vomit, was newish. Nothing in his pockets. Someone had been through those before he came to us.

"Where's he from, Martha?" I asked across the room.

She raised her head from the female body that occupied her. "The landlord of the Fox and Grapes says he was found in the alley between St. Mary's Church and the barracks."

It's a good house, the Fox, and the gentry's servants drink there, as do soldiers on guard at Kensington Palace where the young princess and her mother live.

So it is like that this corpse to be has some money. If not on him for that was took afore we got him, but to his hand somewhere.

I see he is moving his head. He would breathe easier if it was propped up. He is laid on a big table (for do not think we has a table for each body, no they share as they will do where they lie later) and behind him was a little woman. So I move her nearer and let him rest on her. She will never know. And an honor for her, for I know her face now, and it is Charlotte Swithers and she has lain with many men for a farthing and drink of gin. Not that I hold that against her for a woman must live and her husband died from a Frenchy bullet at Salamanca.

My face reaches to the tabletop so we are nose to nose. He has a red scar curving round his cheek toward his nose. I have seen enough scars like that to know what it is: a sabre cut from one of Boney's men. So he is an army man. An Old Soldier.

He might still go, of course. Sometimes these returners have a spasm of life left in them before the puff goes out. I left him while I went down the row, counting the tally. The cholera takes you quickly. I might go myself. Be here tonight counting the dead, and be lined up with them myself by tomorrow.

I walked on down the line, making my tally. I knew some of them. I uncovered one face: Linnet Bird. I covered her face again. She had a child, I wondered where she was.

Before I left, while Martha was counting what she had in her pockets, I went to the Old Soldier. His eyes were closed. Gone, I thought, a waste of my good gin.

On the step a small figure was crouched. Looked at me with big dark eyes. "My mum's in there."

I patted her head and put my hand on my lips. No answer was the thing here. There was half a broken bun in my pocket which I gave her. She took it quickly. "Thank you, ma'am."

She was shivering with cold and a nasty rain was beginning. There was a battered old shawl on her mother which being of no value, I had left where it was, but it would do for the child. I went back to get it.

I plucked it off together with a spotted red-and-white neckerchief that looked better than it might have done. Linnet had a small knife in her pocket. I had missed that before.

A noise made me look back to the Old Soldier. He was half sitting up now. "Where am I? Is this hell?"

Not yet, my fine gentleman, I thought, but by the looks of you, you have a good chance of finding out soon. But Mrs. Trotter has a kind heart as many will speak to. "Stay there, sir," I said, "and I'll have you out."

I went back to the girl on the steps. She hadn't gone, where had she to go? I handed her the shawl. "Put this round you."

"Thank you, missus."

"What do they call you?"

"Some call me Little Bird, missus, but I am Emily."

"Emily, you know Tipsy Larret with barrow?" He was the one-legged man in Farthing Alley who did errands.

She nodded. "I know him."

"Go to say that Betsy Trotter wishes a borrow of it and will settle with him tomorrow."

I went back in and the Old Soldier was sitting up now and groaning. "This is death and I did not know."

I could not carry him, of course, but he got his arms over my shoulders and so got him to the door and on to the barrow. Emily had been quick. So we set off: Me pushing the barrow, the child hanging on behind, and the Old Soldier propped up in it on to Farthing Alley. Penny Court is just behind. I lives in Penny Court. The ground floor back. My old black cat met me at the door and came in with us.

I set him down on the floor, made myself some hot gin and water, and gave the child a sip or two, on account of her needing warming up. The cat accommodated himself on the Old Soldier's feet.

I sat back and considered what to do with him. He was, as things stood, my property. But the moment he got his strength back, he would be his own property.

Every day little matters come up that must be weighed: so much paid out here, so much owed to me here, equal balance, calm of mind, balance being in my favor; happiness, unbalance not being in my favor, unhappiness. Not to be considered. Here I had paid out gin and carriage.

So much this way, so much that. In short, how I was to be paid back?

I thought about this as I cooked us a little supper. The Old Soldier managed a spoonful of broth. He was coming alive again with every minute. Talkative, he became. I've noticed this happens when a person comes to themself again after an illness. I have been a midwife and nurse before I became a Searcher. "I have to thank you," he muttered, dropping off to sleep again.

He was recovering fast. Too fast for some of my plans. He had been drunk and been sick, there was evidence for that, but I saw he had also had a blow on the back of his head. Robbed and left for dead? Or had he got an enemy?

Be careful, Betsy Trotter, I said to myself, he is not what he seems.

The child was asleep. She was older than I had thought, either very small for her age, or aged for her years.

He woke up and licked his lips. I gave him a hot toddy and took some myself. "You feel better, sir?"

"In every way, ma'am." He looked around. "You brought me here?"

"I did, sir."

He shuddered. "Out of that charnel house."

He remembered then; I would see he did not forget.

"Take a little more to drink, sir."

"I will, I will." He drank eagerly. "You will be repaid, no fear of that." He was patting his pockets and muttering of his pouch and his watch.

"None in the world," I thought.

"Your name, ma'am?"

"Mrs. Betsy Trotter, sir."

"A widow?"

"These many years, sir."

He looked round the room. "And not left well provided for."

"Not rich, sir, no"

"But takes in strangers and poor children." He was speaking richly, feeling the gin. "But now you will have a friend at court, Mrs. Trotter." His eyes were closing again. "Jeremiah Flood, at your service. The king's servant, ma'am. The king himself shall say thank you."

"King William?"

His head rolled backward sleepily. "Flood shall save the country."

"Law, sir, not a revolution, not a bloody revolution?"

He was almost asleep; a thick deep chuckle came from the back of his throat. "No, Mrs. Trotter, not a revolution." As he went to sleep, his eyes seemed to turn toward the girl, and he muttered, "Death comes to us all. A child dies easily."

I looked the girl asleep on the floor with my black

cat on her chest. Not that one, I thought. A mother who beat her (for I knew a little of Linnet Bird), starvation and cholera, she didn't die.

"You alarm me, Mr. Flood." The name was one I had heard before.

"Sergeant Flood, formerly of His Majesty's Dragoons."

"You'll have served against the French?"

"That I did, and saw many a good man die and many a knave come through."

And a good man or two hang, I thought to myself. "I have heard of you, Sergeant Flood."

"Jemmy Flood has been mentioned, ma'am, I will not deny it."

"Have you had what you deserve, sir, as your reward?"

He said dreamily, "The ways of the palace are hidden from such as you, Mrs. Trotter."

Fool, I thought, do you think there is only one way into the palace? That you can only go in through the big front gate? There are always back ways in.

Kensington Palace, built by King Billy the Dutchman and lived in it for a while so they say, and haunted by him so they also say. And lived in now by lots of little dried-up princesses and old generals and the Princess Victoria and her German mother. Little old Princess Sophia lives there now, she who held out that her brother, the Duke of Cumberland, did not kill his valet which we all know he did. I know Princess Sophia, but she does not know me. When her maid had a baby by the big red-headed footman, it was Sarah Trotter who came in by the back ways to deliver the child and take the child away with her and none the wiser.

Nor was it the first time for that particular maid. If all her family had lived, she'd have had a fine family. All dead though, bar one. Some children will die however hard you tries to save them, while another one with just the same treatment will live. It's the perversity of them.

In the morning he was up and spry. He had no

money on him, therefore he could not reward me, but he had a lodging in Lirripet Lane and he would come back.

"You might do a service yet, Mrs. Trotter. Perhaps you know a place where I could stable a horse?"

"There is the Fox and Grapes. The landlord there keeps a stable. And a fine lot of broken-down critturs he keeps there."

"Very public, Mrs. Trotter. I am a man that likes a quiet life."

Ah, I thought you might be, I says to myself. "There is my friend Solomon Moon in Fagin Place."

"Fagin Place? And I might need to hire a nag."

"Solomon could oblige, I am sure, sir."

"I am a respectable man, Mrs. Trotter and can pay my way. The Duke of Gloucester is my reference."

"The duke, sir?"

"As I swear."

The child had waked up and was sitting gazing at us with eyes as clear and sharp as my old cat's. She'll know him again, I says to myself.

The Old Soldier hobbled off, back ramrod straight but finding it painful.

"Emily, my little pet, follow that gentleman, and see where he goes. Then come back to me and tell me. And then there will be a bite of breakfast for a good girl."

She slipped through the door without a word and followed him like a little shadow.

When she had gone, I put on my bonnet and went round to Fagin Place.

Solomon was up as he always was. He slept standing up or sitting in his big chair.

"Solomon, you and I have done business together."

"So we have, Mrs. Trotter."

"I have sent an old soldier to you, he will tell you what he wants. It may not be what he really wants. A deep man."

"I have seen through deeper, Mrs. Trotter."

"He's been robbed. It could be, Solomon, that his

bits and pieces may come your way. In the course of
your business."

Solomon said: "They may."

"Keep them, Solomon, and look at them well. He is
a mystery, is Sergeant Flood."

Next day, he came back to me, Solomon did, he was
sitting waiting for me when I came home. The cat, the
child, and Solomon, all in a row.

"You were right, Betsy Trotter, right as usual." From
out of his pocket, he drew a leather pouch. He put it on
the table and put beside it a fob watch. From inside the
pouch, he took a wad of paper. "I paid over the odds,
they had been through several hands before mine."

"And did Sergeant Flood come himself?"

"He did. He brought in a good chestnut and I have
hired him a mare. My best dapple mare."

I knew the broken-down beast.

"And what did you make of him?"

Solomon screwed up his eyes. "Not an honest man,
Betsy, and a liar."

I thought the same. The child had followed him to
the palace stables.

"But that may be to our advantage."

He unfolded the paper on which I could see writing. He held it toward me, but I did not take it. I cannot read easily although I can make my lists of the
dead.

"Here is a map of Kensington Palace, three spots are
marked. One says THE DUCHESS, another says PRINCESS
SOPHIA, and the third says SIR JOHN."

"Robbery?"

Solomon was thoughtful. "A man who keeps a map
of a palace and wants a secret place to hire a good fast
horse has more on his mind than robbery."

"Murder?"

"Murder in a palace is like to be treason."

If ever a man had looked ripe to be hung, drawn,
and quartered and his head parboiled and put on London Bridge, then the Old Soldier did.

Solomon folded the paper and put it away in his pocket. "I have a job for you, my dear."

I knew Solly and his jobs. The black cat leapt away as if he knew them, too. "Emily," I said, "fill the kettle and mind your ears. And you need not hurry back." She went off down the court to the pump with the kettle and was gone some time while I let Solly tell me what he wanted.

"Very well, Solly," I said when he had done. "And I may have a job for you, too."

The knife in my pocket needed sharpening, one of Solly's special jobs.

The young man with the dark curls and the bright waistcoat who was writing down at speed this tale had dried his tears. He was interested in the criminal, in the prisoner about to hang, in the wretched in body. It touched his own heart with fears from his own childhood. He listened to Mrs. Trotter and thought how she told her story as if it was yesterday or today (as perhaps for her it is, he muses) but it must have happened years ago. He had a tender heart especially for stories of poverty and disablement, but he had detected something more sinister about Mrs. Trotter.

John Leftside, footman to the Princess Sophia, is a good friend of Betsy Trotter when he is not half seas over. When he is drunk, he falls asleep and does not wake for hours. There is a good deal of drunkenness in the back corridors of the palace, for the beer is free and the hours are long. Coachmen and footmen are the worst because they do so much waiting about.

There is a little door by a back privy that is never locked, and John Leftside was there, on the ground with his eyes open and a cockroach crawling across his face.

"Johnny, my dear, who is in the palace?"

"Those who must be," he muttered.

Johnny Leftside knew everything that went on; he listened as he waited at the table, listened at doors, looked through keyholes, read letters.

He meant no good to anyone, did Johnny Leftside,

and those who thought he did (like the Princess Sophia and the Duchess of Kent) were wrong. He was one of a pair of matching footmen, chosen for their height, and that was what he was. Johnny Rightside is his pair, and what one does not hear the other does. But Johnny Rightside frequents the Turkish Divan in Bond Street where he meets many gentlemen and hears the gossip there.

"The Duchess of Kent, the Princess Victoria, Sir John, the Princess Sophia? Johnny, do you know Sergeant Flood?"

He put a finger to his nose. "Jolly," he said. "But not to be followed. John Leftside tells you. Come along, Betsy," he says.

Then we retires to a backroom where in return for certain small services I perform for him, he tells me that he has seen the Old Soldier talking to the groom of Sir John Conroy, to the elderly pages of the Duchess of Kent and Princess Sophia. It is the opinion of Johnny that his game is blackmail or abduction or worse of Sir John, he being the lover of the Duchess as is well known, which the Duke of Cumberland cannot abide, her being the mother of the young Princess Victoria.

At this point the young gentleman taking down the story wonders if Mrs. Trotter is telling all here and suspects she is not. He observes all and takes in all, this his nature. He lets her go on.

After this, standing in the stables, I see the Old Soldier talking to the groom who is harnessing the princess's pony. I have seen the princess riding in the Kensington Gardens, and she wears a loose jacket of brown velvet and a large velvet hat that covers her face.

When I saw the horses led round to the front of the palace, I knew where to go. Backstairs wind and creep and are not lit, but you get there in the end.

The princess's room was big and empty. Not even

tidy, and the fire was out. Palace servants are as slack and apt to leave their work as other servants.

The room was well furnished, but the carpet was small, and I have seen richer curtains in citizens' rooms where I have viewed the dead. A table with books and writing pens.

A velvet jacket and a large hat with ribbons lay across a chair. I gathered it to me and hid it under my cloak. This was what Solomon wanted.

Against one wall a long bench lined with tiny wooden dolls, many score of them, all dressed as if for the play in silk and feathers and bright gauze. One lady in silk held two babies, one in silk and one in cotton. One doll dressed like a queen, another like a king. A doll dressed like a bride, another like a widow.

I reached out and took the baby dressed in cotton. It looked like a shroud. I put it in my pocket. The maid to the chambers would be blamed and from what I had seen of her work, she would deserve it.

"So," said Solomon. "Sergeant Flood knows his way about the palace. And Johnny thinks he means to abduct Sir John for the Duke of Cumberland. But Johnny is wrong. Someone else is the victim."

He knew Johnny, knew the duke, too.

"Now we know why the Old Soldier 'as asked me to find him a smooth, fast, very fast nag." Solomon managed a smile, as near as he could. Some might think it not very like. "So it was good I gave him the most docile beast in the world. Anyone might ride her."

And this would be a horse that knew its own way home. Leave it for a minute and it would be off to Solly. He never lost a horse, they were trained so.

I read his eyes. "The princess is to be taken off to her uncle the Duke of Cumberland."

"Would that be treason, Solly?"

"The duke would be a powerful friend." He looked into my eyes. "It might be to our advantage."

"Sergeant Flood is not to be trusted."

Nor was I. Nor was Solly.

"We must look after ourselves, Betsy Trotter. I shall go myself with the pony to hand it over."

"And where will that be?"

"A belt of trees just beyond palace gates. The young lady will ride it with the groom, the pony knackered, and in the confusion she will be taken there and then and ride off on a new pony with the sergeant."

"We are owed a debt."

"And debts must be paid."

His eyes met mine. "Betsy Trotter is a true friend," I said. "Profit, do you think, Solomon?" There is always a profit to be made if you look.

"Profit, Betsy. There must and will be profit."

I have the red-and-white scarf and the knife which is now nicely sharp in my pocket, and I show them to Solomon. They have a use, I say.

He agrees.

We are as one, Solomon, I think. "When is the pony ordered for?"

"A week today."

"Time enough. You will do the arranging? You know how to talk, Solomon."

"Trust to me, my dear."

"And after all, what is a child? Children die easily."

"And go straight to heaven, Betsy, we must never forget that, for they have no sins upon them."

"Bless them, bless them one and all," I says.

Bless you, child. I say too when I see Emily; you have tidied the hearth and kept the fire going, that is a good girl. I put my hand into my pocket. "Here is a present for you."

I handed her the puppet baby dressed in cotton. It looked like a shroud.

She took it eagerly. "Thank you, thank you, Mrs. Trotter."

"But you must be a good girl and do what you are told. Always do what you are told, Emily, and you will go to heaven."

"I will be good."

Then I hand over to her the red handkerchief and

the knife which I tell her are the last presents from her dear departed ma and she will find a use for them.

She was examining the puppet. "What is it wearing, Mrs. Trotter, all so white?"

"I think it is dead," I told her. "It is a little innocent that died and has gone to heaven."

I am a Searcher, sir, I say once more to the young gentleman who has been taking notes and does so again. And I am used to death. I have seen the old and the young die, the innocent and the wicked. I have seen them dead peacefully in their beds and violently on the cobbles. I have seen a hanged man and a violated child. I have seen them die of this and that and there is not one of them that would not die easier with a drop of gin or brandy.

Thank you, sir, and Martha would like a drop as well, would you not, Martha. Take no notice of her, sir, she does not speak much.

Some days went by, and each day I went to the palace and saw Johnny Leftside who was drinking more and more. I was neglecting my work and Mrs. Cant was getting crosser with each day that passed, the cholera not having subsided and her work being heavy.

"I must take the child every day for a walk, Mrs. Cant," I said. "A child must have the air."

I took Emily each day to see the Princess Victoria ride out. Emily enjoyed it and was quick to learn what she should. I could quite love a little angel like that, and I have promised her a visit to the pantomime at Christmas.

"Will I still be here at Christmas?" she asks.

"Ah, who can tell? We none of us know what lies ahead, my dear."

"I thought that," she says.

The young gentleman does not know what to believe as Mrs. Trotter, the Searcher, tells her tale.

Perhaps he has let her drink too much gin. Martha Cant has long since crept out of the gin palace as if she had heard this tale too often before.

But Betsy Trotter goes on.

So one sunny day, a young girl rides out of the palace and under the trees. She was wearing a loose velvet jacket and a big hat that hid her face. Her groom rode behind.

What went on next, Betsy Trotter did not see, but there is an animal scream, muffled shouts, the noise of a struggle, and then the sergeant and the girl on the one horse gallop out of the trees.

"Two of them were seized, but the sergeant got away with the girl." A smile on Solomon's face. "He sped away to the household of his illustrious friend." Solomon's teeth came down in a snap.

"What will they do to him when they find it is the wrong girl?"

Solomon shrugged. "Kill him perhaps. They are all ruffians together."

"And Sir John was grateful?"

Solomon slapped a bag of coins on the table. "And he showed it. He hates the Duke of Cumberland. The duke cannot be touched. The princess did not ride that day."

"It is a pity about the girl, Emily." I say. "What will become of her?"

There are so many things that can happen to a young girl in the streets of London, but Betsy Trotter did her best for her.

The young gentleman has decided that Mrs. Trotter is not telling him all, and he has ceased to write in his notebook. The Princess Victoria is someone who figures in his dreams and he has often gone to watch her ride past. But she is seventeen now so that this story of an attempted abduction and the thwarting of the plot by Betsy Trotter and Solomon took place years ago. If it happened at all, he supposed that the footman Johnny Leftside must have helped them. Stories about the abduction of the princess by the duke of Cumberland and how it was foiled have gone about London long enough, but he cannot use this in his *Sketches of London*. This is a gin-soaked fantasy from the old Searcher.

Next day, says Mrs. Trotter, when I go to the counting with Mrs. Cant, the cholera still going strong, she says to me:

"Oh look, I swear here is the man who was here before and not dead."

"He is dead this time," I say, and I untie the red-and-white handkerchief that is tight round his wicked throat. But I know what has done the real job; I put my hand on his breast where I feel a narrow, bloody knife slit.

"I know how to get revenge. What, let the Duke of Cumberland who had my husband hanged for stealing a horse, let him become king and the little princess die like the little princes in the Tower? Let Sergeant Flood who gave testimony about my husband and watched him drop and enjoyed it, go free?"

The young man puts away his notebook. He has not listened to the Searcher's mumble.

He sees a young girl come forward from the shadows. He looks at her in surprise and question.

"I am Emily, sir."

"You came back?" He has a picture of the young girl, escaping from her captors, making her way to the only home she knew. He has a vision of a young hand drawing something tight around the neck of the Old Soldier, drawing out a knife. And he knows that she will walk through his mind forever, sometimes bearing one name, sometimes another. She will die virtuously, she will die violently. She will be a virgin betrayed, she will be a young wife, she will be a whore, always the betrayed, always the betrayer.

She looks at him with a smile, but does not speak. Perhaps she has forgotten, perhaps none of it ever happened.

She takes the old Searcher by the arm. "Come along, Mrs. Trotter."

They go off together, the Searcher and Emily, to whatever London has in store for them. They are a sad, pathetic sight, he thinks, but terrible, too.

The Stranger

by Michael Z Lewin

As the bus pulled into Jesper, Indiana, the stranger took his Gladstone bag from the overhead rack. Almost alone on the bus, he was the only passenger to alight. As he passed the driver, he said, "Thanks awfully. You gave us a smashing drive." The driver turned his head toward the voice, but the stranger had already begun to descend the steps to the new town.

Four people waited on the curb. The bus would continue in the direction of Bedford and Bloomington, eventually arriving in Indianapolis before dark. The fat man at the front of the line made space for the stranger, but not a lot. Even so the stranger smiled and nodded to the man, and then he nodded to each of the other would-be passengers, all women. None gave him a second glance.

The bus stop in Jesper is on the main street. The stranger considered which direction to walk in and picked what seemed to be toward the middle of the town. As he walked, he shifted his bag from one hand to the other and, later, back again. Finally he found a motel that seemed to be the only accommodation not part of a national chain. It was called the Sunrest and outside the door marked "Reception," he took a breath, lifted his chin, and muttered, "Jolly good." Then he walked in.

A middle-aged couple shared a couch as they watched an early afternoon game show. As soon as they noticed the stranger, the woman turned the sound down by remote control and the man rose, walked to the reception counter, and said, "Do something for you, mister?"

"I believe you can, my good man," the stranger said. "But first may one say this is a remarkably lovely town you reside in?"

The man took a moment to consider this unexpected response to his question. The stranger's voice caused the woman to look, and then rise from her chair.

Cautiously the man said, "You think so?"

"Oh, I do!" the stranger said with enthusiasm. "The more one travels, the more one comes to appreciate the virtues of small, honest towns in the heartland of this wonderful country of yours. The people in such places recognize what's important in life and they concentrate on it. Family. Business. Hospitality. It's wonderful, truly refreshing."

"You talk funny," the man said.

From behind his shoulder the woman's head appeared. "You're English, huh?"

The stranger smiled broadly. "I am, madam, I am. You are remarkably perceptive, if one may say so."

"I've heard your kind of talk on the TV," the woman said. "He is, Glen. He's English!"

"English, huh?" Glen said. The tone of Glen's nasal voice was neutral, but the face was welcoming. "My daddy was over there during the war. He was somewheres called Pontyfrat. You ever been to Pontyfrat?"

"I certainly have," the stranger said. "What an astonishing coincidence! I know Pontefract well."

"Well I'll be jiggered," Glen said. "Did you hear that, Edie? This here fella knows Pontyfrat."

"Welcome to Jesper, mister," Edie said. "So, what can we do for you?"

"To tell you the truth," the stranger said, "it's a slightly delicate matter."

"No credit," Glen said.

"It's nothing like that," the stranger said. "But my circumstances require considerable discretion. Although, if one may speculate, I'd wager that you both know how to be discreet. You strike one immediately as discreet people."

"Yeah, well maybe," Glen said.

"What's this about, mister?" Edie said.

"I am taking a brief holiday, a vacation as you good folks would say. I need to get away from all the hurly-burly for a while, family pressures. You know the sort of thing?"

"We sure do know about family, all right," Edie said.

"And I must say," the stranger said, "I feel I have come to the right place. I *feel* it. Precisely the right place."

"You have?" Edie said.

"Because you've already shown me exactly the kind of discretion that I shall need if I am to spend a week or two in your best room."

The couple glanced at each other. Glen said, "And what discretion have we shown, mister? 'Cause so far Edie and me have treated you the same as we'd treat anybody that come through that door."

"That's it exactly!" the stranger said. "I will need your assurance that you will treat me precisely as you would treat any other resident in your establishment."

"I don't get you, mister," Glen said. "Is there some reason why we wouldn't?"

Edie studied the stranger's face.

"Excellent!" the stranger said with a smile. "No reason. No reason at all."

"Now you mention it," Edie said, "you do look kind of familiar."

"Please, madam, don't scour your memory any further." The stranger tugged at an oversize ear. He scratched his beaky nose. He rubbed the bald spot at the top of his head. "I really do need to remain entirely incognito. No newspapers. No televisions. Just your best room for a week, or perhaps two."

"Lord love me, I've got it!" Edie said.

"Please stop!" the stranger said. "Don't even say it. If you do, I shall have to find other premises, and that will be a great disappointment because we were getting along so well."

"Naw," Edie said, changing her mind and shaking her head. "It can't be. Not here in Jesper."

"Thank you for your understanding and your cooperation, madam. Truly, it is most appreciated."

The best room at the Sunrest was only better than the others because it was farther from the street. The stranger unpacked his few clothes and hung them in the closet. Next he enjoyed a hot shower. Then, with a clean shirt, he dressed again, suit, waistcoat, tie. With toilet paper he buffed up his shoes. Then he sat for a while on the bed.

Before long there was a hesitant tapping at his door. Immediately the stranger rose and opened to find Edie standing outside his room.

"Why hello," the stranger said. "What can I do for you?"

"Sorry to bother you, Mr. ... Hey, is there something I can call you. I don't know what I'm supposed to say."

The stranger raised a hand and smiled. "Please. My friends call me Chuck."

"No kidding."

"And it would be my pleasure if you and your good husband were to do the same."

"Chuck. Wow!" Edie was giggly with pleasure. "And y'all call me Edie, and my husband's Glen."

"How do you do, Edie," the stranger said. He took one of her hands. He raised it and touched it lightly with his lips. "It is my very great pleasure to make your acquaintance. To tell you the truth, I was on the verge of coming to the office to ask you and Glen for another favor."

"You were?"

"But you've come here first. What can I do for you?"

"For me?"

"You knocked on the door for some reason."

"Oh, yeah. That. I wanted to check everything in the room was okay. You got enough towels and soap and stuff?"

"Everything is spiffing."

"Spiffing?"

"Perfect."

"Oh, great," Edie said. "But if anything goes wrong, you run out of paper or you want another towel, anything at all, you let me know, hear?"

"I will," the stranger said. "I won't hesitate. Thank you."

"So, why was you coming to the office?"

"I wanted a word with you and Glen. I'll meet you there in a couple of minutes. Okay?"

As the stranger entered the Sunrest Motel office, Glen and Edie stood behind the reception desk. Glen said, "Chuck, hi. What can we do for you?"

"First," the stranger said, "I want to keep from taking advantage of you."

"How's that?" Glen said.

"Is it not customary when an unknown traveler comes to a motel, for the traveler to make payment arrangements? I don't know how long I shall be able to stay here, of course, but it's only right that I pay in advance for my room tonight." From his wallet the stranger took a one-hundred-dollar bill. "Do you have change?"

Glen hesitated, but Edie said, "Shucks, we don't need that, Chuck."

"Well," the stranger said, "if you're sure." He put the money away and said, "There is also a favor I would appreciate, if you don't mind my asking."

"Y'all ask away," Edie said.

"I'd like some guidance."

"Guidance? About what?" Glen said.

"When I am away from home, what I enjoy, more than anything, is meeting people. Now, of course, in my situation it's rather difficult, but I thought that perhaps you two kind people could introduce me to a few of the local residents."

"You want to meet folks?" Edie asked, eyes widening.

"Only if absolute discretion can be maintained," the

stranger said. "But yes, I'd love to meet some of the good citizens of Jesper. Perhaps people in business like yourselves. Or people who entertain."

Edie said, "So you wouldn't mind going to folks' house for dinner or a little party?"

"I wouldn't mind at all," the stranger said, "as long as—"

"No newspapers, no TV. Am I right?" Glen said.

"Hi. I'm Phil Hoechstadtler, Glen's second cousin and Commissioner of Oaths. Glad to have you aboard."

"It's very gracious of you to extend the invitation at such short notice, Phil," the stranger said.

"Oh hell, no problem with a barbecue. Just throw on another steak. All I got to know is what to call you when it's ready."

"Just call me Chuck," the stranger said. "And make mine medium-rare."

"Come on through, Chuck," Hoechstadtler said. "Everybody is just dying to meet you."

"This is the most wonderful thrill for us," a woman said nervously as they shared the shelter of a maple upwind of the grill.

"Now now, please!" the stranger said.

"No, it is. We read all about England and everybody, and we love them, everyone. Though of course some of them we love better than others."

"And what do you do . . . ?"

"Connie."

"Connie."

"Oh, I'm just a housewife."

"Don't say *just* a housewife. One can hardly have a more complex and intricate task than organizing the daily running of a modern household."

"It can be quite a handful," Connie said. "Especially with three teenage boys."

"Mine are a bit younger than that," the stranger said.

"You got kids?" Connie asked.

"Yes, boys," the stranger said.

"Of course you do. Silly old me." Connie laughed

nervously. "Of course, our house is no palace, or anything."

"So tell me, Chuck," Lenny Kahlenbeck said, "how come you chose a little dump like Jesper to honor with a visit?"

"You do Jesper an unkindness," the stranger said. "I think it's most attractive, and in a beautiful part of the state."

"You been through southern Indiana before?"

"Once or twice. Never Jesper before, however."

"And you really like it?"

"I certainly do, what I've seen of it."

"You . . . want to see around? I sell real estate, so I know my way around pretty good."

"Real estate? Property, you mean?"

"That's right," Kahlenbeck said proudly. "I'm not the biggest in Dubois County yet, but I'm on my way."

"Might that include holiday cottages?"

Kahlenbeck squinted. "You mean a vacation home?"

"That's it," the stranger said.

"You interested?"

"I certainly wouldn't mind looking at one or two."

"Hey, you're talking to the right man if you're looking for property in Dubois County. And take it from me, there's not a better part of the state to invest in right now."

"I read somewhere that you like horses," said an elegantly dressed woman in her thirties. She carried a cocktail glass, but no paper plate of food.

"I can't imagine where you read that," the stranger said, "but it's true. I do like horses, very much."

"I'm Elvira Klingerman," the woman said. She offered her free hand.

The stranger lingered as he shook it. "I'm pleased to meet you, Elvira."

"They say I should call you Chuck, and they say I shouldn't ask personal questions."

"I can see you've been well briefed, Elvira. And, I must say, you are an extremely lovely woman."

Elvira laughed. "They also said you were Mr. Charm. I can see why now."

"I do meet quite a lot of women, but it's such a pleasure to meet someone I can compliment sincerely."

There was a moment when neither of them spoke. Then the stranger said, "Did you ask me about horses for a reason? Do you own some?"

"I do," Elvira said. "Would you like to see them?"

"I would," the stranger said. "Very much."

"Chuck, this here is my wife, Loretta."

"Hi," Loretta said, nearly spilling her drink.

"How do you do, Loretta," the stranger said. "And what a gorgeous bracelet, if I may say so."

"Diamonds and opals," Loretta said.

"It is good, isn't it," Loretta's husband said. "I can tell you have an eye for good jewels. Of course you would, wouldn't you."

"I try," the stranger said. Delicately he lifted Loretta's arm and looked at the bracelet more closely. "Yes," he said with genuine approval.

"I'm Ben Hanna," Loretta's husband said. "I'm a trained lawyer, but I inherited a jewelry business from my old man and I run that, too. It means Loretta gets to wear some real good stuff, and I can write off the insurance because she's advertising it."

"So you might have some pieces that would be suitable for gifts?" the stranger said.

"I sure do. Hell, you've seen this little wrist full of sparklers. Hold it up again, honey."

Loretta Hanna raised her arm unsteadily. At the same time she said, "I think they ought to do laboratory experiments on lawyers instead of rats, don't you? For one thing there's more of them, and for another you can get attached to a laboratory rat."

"Shut up, Loretta."

"Well, excuse my butt, mister smooth talker."

"No more to drink. Understand me."

"Well, I *no habla Engles* anymore all of a sudden."

"Excuse me, Chuck," Ben Hanna said. "You come down to the store, see if something grabs you where you can't say no. Anybody can tell you how to get there. Maybe catch you again later, after I sort out this little problem."

Mrs. Dexter put her arm around the stranger's waist and said, "Hey, tell me the truth, will you, Chuck?"

"What about, Mrs. Dexter?"

"About Margaret. I always thought she was the cutest little thing, but then she got a real raw deal over that captain. And now I hear she's a lush. Is that the truth? 'Cause that would be so sad."

"I'd really rather not talk about that kind of thing, if you don't mind."

"Oh, they told me not to. But tell *me* anyhow. I'll make it worth your while." She winked.

The stranger extricated himself from Mrs. Dexter's grasp. He said, "Please don't."

Mrs. Dexter drew back. "If you're so goddamned happy with that peroxide dress rack, how come you travel alone? Tell me that?"

"Margaret is *not* a lush," the stranger said stiffly. "In fact, she has one of the finest minds you would ever care to encounter. Now, please excuse me."

Near the end of the evening the stranger found Glen and Edie watching the Hoechstadtlers' television. Edie looked up and said, "About ready to go?"

"Yes, thank you," the stranger said.

"Have you had a good time?"

"Very nice indeed," the stranger said. "Your friends are fascinating people."

"I'd have called them just plain folks," Glen said.

"And they are extremely hospitable. Two even invited me to stay in their homes as their guests. People here are most marvelously friendly."

Edie's face wrinkled up. "Does that mean you're moving out of the Sunrest?"

"No, Edie, I'm not. I always feel that I'm not my own man when I'm staying in a house as a guest. Do you know what I mean?"

"I sure do, Chuck," Edie said. "And let me just say,

Glen and me are honored to have you in our little motel."

"You've made me feel very comfortable, and very welcome. And I continue to count on your discretion and cooperation."

The next few days were very busy ones for the stranger, and increasingly Edie acted as social secretary, taking messages and keeping track of when the stranger was available for lunch or dinner, for this excursion or that.

The stranger went out several times with Lenny Kahlenbeck to look at substantial homes in various parts of Dubois and adjoining counties. Isolation, as they discussed at length, would be essential because of the need for privacy. Kahlenbeck offered to help with a hi-tech security system, too, through a cousin.

The area the stranger found most attractive was near Patoka Lake in the Lick Fork State Recreation Area. But there were tempting houses too in Celestine, Riceville, Bacon, and in the ironically named English and Ireland.

By the third afternoon, however, it was clear that the stranger could not be easily satisfied and would not make a hasty purchase.

"But don't get me wrong," Kahlenbeck said. "I respect a careful man, I truly do."

"It *is* beautiful country," the stranger said. "And I certainly appreciate your generosity with your time. I particularly like the modern log cabins. Do you have any more on your files?"

"You've seen everything," Kahlenbeck said.

"But if something else came up, you wouldn't mind my coming back for a look?"

"I sure wouldn't," Kahlenbeck said.

"Good."

"Chuck?"

"Yes?"

"I wondered if I could ask you a little favor."

"What's that?" the stranger said.

"I don't begrudge a minute of it, but I've put in a lot of time with you the last few days."

"And I am very grateful, truly."

"What I was wondering was, would you mind if my little secretary, if she took a picture of the two of us together."

"Oh, I don't know about that," the stranger said.

"It would be just for me, maybe to hang on the wall behind my desk. I know how you want to make sure it didn't get in newspapers or anything."

"Even so," the stranger said. "It's a matter of . . . well, how things are done. What we call protocol."

"Don't you ever have your picture taken with people you meet?"

"Oh, sometimes. For instance, when I'm at a charity function."

"Charity?" Lenny Kahlenbeck's eyes narrowed.

"If, say, a local philanthropist were to make a large charitable donation to one of the causes I espouse. Alternative medicine, for instance, or population control. Well, it would be churlish in such circumstances for me to object to a photograph being taken with the benefactor."

"A donation, huh?" Kahlenbeck said.

"Yes," the stranger said.

"Like, how big a donation is 'large'?"

Having had considerable opportunity to assess the best answer to such a question, the stranger said, "Like, two thousand dollars."

"I see," Kahlenbeck said.

"So you understand," the stranger said affably, "it's probably best all around to forget the picture, because even if you wanted it I'd need the money in cash."

"Cash?"

"Well, think about it. Suppose I took a check. The charity could see immediately where I'd been. And then there would be no chance of my ever being able to buy a secret vacation home here, would there?"

"No," Kahlenbeck said. He considered. "I s'pose not."

"With no receipt, you wouldn't be able to deduct it

as a charitable donation," the stranger said. "But since you'd have the photograph you *could* deduct it as advertising. Especially if it were taken, the two of us together, in front of your real estate office, showing the name in the background."

The photograph was taken the next day.

The price to Ben Hanna, the lawyer-jeweler, was five thousand. If the stranger had worried that Hanna's legal training would make him balk at dealing in cash, he needn't have. Hanna agreed immediately, making the stranger wonder if, perhaps, he had pitched the level of the charitable contribution too low.

Elvira Klingerman made her charitable donations in an altogether different manner, and the stranger agreed to appear in several photographs with her, all Polaroids. The best were taken in the stables.

The stranger declined to dine with Mrs. Dexter, but twice ate with Connie, her three teenaged sons, and her trucker husband. Connie was "just" a housewife, but she was a marvelous cook.

In the late afternoon of his fifth day in Jesper, Edie appeared at the door of the stranger's room at the Sunrest with a boy of about five.

"Hello, Edie," the stranger said. "And who is this?"

"This here is Georgie," Edie said. "Georgie's my grandson."

"Is he really a prince, Gramma?" Georgie said to Edie. "Are you really a prince?" Georgie asked the stranger.

The stranger kneeled so that he could speak face-to-face with his chubby, energetic little visitor. "Am I really a prince?" The stranger winked up at Edie. "No, Georgie, I'm not a prince. Not today."

"My mommy says you're a prince."

"That's very nice of her," the stranger said. "But I'd say that *you* were mommy's little prince, wouldn't you?"

"What do you have to do to be a *real* prince?" Georgie asked.

"Well, gee," the stranger said, "I don't know. I guess you've got to try real hard. Are you going to do that? Are you going to try real hard and see if you can be a prince, too?"

"Okay," Georgie said, and then a horn sounded behind him and his grandmother.

"There's Daddy," Edie said.

The stranger shook Georgie's hand, but the boy pulled away and ran to his father's car. Both Edie and the stranger waved until the vehicle pulled out onto the street.

Then Edie stepped away and faced the stranger. She said, "I know."

"Excuse me, Edie?"

"I said that I *know*."

"What do you know?"

"I know what you've been doing."

The stranger said nothing.

"I have trouble sleeping sometimes," Edie said. "I leave Glen where he's lying, and I watch the all-night news. Last night they had some news from England, about them sad divorces. They showed the Queen of England and all her kids, and the program was about how hard it is on all of them, being royal."

The stranger was ready with a speech about the use of doubles, look-alikes, hired to enable members of the Royal Family to get time to relax away from home, away from the paparazzi.

But Edie said, "You never claimed to be him, did you? Not in so many words."

"No, I didn't," the stranger said.

"I've been thinking about it all day long. Glen even asked me what's the matter, but he knows I'm funny sometimes when I don't sleep, so he stopped asking."

The stranger considered saying he was sorry.

Edie said, "Thinking about it, I can't see as there's a lot of harm you've done. A lot of folks have had a good time because you was around, though I expect there's some that's paid for it. No more than they could afford, I shouldn't wonder."

The stranger said, "Thank you, Edie. You're a generous-hearted woman."

"Oh, no, I'm not," she said. "And I'm also not the only one in town that can't sleep sometimes."

"What do you want me to do?"

"I want you to pack your bags."

"All right."

"And then I want you to go down to the office. I want you to shake Glen's hand, and I want you to pay your room bill. You got enough money to do that?"

"Yes."

"You pay that bill in full, because it would about destroy Glen if he gave you credit and you didn't pay."

"I'll pay the bill in full," the stranger said.

"And then you get the hell out of Jesper," Edie said.

"Is there a bus? Or a train?"

"I don't know, and I don't care. But I want you out of this town before the sun goes down, and don't you stop moving till you're a hundred miles away. And don't you never come back. Most folks, when they're leaving, I say to them, 'Don't be a stranger now.' But you *be* a stranger, mister, or I'll have your hide, Glen or no Glen."

"I'll be on my way inside the hour," the stranger said.

Brotherly Love
An Angel Tale

by Mike Ripley

"Who's an ageing hippy?"

"You are. I thought they'd died out in the last century."

"Say that again," I snarled, "and I'll defenestrate you, if that's the correct term for someone who carries their teeth in their top pocket."

"Okay, okay, calm down. Watch the blood pressure, Angel."

"Then you watch your lip. Just remember, I don't have to be doing this."

"I know. And we appreciate it."

At last the royal "we" had appeared. I'd wondered how long it would be.

Technically, he was right about the last century. It was the first year of the new millennium, that no-man's-land between 1999 (year of religious fanatics and mega-huge newspaper supplements on who had done what and who was going to do what) and—at last—Stanley Kubrick's *2001*. The newspapers were getting ready for that one, too, offering prizes to anyone who could name another film with Keir Dullea.

People had gone ape-shit over the New Year, as you might expect, and I can't say I had a quiet time myself.

The "in" Christmas gift had been a checkbook, even for people who hadn't written a check for ages, because the date lines had all been reprinted 20—. The Jazz Warriors were top of the charts all over Europe, and the newest House release had an electronic drumbeat of 190 beats per minute. All this (except the checkbooks) made my New Year's resolution an early retirement from the music scene. The old B-flat trumpet was upended for the last time on New Year's Eve. That was it, no more jazz for me, I said. "No heart in it anymore?" asked the few friends who noticed. No, too bloody difficult; though I never said it.

I was even sticking to my job (well, four nights a week) as meeter and greeter at the Ben Fuji's Whisky and Sushi Bar in Threadneedle Street. I did it originally just for a weekend as a favor to Keiko, the daughter of the owner, who was called neither Ben nor Fuji, who had got me out of a tight spot in a night club in Chancery Lane (now there was a sign of the times!) one evening by proving to three argumentative out-of-towners that she really did have a black belt in karate.

To be honest, I quite liked the job. I knew enough about sushi without actually eating any, to blag my way through, and with a copy of Sir Michael Jackson's *Guide to Whisky* (29th edition) under my desk in the entrance hall at Ben Fuji's, I could always come up with a nugget about the 350+ whiskies the place stocked.

And business was booming, especially now we were starting the Golf World Cup, hosted in England for the first time. Since the anti-Japanese measures passed by the U.S. Senate in the mid-nineties and the subsequent boycott of anything involving the Japanese, the Americans were not taking part. Consequently, England were joint favorites with the Japanese, although we had Scotland in our qualifying group, which meant the odds were still generous. The World Cup, said to draw the largest television audience in the world, meant a large screen in the bar, showing golf (edited highlights in a window to the top right of the screen showing live action) twelve hours a day with video back-up facility if an act of God stopped play. The sponsors had ensured nothing else would.

It also meant lots of package-tour golfers, many of them Japanese, flocking into and through London, and Ben Fuji's was well and truly on their "must visit" lists. Knowing that the big prize money was put up by the Japanese these days, we also had a regular clientele of British and European golfers, many of them including a visit as part of their preparation for entering the Japanese Open.

Keiko would teach them Japanese food and manners, and I would tell them about Japanese drinking habits, then take their photographs on my Nikon Instanto and get their autographs. (To sell later if they made it.)

It was mostly a load of bull, as Ben Fuji's was hardly a traditional Japanese restaurant. The basement had originally been a "Japanese Room" with paper walls and floor mats. That had given way to a Nintendo virtual-reality golf driving range, which was far more profitable. In any case, European labor laws now prevented waitresses from serving men on their knees.

Basically, my job was vetting—and being nice to—the non-Japanese clientele. No rough stuff was required. Keiko and a couple of the waiters were more than capable of handling that, and one of the sushi chefs could pin a fly to the wall at thirty feet if the mood took him. The official job description was a sort of junior maitre d'. The subtext was more subtle. After their experience in America, every Japanese business preferred a domestic front man, however limited his powers.

So there I was, the acceptable face of sushi in Threadneedle Street.

Not that what happened had anything to do with Ben Fuji's being a sushi and scotch bar. It was just that I was working there the night Sam "Sinister" Dexter decided to call in and get drunk.

I had actually met Sam Dexter once before, though he wouldn't remember.

It had been at a press party to mark the engagement of rock 'n' roll legend Rory D. to that season's hot starlet from the Royal Shakespeare Company (sponsored, that year, by Brahma beer from Brazil—"where the nuts come from"). Rory D., or Rory Dee to be more accurate but less commercial, had played in a heavy metal band I knew called Astral Reich a few years before, and so I claimed lifelong friendship in order to get at the free booze and canapés. To be honest, I was going through a bad patch at the time, and I would have adopted Rory if it had got me into a free lunch.

I was standing at one of the buffet bars, balancing two plates and two glasses (all mine, though it looked like I was waiting for someone) and talking to a couple of Rory's roadies when he swayed across the room and aimed at a waitress clutching a tray of drinks.

I recognized him from the picture above his byline in the newspapers and also the two or three times I'd caught him on a late-night TV show. With twenty-six channels now, *anyone* can get on, but Dexter—"Sinister" to the media world—was usually good for some choice titbits of scandal. Ironically, he could get away with hints and innuendos on TV, which he would never dare print, even as "alleged" rumors, in his newspaper columns since the latest tightening up of the Privacy Charter Act (1993).

"C'mon, darling," he boomed as he reached the waitress. "Stop resting your tits on that tray and bung me some booze. I'm Sam Dexter and famous with it, and I don't intend paying for my drink."

"Why change the habits of a lunchtime," I muttered and the roadies sniggered in agreement.

Dexter made no sign that he'd heard me, and our paths didn't cross for the rest of the party. But three days later he used the line in one of his columns as if he'd said it about Rory D.

Isn't it amazing how long you can hold a grudge?

When Dexter came into Ben Fuji's that night, he didn't notice me. He staggered up to my desk and breathed secondhand alcohol at me and spoke to me, but he didn't *notice* me. I was not there to be noticed. I was there to serve.

"Table for one, my son. At the sushi bar'll do if you've nothing else, but don't cram me in like a fuckin' sardine. Give me two seats and some elbow

room, the most disgusting thing on your menu, four
portions—four, mind you—of that horseradish sauce
shit you serve and let me work my way through the
whisky list. Is that clear? Like me to run any of it by
you again?"

He rocked back a little too confidently on his heels
and produced a packet of cigarettes and a disposable
lighter. The cigarettes were American and a brand I
hadn't seen since they banned advertising cigarettes altogether.

He lit up and ignored me, pretending to examine
some of the prints on the wall. I wondered whether he
was expecting me to ask "Smoking or nonsmoking?,"
but I assumed he knew that no Japanese restaurant was
nonsmoking. As just about everywhere else in London
was, it was actually good for business.

"Table for one, sir, right this way," I said, turning
my back on him and leading him into the restaurant.

I held a menu to my chest, and as I caught Keiko's
eye, I upended it, showing her three fingers of my right
hand. That was our agreed warning sign for a "poten-
tially difficult customer."

As I was doing it, Dexter breathed in my ear: "Do
the *geishas* come in the service charge, or do I have to
negotiate privately?"

I added the fourth finger to the hand code: *We've got
a right bastard here.*

Keiko, all neat in a black two-piece suit, skirt one
inch below the knee as was proper and, as it happens,
fashionable, made her own code sign to me (two
specks of imaginary dust flicked off her sleeve) which
meant she wanted me in the kitchen, pronto.

Actually, she wanted to talk to me in the kitchen,
and no matter how many times I'd deliberately misun-
derstood her that way, she never laughed. This, after
all, was business.

"Okay, Tenshi, who's your friend?" she opened as
soon as the curtain hissed behind us. She called me
"Angel" in Japanese because it is my name.

"No friend of mine, though beings lower down the

food chain might claim an affinity with him," I said, keeping a watchful eye on Mr. Iishi, the sushi chef, who was sharpening his eighth knife of the evening.

"Speak English," snapped Keiko, "that's what we pay you for."

"He's a shit, Grade A."

"Then why didn't you bump him?"

"He's also a journalist, a notorious one and *your* standing orders say I have to be nice to journalists. It's part of your public relations policy. You know, Rule One: Keep smiling, but don't turn your back."

Keiko looked at me over the top of her glasses and shook her head slowly. I don't know why she blamed me for her headaches, though I've noticed other people do, too.

"Keep an eye on him, eh, Tenshi. Let me know if the boys have to deal with him." She straightened her skirt to go back into the restaurant, then remembered the monitor.

Ben Fuji's had video cameras hidden in four strategic points, with two monitors, one in the kitchen and one in the manager's office, which for all intents and purposes, was Keiko's, where there was a VCR. You'd never guess where the equipment was made.

The kitchen monitor showed Dexter sitting at his table, two glasses of whisky and one of iced water in front of him. He was scanning the other diners and leering at the waitresses, all dressed in kimonos and clogs, making them easy, slow-moving targets. Dexter wasn't quite ready to start groping yet, though. He kept looking at the menu and narrowing his eyes. He'd obviously had a long day, and I didn't think he'd spent it at the opticians.

He also did something else. Every few seconds his left hand would swoop near, sometimes onto, the brown envelope jutting out of his jacket pocket. It was the action of a man who thinks he left his wallet in another coat and needs reassuring.

There wasn't time to watch him further. Above the monitor a green light flashed on which meant someone had trodden on the sensors under the doormat outside the entrance. More customers, so I had to get back to my desk. (I'm sure they only have the sensor there to check up on me.)

"Try and get the boys to serve him," I told Keiko, "and get the chef to hurry it up. Tell the girls to keep clear and not to be cheeky. And don't refuse him any alcohol."

"If you say so, but I hope you know what you're doing," she said primly.

I thought I did, up to that point.

Three of them were lurking in the entrance as I made it back behind my desk, and the first thing that struck me was how young they were. One was early twenties, but the other two must have been teenagers, especially the one hanging behind at the back with his jacket collar turned up.

The one who looked old enough to vote (though few people did that these days) approached me, his right hand in his pocket, his left tweaking his nose. Interesting body language. He was a policeman—and wouldn't you know it, they *are* getting younger.

"Do you have a bar?" he asked in a London accent, but a posh one.

"Certainly, sir, but it's for diners only. Will that be a table for three?" I could behave myself when it was called for.

"Er . . . the bar is in the restaurant?" he fumbled.

"Yes, quite correct."

"There isn't a separate bar?"

"No, only in the restaurant. We have a restaurant licence. People eat here. Occasionally."

He stopped tweaking his nose at that and wanted to say something, but held himself back. One of the younger lads behind him whispered something I couldn't catch.

"Do you mind if I just have a quick look around the restaurant before we decide . . ."

I'd had enough of this.

"Is there a problem, officer?"

That stopped him for a second, then basic instinct took over.

"How did you . . . ?"

"The Doc Martens," I said smugly. "Nobody else wears them these days."

He looked down at his shoes, then mentally kicked himself for doing so. They always do, though; it never fails. I could have added that the Marks & Spencer's suit one size too big to cover the gun in the belt holster was also a dead giveaway, but you can go too far.

He recovered well. He held up a finger and said, "'Ang on a minute," then turned to his two young companions, and they went into a huddle.

Then he came back to me, and he had a Warrant Card in his hand.

"Is there anywhere we could have a word?"

"Downstairs." I pointed to the stairs knowing that the virtual-reality driving range was unoccupied. "I'll get cover and join you in one minute."

He looked relieved and said, "Thanks" almost as if he meant it.

I stuck my head into the restaurant and made eye contact with Keiko, then jerked my head toward the entrance. She acted like she hadn't seen me, but I knew she had.

Without making it obvious, I clocked Dexter, who now had four whisky glasses in front of him and was perusing the whisky list for more.

When Keiko joined me, I explained that we had some more out-of-the-ordinary customers, one of whom was a senior policeman, and I would happily put myself on the line dealing with them to avoid any confrontation with the management. That usually worked, and it did again. Keiko said she would get Hiroshi, who had the good English (in fact, better than mine when he wanted to), to man the desk, and I could sort out the police downstairs, which she was sure would take all my charm, diplomacy, and skill *and no more than ten minutes.*

"You'd better call me Tom," said the policeman.

"Oh yeah? And they're Dick and Harry?"

I nodded toward the two lads who were examining the virtual-reality gear like it was Christmas.

The young copper was staring at me.

"That's Gordon and Henry," he said, as if reading it off a card. "I'm looking after them."

I couldn't keep a straight face.

"Come off it, Tom. I've read *Thomas the Tank Engine*."

Then I stopped. I suddenly realized he hadn't.

"You know, Gordon the stuck-up Blue Engine and Henry the wimpy Green Engine with the sad expression ... Thomas—Tom—Gordon and ..."

He blushed then, and turned a killer look on the two teenagers he was "looking after."

"They thought up the names, didn't they?" I asked softly.

"Yes, but that's not important. Look, I need—we need—to know about the movements of somebody upstairs in the restaurant. We need to keep an eye on him without being seen. Can you help?"

"Is this official?"

"Semi-official," he said carefully.

"Then glad to help, officer. Detective Sergeant, wasn't it? Sorry, but I didn't get a chance to examine your Warrant Card very closely."

"It's real, that's all you need to know."

"Fine by me, Tom. Can you tell me what this is about?"

"No."

"I have my employers to think about."

"No."

"Very well, we at Ben Fuji's are always anxious to cooperate with the law and will do so respectfully and diplomatically. Oi! Harry!"

The younger of the two youths looked up from the VR helmet he was examining like a rabbit caught in headlights.

"What's your father do these days?" I shouted as if doing a stand-up routine.

"He's still King," he answered.

Then he bit his tongue.

"Gordon—that really is his name—is a friend from school, one of the few I can trust," he told me. "Thomas is actually Sergeant Dave Thomas."

"Your bodyguard."

"Yes, and I don't want to get him into trouble. I'm not really supposed to be out with just one. I'm afraid Gordon and I rather conned him into accompanying us into the Forbidden Zone."

"London?"

"Yes. We're almost out-of-towners now."

"So why the expedition?"

He gave me another once-over (the fifth by my reckoning) before answering.

"My brother, my elder brother," he started, as if he had lots to choose from, "does not pick his friends as well as I do.

"One of them has talked to the press about a party brother-dear attended last month where there was some silliness involving a swimming pool and various naked ladies in compromising positions."

"Nobody invited me," I said before I could stop myself. "Sorry. Go on."

"Worse still, someone had a video camera and recorded some of the ... er ..."

"Juicy bits?"

"Yes. Juicy bits. God, that sounds disgusting."

He *was* young.

"Anyway, this so-called friend has sold the tape to an absolute shit."

"Sam Dexter."

"Why, yes. How did you know?"

"I recognized him from your description."

He smiled at that, something he rarely did, if the newspapers were to be believed.

"Does your brother know?" I prompted.

"No, and he wouldn't know what to do if he did. Anyway, he's on tour at the moment."

He said it as if he were talking about a second-rate rock band doing one-night stands around the Midlands.

"So what did you have in mind?"

"Well, Plan A was to stop my brother's dippy friend from selling the tape. God knows, he doesn't need the money; just doing it for the mischief. But we were too late. He'd done the dirty deed by the time we got there. Fortunately, Dexter had gone straight to the local pub to celebrate."

"Does he know what's on the tape?"

"Yes. He insisted on a viewing before buying."

"Can I ask how much?"

"Thirty thousand quid, he said, and he felt pretty shitty when I called it thirty thousand pieces of silver," he said proudly.

I'll bet. I could feel lower than toenail dirt for that sort of money.

"So you followed Dexter?"

"Well, Thomas—Dave—did, at least into the first three pubs. Then he took a cab here. He has the tape in his pocket. I saw it."

So did I, in a brown envelope.

"And just how were you going to relieve him of it?" I asked gently.

"We never actually got down to detail on Plan B," he said seriously. "Gordon thought we should borrow Dave's gun and mug him, but I don't think Dave will go along with that. So, really, we haven't got a plan. We just need to keep an eye on Dexter and wait our chance. Would you help us do that?"

How could I refuse?

"I tell you what; you stay here and I'll check out Dexter. There's no way you can show your face in the restaurant without him seeing you, and if he thinks you're after him, it will just convince him he's on to something big."

"Good plan. Thanks. How can I repay you?"

"I'll think of something."

I didn't have to go far to get a situation report on Sinister Dexter. Keiko was waiting by my desk.

"He is a pig, that man. He is griping everyone. Not only my girls, but customers, too!"

"I think you mean 'groping,'" I said calmly.

"Whatever. Get rid of him, while he can still stand."

Now I only usually listen to about forty percent of what Keiko says, but as she once bested me in a nine-hour sake drinking session, I do respect her views on male alcohol consumption.

"How pissed is he?" I asked seriously.

"Weaving in the wind. Another three or four scotches and he'll start griping the men."

I knew it was worth listening.

"Keiko, you've got it. I want you to keep him here and keep the table next to him free."

"No problem, I wouldn't put anyone there."

"Good thinking. Now tell one of the waiters to drop something or spill something on Dexter's table. Then we want lots of profuse apologies and take him the bottle—the bottle, mind you—of the Tobermory Malt, the twelve-year-old."

Well, that's what it said on the bottle, but I know it to be a single malt that had gone overproof and now clocked in nearer sixty percent than forty percent alcohol.

"Give him the bottle . . .?" Keiko started, but she was talking to my back as I headed for the office.

"Glenda?"

"Perhaps. Who wants to know?"

"Angel."

"Darling! Long time no . . well, no anything, really. Whadderyerwant?"

"I want you to seduce somebody in a Japanese restaurant and pick his pocket and within the next hour."

"Seems reasonable. Have I time to put my face on?"

"Got any money on you?"

"Not a cent, but Sergeant Dave has." Henry smiled.

"Has he £250?" I asked, swapping my dinner jacket (Keiko had insisted) for my leather bomber.

"I'll ask."

Henry and Sergeant Dave went into conference.

Gordon was fully plugged into the VR machine, whapping balls down a fairway somewhere.

"He wants to know what you want it for," Henry came back.

"I'm hiring somebody to pick Dexter's pocket and get that tape for you."

"In that case, I'll get the cash."

No questions, no arguments. Who says breeding doesn't tell?

"You didn't have to come," I told them for the tenth time.

"Listen, Angel, if that's your name, I'm going to have enough trouble accounting for £250 without receipts as it is. If you just drove off into the night with it, I'd be back on traffic duty."

"You have a point, Sergeant."

"Plus"—Thomas put his face up to the open glass partition—"I'm not supposed to be farther than five feet from his nibs even when he's peeing. Where the hell are we anyway?"

"The Barbican."

"Do people still live here?"

Now if "Henry" had said that, it would have made headlines. Instead he chimed up with: "This is a taxi, isn't it?"

"It was," I said over my shoulder.

"A Fairway."

"Do they still make them?"

"No."

"Is it old?"

"About twelve years. You still see them around."

Ordinary mortals do, anyway.

"It's not a real one, though. I mean a licensed Hackney Carriage?"

"No, it's delicensed," I answered patiently. After all, the kid still probably went train spotting.

"He's called Armstrong Two," I said. There was a half minute of silence from the back.

"Why Armstrong *Two?* What happened to *One?*"

Bright lad.

"That's a long story."

The one advantage Armstrong Two had over Armstrong One—apart from being in one piece—was the mobile phone fitted in a dashboard mounting. I used it to call Glenda when we were close.

"Be outside and ready to jump in exactly two minutes," I told her when we were five minutes away.

"You've got to be kidding, Angel, I'm nowhere near *dressed* even."

"Good, that'll speed things up."

"Oooh—you smooth-talking fucker, you."

I hung up and pulled Armstrong over to the curb, got out and, walked to the boot where I keep various emergency-only items.

I moved round to the nearside passenger door and opened it.

"Take off your jacket," I said to Henry. "And put these on."

I handed him a sweatshirt three sizes too big for him (advertising a now bankrupt chilli-to-go and carwash in Bangor, Maine) and a baseball cap (adjustable—one size fits all) plugging the Romford Spartacists, which was a gridiron football team, not a political movement.

Henry complied with enthusiasm.

"This is so Glenda won't recognize me, isn't it?" he chirped, crumpling a suit jacket that probably cost half an Armstrong.

"That's right, and just hope she doesn't."

He looked at me quizzically.

"Trust me on this one," I said.

"Do you *know* who you've got in here?" Glenda hissed out of the side of her mouth. As she was sitting in the rumble seat behind mine, I could hear her perfectly well without her spitting in my ear.

"Shut up and forget it," I hissed back.

In my mirror I saw Sergeant Dave Thomas reach for his wallet.

"Payment on results," I said loudly. "That's the usual way, isn't it Glenda?"

She straightened up in her seat and made a futile effort to drag her short skirt down a centimeter. If she'd succeeded that would have made it only seven inches above the knee.

"Haven't had any complaints so far, Angel," said Glenda.

Henry, Thomas, Gordon, and I were in the manager's office looking at the restaurant on the video monitor. Glenda was out there doing her stuff, and it was Academy Award–winning stuff.

Keiko had done her bit, organizing a minor accident, groveling apologies, and then a free (or at least to-be-paid-for-later) bottle of the Tobermory head-banger. And Dexter had gone along like he'd read the script. If his pupils hadn't been so dilated, there would have been a glint in them saying he was going to finish the bottle just to show them. Whoever "they" were.

Glenda had tick-tocked her buttocks into a chair at the table next to him, fluffed up her auburn curls, smoothed her skirt, and picked up a menu. Dexter was at her like a shark coming out of Lent.

He persuaded her to try a whisky as an aperitif. Then as an alternative to sake. Then just for the hell of it. Then to finish the bottle.

Glenda, who could drink me under the table and carry me home (and, indeed, has) matched him drink for drink and then—master stroke—ordered champagne. Even without sound, we could feel Dexter say, "And why not?"

When I lip-read Glenda describing the basement room with its virtual-reality golf range (about which I'd briefed her) and then pantomime that she needed to use the toilet, I knew he was hooked. Glenda stood, played with the hem of her skirt and the string of large (fake) amber beads balanced on her bosom, fell back a pace, and allowed herself to be steadied by Dexter's outstretched, sweaty hand.

"Nice touch, that," I said, admiring a professional when I see one.

I realized no one was listening; they were all looking

at the monitor as if they'd never seen anything like this before. Then Henry looked at me, dead serious.

"You're getting a kick out of this," he said, deadpan. "And I've been wondering why, because there's nothing in it for you. In fact, you haven't even asked for anything. You're helping us just for the hell of it, just to stir things up. You don't really care one way or the other, do you? You don't have problems like this, do you? You're like one of the old hippies who just drift through life in your battered old delicensed taxicab, just to be a rebel, thinking it all a bit of a bad joke."

The kid was getting too close for comfort.

"Who's an ageing hippy?" I snapped.

It got triple x-rated (as they say now on TV) pretty quickly once Glenda and Sinister made it to the virtual-reality room.

The VR driving ranges had semicircular control panels raised on small platforms like a conductor's rostrum. They contained all the electronic gizmos needed to run the ranges and to protect them from the helmeted VR golfers; they were leather padded.

Glenda realized the erotic potential of the podia immediately, and as Dexter bent over to examine the virtual-reality helmet, Glenda goosed him something rotten.

"I say!" said Gordon, glued to the screen.

"Ignore him," whispered Henry. "He's very young in many ways."

"I'd forgotten he was here," I said, fiddling with the VCR controls.

Dexter couldn't quite believe it either. He swung round and walked into Glenda's open arms. Glenda backed him up against a podium and planted a smacker on his lips, her hands disappearing inside his jacket. Without unplugging her lips, she slipped his jacket off and held it with her left hand while her right went to his groin.

Sergeant Thomas and the green-and-blue engines were watching her right hand, as was Dexter. I was watching her left as she freed him from the jacket and then hitched it round until she was near the pocket with the envelope. Dexter's hands and mind were fully occupied in trying to push up her skirt. That short, leather skirt, which had flown up like a Venetian blind in the restaurant, now seemed to be glued to her long, high-heeled legs.

Just as Glenda's red fingernails closed around the envelope, Dexter decided the skirt problem needed a better perspective, and so he took an unsteady step backward.

The problem was he kept going, the back of his thighs hitting the edge of the podium and tipping him backward. Glenda, probably thinking he had realized she was doing a lift, dropped the jacket and removed her support from his back. He toppled over, hit the floorboards and bounced slightly before coming to rest. I hoped the alcohol had acted as enough of a muscle relaxant to prevent serious damage.

Glenda looked down at him in amazement from the control panel. She stamped one of her high heels so effectively the four of us jerked back from the monitor, as if we'd heard it. Then she pulled off the curly auburn wig and flung it over Dexter's face.

"Bloody hell," said an aristocratic voice. "She's a man!"

"Welcome to the world, Harry."

I had to introduce him to Keiko and the staff; that became part of the deal though they were sworn to secrecy. We did it in the kitchen so the punters couldn't see, and it went down well all round. He said he knew their emperor and what a jolly nice bloke he was. They said they didn't but, of course, they'd take his word for it.

Then we paid off Glenda, and I offered to drive her home, but she said she never finished her dinner and sushi was *so* erotic ... On Henry's instruction, Sergeant Thomas put enough cash behind the bar to ensure she wouldn't go hungry.

It was my idea to pile Dexter into the back of Armstrong. Sergeant Thomas (and Henry) knew he lived in

Finchley, and a Euro driving license in his wallet confirmed the address and that he had enough cash to pay
even my exorbitant rates. (I also took the trouble to remove £90 for his meal and one of these days I must remember to pay it into Ben Fuji's.)

"If he wakes up," I said, pulling on my leather
bomber jacket and smoothing my hair flat with hair gel
(hair gel was back in a big way), "I'll just play the ag-
grieved musher."

"Pardon?" asked Gordon politely.

"Cabbie. Ferryman. Hackney Carriage operative.
Hatless Chauffeur."

"Oh," he said vaguely. It was way past his bedtime.

I took Henry to one side as I closed Armstrong's
boot. The street was deserted, but he had turned up the
collar of his jacket, and he still wore the sweatshirt and
hat I had given him.

"You want these back," he said, starting to peel off
his jacket.

"No, no. Keep them. I'll add them to the bill."

He fixed me with his eyes. I'd read somewhere
they'd been trained to do that.

"There will be a bill?"

Sergeant Thomas hovered close behind him, so I
dropped my voice.

"We ageing hippies aren't into money, man. Can you
dig that?"

He smiled and for once the newspapers were right,
he didn't smile enough.

"You've got the tape?"

He patted the inside pocket of his coat.

"And you'll turn it over to your brother?"

He waited five careful seconds before answering.

"I'll bring it to his attention."

They were taught not to tell lies as well.

"Are there any copies?"

"No." He was confident. "There wasn't time."

"Good. Then this is the one we put in the envelope
in Sinister's pocket."

"What's that?" he stared open-eyed at the cassette I
offered him.

"I taped the scene in the basement, right up to Glenda revealing her ... er ... credentials."

"Christ, he'll have a heart attack," he said gleefully, grabbing it. "I hope he doesn't watch it before he gives it to his editor."

Then he flashed a look at me.

"Are there any copies?"

Good thinking, kid, you're coming on.

"No. But Dexter doesn't know that."

Henry's face bisected.

"Way to go, Angel. You used to say things like that, didn't you?"

He put the new cassette into Dexter's brown envelope.

"May I do the honors?" He indicated the slumped figure of Dexter, snoring loudly, stretched across Armstrong's backseat.

"Be my guest."

He turned, then stopped and offered his hand. I wasn't sure whether I should bow or not. So I didn't.

"Thank you, Angel, if that's your name. I still don't understand why you've helped us, but I'm grateful, and if there is ever anything I can—"

"Don't worry, I'll call."

He looked puzzled.

"I know where you live," I explained.

He smiled again and pulled me closer as we shook.

"You know, I was going to ask you for Glenda's phone number for my uncle," he whispered. Then he squeezed my hand. "I still might."

It was my turn to grin.

Sergeant Thomas hadn't finished with me, though. As Henry put the new tape onto Dexter's comatose person, Thomas took me to one side as only policemen can.

"I don't have to remind you, sir, that—"

"No you don't; it's okay."

"And I hope you'll give me your address so that—"

"No way, Mr. Tank Engine. You'll just have to trust me."

He sized me up.

"Well, we have to trust somebody, I suppose."

"That's the spirit, Sergeant. And should I ever have my collar felt, you won't mind if I mention your name, will you? Of course, I won't say how we met."

Mr. Nice Policeman was in danger of giving way to Mr. Nasty. There's a Jekyll and Hyde gene in all of them.

"So that's your price, is it?"

"Partly, Dave, partly. And I may never call it in. I may not have to, seeing as how you've already noted my registration number and will no doubt put it through the police computer tomorrow."

Even in the streetlight he blushed.

"Don't worry, Dave, always C.Y.A.—cover your arse. That's all I'm doing."

"So what else do you get out of it? Come on, I want to know."

"Well, Sergeant, look at it this way. You like young Henry, don't you?" He nodded. "And he's going to go far, isn't he?"

"I . . . er . . ."

"Put it this way: If you were a betting man, would you put money on *his* being the face we see on our stamps in a few years' time?"

"Possibly."

"So would I. And I'll be able to say I had him in the back of the cab once."

Lex Talionis

by Jessica Palmer

Be it known—ye who believe that he does not love England, who think him little more than a puppet of the French Charles—that King Richard II in the third year of the Boniface's reign will never be governed by the Frankish king. This Richard loves his England well, even if he loves me not at all, and places my soul in mortal peril in his service.

Tallows flicker and flare. Hundreds of candles, made of precious beeswax and more than would grace the king's hall, light the damp walls. Their fluttering illumination bounces off the craggy face, sparkling in a myriad of colors. Such delicate beauty belies the demonic trade that takes place within radiance's embrace, and I blaspheme by my presence in this odious den.

Again, I wish to flee, but my feet and my body are not mine to command. The sorcerer's apprentice takes the cloak from my tremulous fingers and then lumbers away between boiling tub and bubbling vat. No creature made of the union of man with woman, the wizard's assistant is a homunculus, born of human seed and horse manure.

This I well believe, for a foul odor follows the mannikin, who is small and as-yet unformed, its face blank and without features.

Unimpressed by my presence or my station, as if I were little more than a scullery maid, the conjuror turns his back on me and pours blood on a writhing spider he has impaled upon a wooden board.

Inside, I smolder at the insult. For I am Philippa, the countess of Oxford—granddaughter of Edward III. Daughter of his youngest and favorite child, Isabella, and Ingelram, the earl of Bedford, Count de Soisson, and the sire de Coucy. Cousin to current king, Richard.

The necromancer wipes his hands on his robes, defiled and stained with who knows what loathsome substances. Like his faceless assistant, the man reeks more than any court physician who wears blood and vomitus as an emblem of his craft.

From under bristling brows he examines me as I ponder the poor spider.

"A small service," he says, "done for a friend."

I shiver as he explains its import, and I wonder what "small service" will he do for a king.

So what, you may ask, has brought someone of my gentle birth to this pretty pass and to a place where I must consort with the devil's disciple?

'Tis no glad thing to be cousin of the king. Well I loved my grandfather even into his dotage as he loved us, my royal mother and me. Named after his queen, I benefited from his largesse. Upon my birth, I was given silver service of six bowls, gilded and chased, six cups, four water pitchers, four platters, and four-and-twenty each of dishes, salt cellars, and spoons. 'Twas a handsome gift.

After King Edward's passing, my mother and I were reduced to penury, near to begging for each meal, each coin, each small measure of cloth. The niggardly treatment by the young Richard's regent and his councilors caused my mother's early demise. Of this, I am sure.

Before me, the alchemist bends to examine the onyx I was commanded to bring. According to his instructions, its face has been carved with Andromeda's head. A fine filigree of silver and lead—he was very specific about this—surrounds it, and it has been made into a brooch. A princely gift.

The scorched crucible swings creakily over a guttering flame held in the palm of a gallows hand. The ragged ends along the wrist curl inward, and the stench of putrefaction and decay waft through the air mixed with acrid smoke.

The room around me floats and drifts.

No, there is little cause for love between Richard

and myself. Less thanks to my husband, Robert de
Vere, to whom I was betrothed at the age of four. Said
Robert is the king's favorite, and one would think that
such happy circumstance would warrant security for
one's person and one's property.

Not so.

The villein in the field has more freedom than I.
Richard is a choleric man, and I have lived many years
under his shadow. His eyes and ears are everywhere,
even in my bedchamber. Naught that I say goes unre-
ported. Someday I fear that my anger, my ire, will be-
tray me.

Richard waits like a cat outside a mouse's hole,
ready to pounce upon my least infraction, ready to strip
me of my title and my rights as he has already stripped
me of my dignity and my pride.

King Richard has long suspected that 'twas I who
brought the appeal against Oxford through my uncle
Gloucester and the Lords Appellant.

And why shouldn't I? I who have been so wronged.

I am not like the king's wife, Queen Anne, fragile
and forgiving. The blood of Plantagenet flows in my
veins and more vigor courses within my breast than
that.

'Twas my royal cousin who came between my husband and myself, arranging trysts between my lord and
his Bohemian whore, lady-in-waiting to the queen.

Lady, did I say? Nay, no lady this. A harlot, a Jeze-
bel.

'Twas Richard who touted this execrable behavior,
parading my shame before the world. 'Twas Richard
who asked the schismatic Urban for a divorce on behalf of my husband, and the Roman pope granted it,
knowing my father cleaved to Avignon's Clement.

My beloved husband escaped Gloucester's clutches
at Radcot Bridge, fleeing to Flanders to stir up trouble
with the duke of Geulders in Richard's name.

The king is separated from his favorite, and I left
neither widowed nor wed. Should Robert set foot upon
English soil, his head is forfeit, but that is not enough,

for it resides upon his shoulders still, and I will not rest until I am avenged.

And the king blames me! But I ask you: What mercy has Richard shown to me or my good name?

Yet all tools, no matter how repugnant, have their purpose. I no less than others, and Richard despite the opulence of his court is a practical man. The king has not forgot that my father is the sire de Coucy and has Charles's ear.

Little do I recall my father, only that he was a large man, dark and well-graced, comely in form and practiced in the arts of chivalry.

Friend and foe alike speak well of him. Even my grandsire was smitten with him during his imprisonment here in England—when Ingelram and the late French king, Jean, resided unwilling in Edward's hall—giving his youngest daughter's hand in marriage to someone he would normally have called enemy.

Froissart noticed Ingelram, his future patron, then and said: "The young lord de Coucy shined," and later, he would call my sire "the most gracious and persuasive lord in all Christendom."

Never in King Edward's life was his trust in Ingelram betrayed, although it did not last long beyond his passing.

The wizard mumbles in some strange tongue, but I will not listen. Arms wave. Fingers waggle. Black sleeves fall back to expose skeletal limbs as though their possessor were consumed by evil from within.

Bats fly above my head, and a magpie casts its evil eye over the proceedings. Leeches squirm in a silver bowl beside me. Spiders crawl within confines of a jar. Next to my head newts swim in an open tank of murky water. A salamander scrabbles inside a crystal dome; the sharp scratching sends chills down my spine. Obscene beasts pace in the rusted cages around me, watching all. Rats, poisonous toads, and other animals, more fantastic. Creatures that I cannot name. As if they understand his words, they grow more agitated as he speaks, and I wonder what fell fiend will he summon from corruption's depths.

I shield my eyes. I will not look, and I finger my
Book of Hours, praying to the Blessed Virgin to protect me. I call the image to mind of my confessor, so
different from this specter before me.

Crocks containing powders of the purest white, rich
yellow, and sparkling silver and gold line the walls.
The nomenclature of each is written in Latin in fine
hand. Vile names that roll off the tongue like some
profane liturgy, and the fetor that emanates from the
shelves is worse than the middens in high summer. Not
unlike to the smell of the kennels where the huntsman
stores the many strange medicines and ointments used
to cure the wood madness and other such ailments that
afflict the hound. But this smell is sour, almost metal-
lic, like the chemical odor that attaches itself to the
apothecary. Herbs hang in straggling vines from the
unseen ceiling above our heads, lost in the umbra that
not even the tapers can reach.

And I must swallow hard to keep down the wine I
called for upon arising, which even now sours in my
stomach.

Never one for frontal attack when what can be got
can be got by guile, Richard sent the young Mortimer
to talk to me. Like his master, the earl of March and
Ulster, and heir apparent to the throne, he did not approach me directly. Instead he came upon me in my
apartments, alone, sidling up to me like a crab to bring
me communication from my liege and lord.

Mortimer spoke with the soft, smooth words and fair
speech.

"Your cousin, the king, sends greetings . . . begs favor . . . he would regard this small service a token of
your esteem."

And behind the pretty words, the implied threat: "Or
sacrifice your title and your lands." If not my freedom
and my life.

'Twas Mortimer who told me of the conjuror, even
arranged this meeting and sent me here, to the peril of
my very soul.

How many times must I prove that I am loyal to my
country and my king? and what choice have I but to

obey my sovereign? Even though it means consorting with the devil himself.

To this man my king has commended me, condemning me for all eternity and setting me against my kith and kin. And I will do what Richard asks, returning even to Satan's chambers a second time if I must. No puling, cowardly female am I. Damned though I may be. I know naught of France. England is my home, and I will defend her.

Yes, Richard loves his England well and must have peace. For this end our king would send me to the great parley at Amiens. Not that I, of the fairer gender, may join in the talks, but that I walk unnoticed among the greats. My uncles, Lancaster and York, think that they take me with them to persuade my sire, but I know the darker purpose, reflected in these dank walls and stirred in the sorcerous vial.

The alchemist's great athanor belches great clouds while the alembic sizzles and hisses. The pestle and mortar are caked, blackened, and grimed. A tapestry, festooned with webs, proclaims its sad motto: *solve et coagula.*

I have seen naught of that noble principle here. Only the charlatan who would suspend gold in wax or paint nails so that it appears to the uninitiated that baser metals have turned to gold.

A human skull perches atop a stack of parchment, restraining the many scrolls against the breeze that continually drifts around the cavern, clearing noxious vapor and fumes.

Yet I grow dizzy. The chamber seethes with many whispering voices, and I am surrounded by a buzzlike whine of many midges or the whir of fay creatures darting around my head. The room swims in and out of focus. The colors on the glittering wall run, to gather in a puddle on the floor.

How many days have come and gone since I passed beneath this portal?—though I know it can hardly be more than a few scant hours.

The necromancer retrieves jars from his shelves, a

pinch of this, a bit of that, sprinkled into his boiling cauldron.

Sanguinaria canadensis, and I easily recognize the word for blood even if I had not recognized the plant, blood root, or King's root.

And I wish I had not listened to my lessons quite so well. 'Tis a fell concoction indeed. *Cystisus scoparius,* simple broom. *Pentenilla canadensis,* cinquefoil. *Canium maculatum,* deadly hemlock. *Heliotropium europaeum. Solanum nigrum,* nightshade!

The potion boils. The air grows thick. The mist around the crucible seems to glow with a venomous green light, and I can see faint ghostly images— twisted demons—which materialize above the cauldron and dive into its churning depths.

The steam he captures in a crystal dome, murmuring all the time. It drips oily and grim, dribbling into a golden bowl that holds the brooch. His dwarfed assistant shambles to his side, taking the vessel from his master's hands.

The magician grins, and I steel myself.

"The brooch must remain in this potion for seven days and seven nights. I will communicate with you when it is ready."

Dismissed.

Even before its transformation, I quailed to touch the jewel even when it was wrapped in silk, but now that it has been soaked in this lethal brew, I tremble to think that it must be sewn, well hid, within my skirts.

So I will go to France in good estate, as befitting one of my station. And I will enjoy myself. I will carry myself joyously to capture the heart of the "Most Christian King" until I get close enough to do that which is commanded of me.

Let Our Father in heaven above judge me, for I have no choice. But if accursed I be, then perhaps I will do one other thing, one small service. Just for me.

Those who know me would have said that Richard chose his emissary well. Loyal to the English throne, I had no cause to love the French king. Forsooth, I have little love for my father who at Edward's death withdrew his support, becoming the sworn enemy of my liege and lord and leaving me to face the wrath of Richard and his regent alone.

Since then, I have walked the sword's edge of intrigue, and I took to this skill as the hawk to the hunt. Mayhap, it comes naturally for any who were raised as I was in court where scutage pays more than bravery; hubris wins over humility; and the spurious and sycophantic must inevitably defeat probity.

To appease my father, Richard did not send me in mean estate. I was accompanied by many wagons and wains laden to bursting with gem-encrusted robes, rich carpets, and tapestries that bore Richard's insignia, the white hart.

Wearing slippers of softest Spanish leather, I danced with the many glamorous knights arrayed like blushing bridegrooms. I performed many a delicate leap or capering quadrille trying to catch the king's eyes.

In my dress embroidered with thread of gold and sewn with fine emeralds, I glittered a jewel among jewels. Not even the duke of Burgundy, Philip the Bold—in his doublet of black velvet, its sleeves thick with roses of sapphires and rubies, surrounded by pearls—could outshine me.

I was coquettish; I was gay, and few would have guessed at the deadly gift I carried upon my person.

The French were also eager to make peace. Four companies of one thousand kept guard both day and night. No subject was permitted to speak of combat upon pain of death. No one was allowed to sortie at night without a torch, and any page or varlet who provoked a quarrel was sentenced to immediate death.

We were received with the greatest honors, and the talks opened with ceremony. I gazed on blandly as Lancaster knelt three times in ritual homage and was welcomed by Frankish Charles. All the great lords gave banquets, each more splendid than the next. Minstrels played lutes, harps, and reed pipes, making merry music while we feasted on partridges and fat capons, sitting below a great white confection, a swan of spun sugar. Knights served their liege on horseback.

My father deported himself well—a fine figure of a man. Froissart did not lie, but my father was a stranger to me.

Then it was my sire's duty to provide the grand repast for king and company. With neither mother nor sister to take precedence over me, I sat as my father's lady at the head table next to the Frankish king.

There was duck, rabbits, roast pork, sweet jellies, and cheeses for the first course, and I made sure that I kept the king's cup full.

Before the main course a great pastry was brought in and cut with due ceremony, releasing over one hundred white doves, symbol of the peace this parley hoped to attain. In a flurry of white feathers they flew to the rafters to roost, adding their throaty chorus to the voices of the castrata who serenaded our meal.

Ingelram rose to arbitrate between Lancaster and Burgundy, and I saw my chance. Quickly, I withdrew the foul gift from the folds of my golden gown and pressed it into Charles's hand, whispering into his ear that it was as a token of my king's affection, the brooch's tainted tooth biting through the soft flesh of the palm as I did so.

Quite happily drunk, Charles accepted my flustered apologies. He raised his flagon to me with a toast, quickly covering my embarrassment, and quipped most gallantly; "Done, pierced to the heart by the beauty of Coucy who does credit to both realms."

Blushing furiously, I pinned the jewel to his tunic so that it was veiled by royal robes. My father returned, and my job was finished.

The talks were doomed from the start. I knew this before I left, even before the necromancer placed the crystal vial in my hand.

The French wanted Calais raised in exchange for the old King Jean's ransom. Richard was desirous of peace, but in no mood to parley over a matter so dear to his heart and necessary to his exchequer. My uncles refused to accede, saying they must return to speak with my cousin, the king, before they could agree to any terms.

Sometime during the negotiations, King Charles fell into a fit. His face flushed and red, he raged at unseen devils, and I shuddered to see the poison work. Spittle foamed from his mouth, and he shrieked as if all the legions of hell pursued him. The leeches came and went. Malodorous physicians plied him with a drink made of ground rubies meant to decrease fever of the mind that seemed to have taken ahold of him.

There were whispers of sorcery, and only I know the truth.

I kept my peace.

Once I was allowed into his chambers to see him, at which time I ensured that the brooch was still on his person. Few thought it ill that the king's cousin should secure such a royal gift, blessed as it was—or so I said—by the pope. No one quibbled o'er Avignon or Rome where tribute was concerned.

They tell me that King Charles fights his own knights, falling mad like a frothing dog from his saddle, recognizing no one, not even his wife. He plays like a child, a toy king. With his young brother, Louis, he invents games, each more ghastly and macabre than the one before. Les Bals des Ardents.

The brooch works on him still, eating away at his mind and soul, and I wonder at this deed my king has made me do. What magic was this that would rob a man's mind and leave him still living, an empty shell? Surely, 'twould have been nobler to kill him.

Still you could say, I have done my job well, and for this I have exacted payment—payment in kind. Pray God—if I may pray to God anymore—that Richard never knows. I have endangered not only this life, but the next one. Yet if I have imperiled my immortal soul by my trafficking, then I will be condemned as a sheep rather than a lamb.

The second time I attended the enchanter in his dark dungeon, I asked him to do me a small service as he had done for others in the past. True to his craft that spends life's blood and breath in the search of gold and greed, the sorcerer was willing, caring little of its recipient.

I gave him a large pearl my mother had given me. She would understand. 'Twas a small enough price to pay for vengeance upon both those who had plotted my ruin.

Only asking the necromancer to wait until I was quit of England's shores and far from the Brabant home where my husband now resided.

They say his passing was agony—impaled by a boar, like the spider on a board. His entrails drawn and drowning in his own blood. The deed is done, and unwittingly my royal cousin has shown his gratitude for my "previous service" by getting a writ to rescind the divorce so that the titles are mine. The lands are mine. Restitution has been made in full.

This, the final insult, I can stand. I care not that Richard has brought my husband's body home with pomp and honor. Or that the knave rests in the chapel. Richard places a ring upon the dead man's finger, and many hours has the king gazed longingly on that dead face, thinking himself alone.

He is not.

Hidden by the shadows, I smile behind my pomander. Nauseated by the stench of decay, still I will not move. Morgan le Fay once defeated a king using woman's wiles and wizard craft, and I, abandoned wife, rejected lover, have emulated her. Damned to perdition's flames, perhaps, but victorious at last.

Queen Alienor's Favor

by Paul Dorrell

The queen sat with three of her ladies beneath a tall window through which streamed the late afternoon sun. Her impatience showed in the lift of her head as I entered, and setting aside the embroidery on which she had been working, she stared at me with that terrifying directness I was to know so well. She was then little short of seventy, yet her face was as smooth as that of a woman who has not yet borne children, and she held herself erect as any knight.

One of the women muttered something in that confounded Provençal dialect—I never could master it despite all my years in the service of that monstrous, wonderful family—and they all laughed. It was not the laughter of empty-headed ladies such as I had known till then, women who deluded themselves that they ruled their men by subtlety. These were different, as were all those at Fontevrault and most who surrounded the queen. *They* had learning. It was a new world to me, and often very shocking, a society of southern manners and southern expressions.

"You may sit, Sir Ralph." She gestured imperiously toward the stool near where I stood.

"My lady . . ." I did not know what to say more, and so I merely sat and waited on her.

"I have heard that you are a man of considerable courage—and physical strength," she said.

Again, her women laughed, their eyes darting over me with no hint of demureness or shame. I had not even had time to take off my stinking clothes after the ride from Chinon, being summoned to the presence before I had even dismounted, and my mail was splashed with mud. Beside these lovely does, I felt clumsy and unappealing. My tongue would not move, and so I simply bowed my head.

"But not a man of many words!" she continued. "Perhaps that is as well. There are more than enough chatterers in my retinue, and we shall be together a great deal from now on—that is, if you do not find it too demeaning to serve mere women."

I remembered then King Richard's amusement when he told me of my new duties, in the dowager queen's personal guard. Both of us had spent most of our lives with fighting men, and I had served under his command for some seven years in which I had seen why he came to be known as the Lion-Heart. But he knew also his mother's court in Aquitaine where women were held in high esteem. I, on the other hand, had known little of their kind since the day I left my father's keep in that awful rain-soaked corner of Ireland that was my destined inheritance. Fontevrault itself was truly a woman's place, even though the order accepted both sexes, for it had been founded as a place of refuge for those whose husbands abused them. Its reputation had spread throughout Europe, and my alarm must have shown.

"So, you've no taste for feminine company." He had laughed. "Well, don't think you'll have a soft time with my lady mother."

As I looked at her, I saw how alike they were. Both had the same long, straight nose that added to their autocratic air; both had a merry devil in their eyes; and both had that set of jaw which, when relaxed was attractively firm, but when fixed showed proof of their inborn ruthlessness. As to their hair, my lord Richard's was red gold, but I had not seen his mother's, hidden as it was beneath veil and wimple. Perhaps it was white now, as would accord with her age, but I could not believe that to be so.

"You are aware of our mission?" the queen said.

"His Majesty told me something of it, madam," I replied.

"Oh! Don't be so cautious, sir. Harsh I may be, and

demanding, but I am not stupid enough to expect total ignorance in one who lives close to power. Besides, your face shows that you grieve for the crusading life you would lead beside the king."

"I know that I am to accompany you to Navarre, madam, to bring back King Sancho's daughter as Lord Richard's bride."

"And sharp grief that'll bring to the king of the French." She spat out that title with disgust and contempt. "I doubt he'll let my son marry the princess Berengaria without some trouble—Richard is still betrothed to his sister—which is why I must have good men beside me. But I'll not have a son of mine married to that over-stewed dumpling, Alice. The man who will take Jerusalem must have a queen worthy of him."

I continued to sit silent, stunned at her lack of concern for the niceties that should have ruled our encounter. Not only was she Duchess of Aquitaine, the one-time wife of one king, widow of another, and mother of a third; she was also the richest and most powerful woman in the world. But it was her certainty of her position that allowed her certain laxities, and even those who loved her most were terrified of her.

"Ah yes! The King of France, who calls himself Augustus." Her voice was like a dagger. "We know that he plots against us even now. Ysé . . ."

She gestured to one of her ladies, a beautiful, fragile creature with wide, brown eyes and a generous mouth, who rose and took a paper from a table behind the Queen, handing it to me. The language was not French, that much I knew. The characters were not even in true script.

"It was found on a man killed by robbers not far from here. Do not be concerned that you cannot read it. It is in cipher. But look beneath the writing," said the Queen, tetchily pointing to the picture drawn there.

It showed a tree with many branches and roots. At its summit was a crown, and at its base a lion with its mane caught in its toils.

"The tree is the King of the French who reaches everywhere," explained the woman Ysé, "and the lion is

King Richard whom he would destroy. As yet, we do not understand the message, but one of the brothers here is working to find its meaning. All he has managed so far is '. . . above all remain unseen.'"

"Subtle always." The Queen laughed. "He has the nature of a fox lying in the bracken."

That was very much what many said of him, and exactly what I had seen in his eyes on the only occasion when I had seen King Philip before. I was in Paris at the time, trying to acquire some learning. As evening fell one day, I was wandering along the rue de l'Estamperie when I saw a man leading two horses draw near the door of a modest house. From the entrance slipped a man wearing a hood and cloak, and above, at a window, I saw a young woman. She stood there a moment and raised her hand in good-bye as she looked down on him.

A hand drew me into the shadows before they saw me, and I faced an old woman.

"Best not let the king know you saw him in the chicken-run," she said and laughed softly. "Master Reynard has great care for secrecy."

"Why?" I protested. "All kings have mistresses."

"But this king has a sidling nature."

She was gone, and I paused only for one last glimpse of the sovereign. He faced me full on, and I saw the reddish hair and the sharp eyes. Even to this day, I cannot be certain that *he* saw *me*, but I felt a chill pass through my bones.

"Sir!" The anger in the Queen's voice recalled me to myself, and I was compelled to explain.

"How unlike his father he is." She sighed. It seemed that even now there was regret for the failure of her marriage to Louis, his father, the man to whom she could not present an heir.

There was little discussion after that. I was informed that my first duty in her service would be to accompany her to the king's residence at Chinon where they would say their farewells before he departed to the Crusade and we made the journey across the Pyrenees to Navarre, a formidable effort for anyone, let alone a woman of her age.

As I bowed to take my leave, a terrible scream tore at the air, like a soul in Hell itself. I felt myself go pale, but the queen was unperturbed.

"That is poor Agnes, one of our sisters. Her wits are turned, I'm afraid, ever since the death of her brother—he was burnt for heresy, for Catharism." She sighed as she waved me away.

Ysé accompanied me. She had all the rich promise of the South about her, and when she spoke, her voice was strongly accented.

"If you have need of anything, you have only to let me know, sir. Your rank and your position here entitle you to much, and the Queen is generous to those who serve her."

A man lolled on a stone bench against a wall, strumming almost silently on a psaltery and mouthing words I could not hear but whose shape I took to be once again of Provence. The golden light from the window fell on his hair, and in the Queen's garden I saw ladies and their companions strolling in intimacy. It was a moment of purest pleasure, a sight of a way of life I had never imagined, where harmony and love ruled.

But the moment was shattered as a door flew open, and with a great scuffling three women, sisters, burst into the antechamber, two of them trying to restrain the other. Her veil was pulled to one side so that I could not see her face.

"You shall burn, cruel ones!" she screamed. "You shall burn in Hell, as surely as my brother burnt in the square in Paris."

"She imagines everyone to be her brother's tormentors," said Ysé. For a moment, neither of us noticed that she had grasped the sleeve of my mail, so firmly that the impress remained some moments on her fingertips.

All the rest of that day, and late into the night, the poor woman's screams could be heard through the community of Fontevrault, rising even above the singing of the offices in the great abbey.

* * *

I should have set a guard permanently on Brother Leo, the old monk charged with solving the cipher, but sweet-natured though he was, he freely confessed to the sin of pride in certain matters. He would have none of it, and for this paid with his life.

It was only two days before our departure, and the place was in a constant turmoil. The Queen had pressed Brother Leo incessantly, and he had worked every night into the small hours until eventually his face showed that he was near done with the task.

As I left the Queen's presence after presenting my report, I saw Ysé, head cocked to one side, standing near the main staircase. She turned a moment, then put a finger to her lips. I waited, and after a moment I too heard the footstep, light and careful. Not one footstep. Two. Even as Brother Leo appeared, he seemed to stumble, grasping backward as he fell. His neck twisted at a strange, exaggerated angle as he struck the floor, and I had no doubt that he was dead.

Ysé stood there only a moment, then rushed up the stairs, ignoring my cry. Above, I heard a door bang shut and a key turning in a lock, and then she returned.

"You could have been killed," I shouted.

She replied quietly with great calm, "My life is given to the Queen's service, sir, but I thank you for your concern." Then bending to the body, "See. He has still a paper here."

What she took from his hand was a torn corner, the part of the ciphered document with the drawing on it. By now voices and running footsteps were approaching, and she hastily hid the fragment in her sleeve.

The Queen was subdued when finally we sat alone with her; it seemed to me that she suppressed a shiver.

"Oh, he is sly," she murmured.

After that, though, was a time of ease and happiness for me. We went first to Chinon, where mother and son made their farewells with a strange mixture of stoic hauteur and cooing affection. Then King Richard went off to war on the twenty-fourth of June, 1190, with his banners dancing and much singing of hymns, the very image of the brave warrior he truly was. You will hear many times of his cruelties, and he was cruel, a butcher at times; you will hear of his vanity, and he was vain, but he knew also how to win a man's undying devotion; you will hear of his foolhardiness, but he would never ask anyone to take a risk he himself would not take. My heart *did* sink when I saw him ride off. I wished that I could be with him, and had I not passed into the train of his lady mother, a being even more extraordinary than he, I should indeed have felt that my life had gone for nought.

But she was magnificent! She drove us hard, seeming always to be the last to tire, and never once did she complain of the cold of the mountain nights or the burning heat of the day as we crossed the Pyrenees.

For my part the journey was rendered more than bearable by the presence of Lady Ysé, though she outshone me in thinking and knowledge. I am afraid I was never truly gifted for study of any kind other than what concerned horses, armor, and other such typical interests for one of my birth. I was clumsy and mostly tongue-tied, yet I realized that she had some stirring for me, too.

And we had considerable time together in the Navarraise capital, Pamplona. Much of our time was spent in the antechamber of King Sancho's private apartments. We would often hear the voices of the two great ones raised in anger as they wrangled over the terms of the settlement that must be fashioned. Little talk of the heart's true affection in such matters.

I do not know if Lord Richard could ever truly love a woman. I suspect that he had shut himself away from all such feeling, having seen the anguish of his parents' life, the cruelty of his father, King Henry, who kept her prisoner for fifteen years. There are those who will tell you that he loved men, but I never saw any real proof of this. Rather, I think that he found in most men something he could never share with women other than his mother, and to some extent the princess Berengaria. Only they dared to meet him as his equal.

That he admired the younger woman, I know. He

had met her some years before the decision was made on their marriage, and though there was never any question of the love such as is sung of by the troubadours, they nevertheless found real pleasure in the meeting of their minds, and they had a deeper understanding that I was not fully to understand for some time.

In spirit, the princess of Navarre was very much like Alienor, though she never had the lightness in her that made the queen so winning. I suppose that similarity is the reason they could never be truly friendly, even with so many common aims and interests. Moreover, the older woman would always have the advantage in beauty, and Berengaria herself, at twenty-seven, was not young by now, with somewhat heavy bones. Being of a very studious nature, she had passed most of the time in her maiden years immersed in books of every kind, and, like Queen Alienor, she could read and write in both Provençal and Latin; she knew more of philosophy and religion than most of the famous clerics and scholars of our time. Admirable though this erudition may have been, it had not greatly benefited her looks, for such sedentary pursuits had made the flesh settle too much, so that she had a somewhat bovine appearance. And she had a passion for eating, particularly for sugared almonds from vassal Moorish princedoms. I shall ever remember her best as seated with a book whilst absentmindedly munching on sweetmeats. But she was a good, kind woman who always strove to please those around her and knew too well in whose shadow she lived.

Enough of this. For the most part affairs of state make dull reading. Suffice it to say that we eventually left Navarre as autumn first began to turn the color of the leaves, and it was whilst we were once again in the mountains that the first attempt was made on the life of the princess.

The town seemed almost to be sliding off the side of the rock, and indeed there were places where the ground beneath the walls had fallen away, leaving breaches in their defenses. Obviously the place was too poor to attend to such repairs as must be necessary, but the main square was pleasant, and a market was set out there as we made our way to the tower of the local lord. A woman ran up to our train, holding a small covered dish.

"I have a gift for the princess of Navarre," she called, and when she was pointed to Berengaria, she moved close and stretched up, taking off the lid.

The princess' eyes lit up as she saw the almonds, so smooth in their colored sugar coating. I swear she had never seen anything more tempting. She reached down to accept the gift, and at that moment the Queen dashed it from her hand. For a moment all was still in the square. Everyone stood there, shocked. A dog rushed over and licked curiously at the sweetmeats, then whimpered briefly and keeled over, kicking for a moment before its life was gone.

Panic and rage erupted then. The woman, who had been standing there as if turned to stone, now ran, darting between all who tried to stop her. I led the pursuit, which brought us to the edge of town. Only just in time did we rein our horses to a halt, for here what path there was had crumbled to a disarray of rock and dust on which the would-be murderess stumbled and slid toward a gap in the wall. As she fell, she grasped at the stone, and a huge section went with her. When we found a place to look down in safety, we saw only her tomb.

She would never be put to the question.

"Small matter," said the Queen. "We know well enough that King Philip is behind this." In her hand she held the bowl the woman had presented to the princess. Etched in the bottom was the same insignia as on the document I had seen at Fontevrault.

"Not only is his royal pride wounded that my son should decline to take his whore dumpling of a sister to wife, but more, he fears as does the emperor, that this will be a Cathar marriage. With the power of the Church so challenged, what might happen to their rule? They think that our southern ways of tolerance and curiosity are the heresy itself. Well, Sir Ralph, you must decide whether you wish to continue serving me— perhaps I *am* truly anathema."

"That can be no concern of mine, madam," I said. "But I am committed to your service and shall be with you as long as you shall wish it."

She smiled then, and, strangely, it was the first time that she looked old. For a few moments that fiercely maintained loftiness was relaxed, and she looked for all the world like any southern Mémé.

"Go now," she hissed urgently, looking away from me. "You need to rest, for I shall drive us hard tomorrow."

As she turned back to me, waving her imperious hand, her voice and her eyes regained their steel. My stern mistress was back, and I was glad.

On then to Pau we rode. Already the season was falling toward winter, and the winds were beginning to bite at our flesh on the open tracks. We stayed two days, enough only to gather provisions and make some repairs to our baggage train. Our amusement, brief as it was, was provided by a company of tumblers, jugglers, and the like. One of their number in particular amazed us all with his acrobatic tricks and his sleight of hand, making coins appear from the ears and mouths of the children who gaped all round him. The Queen and the Princess each gave him two gold pieces, and he bowed cheerfully, sweeping his arm wide.

From then on, we made hard for Fontevrault, wishing to be secure before the worst of the winter set in. Once arrived, I saw little of the Queen for some days, for she shut herself away with vast piles of papers that demanded her attention. Nor did she neglect to count the coins in chests of levies from her subject lords. She was not rich merely through inheritance, but also through careful surveillance of her revenues.

Although the monks and the nuns of the order had strictly separated cloisters, there was nevertheless a considerable amount of mingling between them in the other buildings, particularly in the Queen's apartments, which were filled with a constant stream of visitors, both nobles and clerics. Those churchmen from outside who did visit the community were often scandalized by the freedom of our society, but, of course, they controlled their tongues in the hearing of this woman, particularly when they were sharing her table. How often I have seen a fat prior chewing on a portion of chicken swimming in rich sauce whilst proclaiming the virtues of self-mortification!

At the end of November a train of monks from Dinan stopped to rest amongst us. They were on their way to Marseille where they would embark for Outremer, on one of the last ships before the winter, to give spiritual succour to the soldiers of the Cross. Naturally, Queen Alienor received them sumptuously, despite the fact that they were of the Cistercian order and some had actually known Bernard of Clairvaux, who so railed against her in his lifetime. With them she came as close to deferential as ever I saw her, and as near as I would guess, she could ever be to bowing to anyone. Evidently it was true what people said of the terror she felt of Bernard, and even all those years after his death, it seemed she felt his shadow amongst his followers. For that reason, I believe, she left them pretty much free to wander at will.

Actually, they showed too fine an appreciation of her hospitality, and I saw her patience wearing thin beneath her polite smiles, for they gave no sign of setting out again. Nevertheless, she continued to entertain them in her hall, and so they were among us on the night that Ysé and I, having won approval of our families and the queen, celebrated our betrothal. It was a splendid meal that, and the wine flowed even more freely than usual, the monks, with one exception, becoming rowdy and lapsing into bawdy song such as would have horrified the revered abbot of Clairvaux. I thought that the quiet one must be disapproving of his fellows' looseness of behavior and laughed inwardly as such meanness of will. Yet there was more, an unease I felt but could not explain.

Eventually, the noise was so great that the Queen

rose to retire to her chamber, and the Princess with her. With them, of course, went the other ladies of the direct entourage, including Ysé. As they approached the door, I looked across and saw the face of the morose brother which until now had been bowed low.

It was the tumbler we had seen in Pau!

As the realization struck me, I cried out and pointed at him. All turned this way and that in alarm, but the confusion was so great that he was somersaulting across table and floor before anyone could catch him. As he landed on his feet before Berengaria, a knife fell into his hand from the sleeve of his tunic. He raised his arm to strike, but Ysé threw herself in the path of the blade, hitting at him as she did so.

It struck true and deep. My lovely doe was dead even before her body hit the floor.

By then there was no escape for the murderer, and he seemed not to care. He even smiled as guards seized him. He would answer nothing, no matter how the queen raged at him. All he would do was reply with defiance: "What I did was for my God. I curse all heretics. May they die in torment."

Though perhaps I had good reason, I could not bring myself to take part in what ensued for him, for I never could stomach torture. That one may kill in the heat of passion or of war, I accept and understand, but not this willful bloodiness. Nor, I felt then and feel now, would it have been the wish of Ysé. It brought no one any profit, anyway. Such was his fanatic strength, I am told, that he did not cry out once, nor utter the slightest sound except for a long sigh when his life gave out.

Round his neck on a thong was a medallion with the insignia of the tree and the lion.

Alienor's advisors urged her to treat others in the same way, particularly the monks, but she would have none of it. She always had a horror of such practices, as also of imprisonment. She did preside over the interrogation of a number of men and drew the conclusion that the visiting Cistercians at least were innocent, that the man had insinuated himself amongst them. There was one question above all remaining to be answered.

The woman in the mountain town and the false monk both acted under the direction of someone, perhaps the same person who had silenced Brother Leo. But who might that be?

On the following afternoon Ysé lay on a bier in the nave of the great abbey, candles set to either side of her head. I knelt at her feet, unable to keep back the tears that seemed not to come from my eyes, but from some place deep in the pit of my stomach. The touch of a hand on my shoulder, gentle though it was, roused me with the force of a blow, and I whirled, reaching for my sword, which, of course I had not brought into the church with me.

It was the Princess.

"Your Highness," I said, "you should not be unguarded."

"We are in God's house. He will protect me," she answered.

She turned then at the soft footfall of a sister who moved toward us. The face lifted. It was poor mad Agnes, her eyes wild and her veil again askew, but now I could see her face. It was King Philip's mistress, the woman he had been leaving that time in Paris. As she reached us, the madness went from her eyes. There was instead a firm intelligence there and a fixity of purpose in the mind which she had kept hidden while seen by all. She laughed as she loosened the silk cord from which hung her Cross, wrapping an end round each hand.

I lunged, and she sneered at me.

"Would you strike me in this place, which is for the protection of women?"

I was so taken aback, I paused a moment, giving her an advantage, then reached out again, but she darted to one side, slipping a coil round the neck of Berengaria. The Princess managed to grasp the cord before it was fully tight, and for some moments they struggled thus, the nun cool and deadly as she sought to finish her work.

"You thought I was mad, grieving for my poor

brother! I tell you, I laughed in his face as the flames fed on him. As I serve only one earthly king, I serve only one heavenly king, the true God, and he is not yours."

"We are not heretics!" I shouted, but she paid no attention.

As I struck at Sister Agnes. Berengaria broke free, choking and rubbing at the bruise on her neck. The murderess stood a second, her eyes filled with hate, then ran toward the high altar. Hearing me in pursuit, she stopped to seize a massive candlestick from the holy table itself. So heavy was it that she needed both hands to heft it, but with the strength of frenzy she managed enough force to launch it at me, striking me full in the chest. I fell in agony, and she darted through a doorway on the southern side.

As I struggled to regain my feet, there was a commotion at the far end. The Queen and her guards stood there at the west door. One of the men pointed above me. There stood Sister Agnes in the little gallery that runs high above the apse, looking down on the altar. She seemed to kiss one palm, then stretched her hands out to each side as the guards ran up the nave.

"For my king and the true Church!" she shouted. "Lord, into thy hands I commend my spirit. Grant me rest, and to your enemies eternal damnation!"

With this, she threw herself forward and fell to the stone floor with a thud and a snap of bone. When they retrieved the body, they found her skull was smashed, and blood and brains smeared the back of the altar cloth.

Clenched in her hand, so tight that it had not loosened even at the last, was a ring with the now-familiar engraving.

From the street the sounds of the city drift in through the high windows. Strange foreign sounds, foreign voices, all muted by the thickness of the walls. If I make a great effort, I can turn toward the nearest window and see across to the building opposite, another window, though smaller and square as opposed to the arched openings here. Sometimes there is an old man there, a Jew with a long white beard, reading what I imagine to be a sacred text. I could wish that I had been able to talk to him, to learn something of the truth of his beliefs rather than the fantastical stories one hears from childhood. The mania of religion has caused too much grief in this world, as I know to my own cost.

But I shall not have that opportunity, nor shall I walk the streets of Jerusalem as I had hoped, to see where once the Christ trod. My legs would crumple under me were I to try to stand. The poison in my veins makes its progress slowly but unfalteringly, and the heaviness possesses me ever more. There is little time left.

Brother Michael, with whom I struck up a friendship on the sea crossing, sits by me here, so patient, truly what I would call a serene man. He notes down everything I say, just as I say it. I hope that one day, perhaps centuries from now, this account will be found and others may know a part of the truth of those I served and loved.

My lion-hearted Lord Richard and Queen Alienor lie now in their royal tombs at Fontevrault, and close by are the bones of Ysé, but my resting place will be here in Outremer, this foreign land, this place of heat and constant war, and of Our Lord.

There is little left to tell. Eventually the princess did marry the king, as Alienor wished. That remarkable woman made the long journey to Messina with Berengaria, but all her plans came to nought, for there was no child from the union. Perhaps the Navarraise was barren; no one has ever been able to say. Richard survived his crusade, but met death at Chalus, struck in the shoulder by a crossbow bolt whilst laying siege to the tower in a stupid quarrel over ancient gold, behind which, as ever, lay the hand of the fox-king. Chalus fell before he died, and as they carried him to the tower, he pointed at the sun standing above a mighty tree.

"See how proud King Philip now wears his crown," he said and laughed.

The Queen grieved for the rest of her life, and small comfort she had from her son John who then took the throne. But she remained the most splendid woman in Christendom, right to the end of her days.

As for Berengaria, she lives still, a stout dame so they say, of forty-five odd years, with still the passion for those sweet almonds.

I never again looked on a woman with any passion or desire, and after the death of the Queen, no light seemed to come into my life. My desolation was observed by one of the brothers of Fontevrault who urged me to find my peace by making the journey here to Jerusalem.

Such irony! I have found peace now, and it approaches fast. Eternal peace. The king of France has at last had his revenge on me for the defeat of his plot and for the death of his mistress.

It was shortly before Christmas last year, whilst I prepared for my pilgrimage, that he came to Fontevrault in great pomp. Even before the queen's passing, he had seized most of her and Richard's territories, John being too dilatory and devious to act as he should, and now the French king wished his triumph to be seen by all. He knew how Alienor loved Fontevrault, in truth her proudest estate, and so he held a feast there.

Wisdom should have dictated that I not go to the hall that night, but I was curious to see him once more. At first he was animated, jovial, and paid me no attention, but as he sank in his cups, his face showed vicious, and he kept staring at me, narrowing his eyes as if searching for a hidden answer or a discarded memory. Finally, he summoned one of his guards, pointing to me and muttering low.

Perhaps he hesitated to lay hands on me there. Not only was this a holy community. Also, by a strange move of fate, we had become, though remotely, kinsmen when poor, mistreated Alice was finally given in marriage to my distant cousin, Count William of

Ponthieu. Perhaps, vulpine as he was, he enjoyed the sport of tracking me. Whatever the cause, I managed to slip away as the minstrels took their places and did not delay to take what baggage I could before riding into the night. But pursuit was fast behind me, and I must have been followed through Europe and across the sea.

As I stepped ashore, the man behind jostled me as though burning with the true pilgrim's zeal, but even before I felt the sharp prick in my arm, I think I understood. I did not even turn to see his face, nor cry out for help. Indeed, it was only when I fell, as my feet touched at last the dust of the Holy Land, that anyone knew I was stricken. They brought me here and did what they could, but I told them there was no cure. I knew that more surely than anything since the passing of the one I loved most.

And so, on this fifth day of February in the year of Our Lord 1205, in the hospital of the Knights of Saint John in Jerusalem, being fifty-four years old, I, Ralph of Ponthieu, knight, beg the indulgence of my fellow men and give myself to God for the last time. May He grant that, should I enter into His Heaven, I shall meet once again the lord Richard and Queen Alienor, and my lady Ysé.

Balmorality

by Robert Barnard

I am going to write down a true account of the Merrivale busness without help from my secertary because I know if it comes out I shall get blamed, especially by Mama, who blames me for everything that goes wrong in her circle, in Society in general—even, I sometimes think, in the country at large, as if I were somehow responsable for the national debt, the troublesome Afgans, and the viragoes who advocate votes for women. Nothing I say would influence Mama's opinion, in fact nothing anybody says does, but perhaps an account in my own hand, without the intervention of my secertary, will convince posteraty that I was entirely blameless. Here is the whole truth of the matter.

The story begins in a corridor at Balmoral Castle, built in a baronial but incomodious style by my revered father when I was no more than a boy (but learning!) In Scotland the summer nights are short, and the twilights almost seem to murge into the first lights of dawn (especially for those who have brought their own supplies to orgment the meager rations of wines and spirits). I was, I must admit, in a pretty undignified position for one of my standing. I was squeezed into an alcove, perched on a sort of bench, shielded by heavy velvet curtains. Not a comfortable position for one of my gerth. I would very much have prefered to stand, but I tried that and found that my shoes pertruded under the bottom of the curtains.

So far I had seen nothing I did not expect to see. I had seen Lord Lobway leave the comforts of his martial bed for the delights of Mrs. Aberdovy's. I had seen

Lady Wanstone tiptoe along to comfort the loneliness of the Duke of Strathgovern. I have corridor-tiptoed in my time, or been tiptoed to, and I do no condem. I have nothing against adultary provided it is between consenting adults. Seducing a young girl is the action of a cad, unless she is very insistant.

What I had not seen was the figure of that frightful fellow John Brown. Now please do not misunderstand me here. I did not for one moment expect to see the awful gillie going to my Mama's bedroom. I do not suffer from the vulgar misapprehension about their relationship. In any case Mama's bedroom is at least a quater of a mile away, otherwise I could not have been hiding in the corridor! No, the door I was watching was that of Lady Westchester, and the reason was two-fold: if I could catch John Brown out in a nocternal assingation with the lady, I could take the story straight to Mama (I already had my sorrowful mein well prepared) and that would perhaps see the end of his embarassing presence at her court; and secondly I have a definate interest in Lady Westchester myself, and I object to sharing her with a gillie. Her husband has been very willing to turn a blind eye (and even, since he sleeps in the next room, a deaf ear!) but I wonder whether he would be willing to do likewise for the repulsive Highlander? For when I heard Lady Westchester, in intimate converse with her best friend Mrs. Aberdovy, say "He's so delicously ordinary!" that, I concluded, was who she was talking about. I had seen her fluttering her eyelids at him when he helped her to horse. And which of the other servants mix with Mama's guests on that level of familiarity (or impurtenance)? When she begged me not to trouble her that night (I had not noticed it was any trouble) then I concluded that her assingation was with one infinately lower than myself.

Dinner had been oxtail soup, sole, foie gras, turbot, snipe, crown of beef, game pie, steamed pudding, and one or two other trifles I had just picked at, but dinner was hours and hours ago. I was just beginning to feel hungry when I heard the sound of a door opening. I peered through the heavy folds of velvet. It was not Lady Westerchester's door. I was about to withdraw into my alcove when I saw a scene in the open doorway that gave me furously to think. The door was Colonel Merrivale's, and coming out was a little bounder called Laurie Lamont, whose presence at Balmoral I found it difficult to account for. But what made my heart skip a beat was that I could see clearly that Merrivale was withdrawing his hand from the inside pocket of his jacket, while Laurie Lamont's hand was withdrawing from the pocket of his trousers.

Not an hour before Merrivale had been winning quite heavily off me and other gentlemen at poker.

Lamont scuttled off down the corridor and away to his room in some obscure corner of my Papa's Gothick pile, and I remained considering the scene I had just witnessed and hoping that the gastly gillie would make his appearance soon. I had waited no more than a few minutes when I heard footsteps. Looking out I saw that it was my own man! I shrank back, but the footsteps stopped beside my alcove.

"I would advise Your Royal Highness not to remain here any longer."

Well! He had barely paused, spoke in a low voice, and then continued on down the corridor. After thinking things over for a few minutes I emerged rather nonchalently and returned to my suite of rooms. Where my man awaited me.

"How did you know I was there?" I demanded.

"I am afraid, sir, there was a certain swelling which disturbed the hang of the curtain."

He has a clever way of putting things, my man. He meant there was a bulge. He is fair, tall, with an air that is almost gentlemanly and an expression that I have heard described as quizicle.

"Where had you come from anyway?" I asked.

"I was myself watching from another of the alcoves," he replied. I looked with distast at his discusting slimness. "I too had had my suspicions roused in the course of cards this evening."

I did not enlighten him as to which door I had in fact

been keeping an eye on, or give any indication that the scene in the doorway had come as a complete bomshell to me. As he relieved me of my clothes I let him continue.

"You remember, sir, that you summoned me to prepare some of the herbal mixture that you get such relief from, after too many cigars?"

"Shouldn't be getting short of breath these days," I complained. "I've cut down to just one before breakfast, and the odd cigarette."

"I rather fear that without noticing you have increased your consumption *after* breakfast, sir," he said. I allow my man great lattitude. He is invaluable in all sorts of little arrangements. "Anyway, the fact was I was in the card room for some time, during which Colonel Merrivale was winning quite heavily."

"Too damned heavily. I'm well out of pocket."

"Exactly, sir. And I noticed this Mr. Lamont. He was deep in converse with the Countess of Berkhampstead. She was telling him about her various ailments, and was so engrossed—predictably so, if I may venture to say it—that she was noticing nothing about him. They were by a mirror. By testing I realized he could see the cards of two of the other players. And I got the idea that he was making suttle signs to Colonel Merrivale."

"The damned rotters!" I exploded. "At Balmoral too! Windsor would be another matter, but Balmoral! I know Merrivale. He's brother to one of the Queen's Scottish equerries. Who is this Lamont fellow?"

"I have made enquiries about that, sir—talked to his man. He is active in civic affairs in Edinburgh, it seems. Has been pressing the case for a fitting monument in the city to the late Prince Consort. He has been agitating in the City Council and the newspapers for an opera house, to be called the Albert Theatre."

"It will never happen. The good burgers of Edinburgh are far too mean."

"It may be, sir, that he doesn't expect it to happen, and that that is not the point. He has, after all, been invited to Balmoral . . ."

"True. Mingling with those very much above his station."

"Quite, sir."

"Mama is too gulable. It's too much that people get invited here at the drop of the word 'Albert.'"

"I suspect it has been noted, sir, that the name is a sort of open sessamy."

"The bounders have to be exposed."

"Quite so, sir. But how?"

"I can charge him publicly with what I saw."

"Hardly conclusive, sir. And I see a difficulty: you were playing poker, for money, at Balmoral, sir."

He was his usual impurturbable self, but I huffed and puffed a bit, though nothing like as much as Mama would have huffed and puffed if she knew we had been playing poker for high stakes in what is vertually my late Papa's second morsauleum.

"Ah yes, well ..." I said finally. "Might be a bit awkward. Though when I think how the Queen goes on about the company I keep ..."

"Perhaps we should sleep on it, sir. By morning we may have thought of something."

"Nothing to do but think," I muttered, as he pulled my nightshirt over my head. I leapt between the sheets, burning my leg on the stone hot water bottle. "I'm not used to sleeping long. Alix would have been better than nothing."

For my dear wife has no love of Balmoral, and generally siezes the time of our annual visit for a trip to see her relatives. I make no objection. If her relatives had been German, Mama would probably find her visits to them admirably fillial, but as they are Danish she says she is being selfish.

Well, I spent a lonely night warmed only by hot water bottles, but I can't say that in the morning I had come up with any great plan. All I could think of was whether John Brown was in with Lady Westchester, and what they were likely to be doing. Mind you, I don't think my man expected me to come up with anything. When he said "we" he meant I. He's got rather a good opinion of himself.

"Well, sir," he said next morning, as he shaved the bits of my face that needed shaving, "it's a beuatiful day, and apparently the vote is for a croquy competition."

"Damned boring game," I commented. "Bonking balls through hoops."

"But you do play, sir."

"Oh, I can bonk with the best of them."

"Because I thought just possibly something might be made of it."

And he wisked off the towels just like the johnnie in the opera, and confided in me his thoughts.

The Arbroath smokies served at Balmoral are, I have to admit, unparalelled, and the kedgeree not to be despised. The sausages, bacon, and black pudding are inferior to what we have at Marlborough House, but the beefsteaks can be admirable. I breakfasted alone. If I take a small table and look royal everybody knows I am brooding on affairs of state and I am not disturbed. When I had eaten my fill I lit up my second cigar of the day and strolled out on to the sun-drenched lawns. It did not even destroy my good humor to see John Brown setting up the hoops and pegs and three separate croquy lawns. Somehow I knew things were going to go according to plan.

Lord John Willoughby had been recruted to further the plot. Lord John is in fact alergic to croquy, but he was a fellow loser of the night before, and he was to be used as an apparantly casual bystander. He had been approached by a deputation consisting of my man, and he had joyfully gone along with the idea. Those villians Merrivale and Lamont had been organised by Willoughby into opposing teams, and when I strolled up to Merrivale and said, "Give me my revenge for last night, eh?" Lord Rishton willingly dropped out of the game and transferred to another team, which left me partnering the loathsome Lamont, with Merrivale's partner the delectible Lady Frances Bourne, whose only fault is her unshakable faithfulness to a damned dull husband. Still, if I couldn't partner her in any other sort of games, croquy it would have to be.

Willoughby, I'll say this for him, has a sense of humor. He arranged it so he stood on the sideliness of our game talking to Lady Berkhampstead. He was, too all intents and purposes, totally absorbed in her twinges of this and agonising attacks of that. I let the game proceed until I was well-poised to shoot my red ball through the fourth hoop and Lamont was rather poorly placed for getting his yellow ball through the third. Then, as he was standing beside his ball shielding it from the gaze of spectators, I gave the sign and both Willoughby and I stepped forward.

"That man moved his ball."

Laurie Lamont looked astonished, as well he might.

"I haven't touched my ball, sir. It's not my turn."

"I'll have no partner of mine cheating," I said.

"I saw him," said Willoughby, coming up. "He shifted his ball to a better position for his next shot."

"And where there's cheating, there's money on the game," I said menacingly. "I wouldn't mind bet—I strongly suspect that they've got a wager on this."

I looked meaningfully at Lamont, then equally meaningfully at Merrivale. I wanted both of them to understand *exactly* what piece of cheating was in question.

"And since no one would suspect Lady Frances of betting, I think we can take it that you, Merrivale, are the other culprit. Betting on a game of croquy in the grounds of the Queen's Scottish home! And cheating! You probably even have the wager on you, I'll be bound."

I knew they did. Lamont had his on him because he's one of these tradesmen chappies who won't leave loose money in their rooms even when they're guests of their sovereign. Merrivale had his on him because his man had been persuaded by mine to slip it into the inside pocket of his jacket that morning.

"I absolutely protest, sir," he now spluttered. "I have no money on me!"

He opened up his jacket, and pertruding from the pocket was an envelope. I extracted it and counted the money.

"One hundred and fifteen pounds. And no doubt you too have a hundred and fifteen?" Lamont squermed and kept his jacket tight-buttoned. I held out my hand and he took out the money. "Two hundred and thirty pounds. Well, well, well!"

It was the sum Merrivale had won the night before, shared equally with his accomplice. I pocketed it.

By now there were several bystanders, all curious to know what was going on. Lady Berkhampstead, interrupted mid-twinge, was loudly demanding to be told what was happening. I pointed to the castle.

"Betting at Balmoral. I never thought to see this day. You sir—" I turned to Merrivale—"I would have expected to know better. You sir"—turning to Lamont—"I had no expectations of. I count on hearing that you have both left the castle before nightfall."

There was a moment's pause. Merrivale spluttered, then the pair of them slunk in the direction of the castle, their tails almost visably between their legs. I walked over in high good humor to watch one of the other games.

"Just a little contratems," I said airily. "Regard our game as scratched."

That evening, when my man was poking and prodding me into my evening wear to make me presentable for the dreary horrors of a Balmoral dinner, he said, "Colonel Merrivale's young daughter has been taken ill, and Mr. Lamont's mother. Quite a coincidence, sir."

I grunted my satisfaction, and in an interval of prodding said, "That'll teach the Queen not to invite just any little squert who happens to suck up to her on the subject of Papa. I wonder if I should rub it in that she ought to be more careful who she invites?" I saw an expression pass over his face. I am very quick on the uptake. "Well, perhaps not. Perhaps I may just write an account of the whole busness for posterity."

"That should make fasinating reading, sir."

My mind going back to the start of the busness and my concealment in the alcove, I said, "Lady Westchester has intimated that I would be welcome to-night. Don't know that I shall take up the offer.

Damned unpleasant not knowing who I'm sharing her with."

"I happen to know, sir, that the reason Lady Westchester was . . . unavailable last night was because her husband especially requested the favor of a night with her. The sort of ladies his lordship habitually consorts with are in particularly short supply in the Balmoral area."

"Really?" I said, rather pleased. But then I pondered. "That doesn't explain the other thing, though."

"Other thing, sir?"

"I heard her say of some man that he was 'delicously ordinary.' I'm damned sure she was talking about John Brown."

There came over my man's face that smile that people call quizicle.

"Oh that, sir. Is that what you suspected? Her ladyship has been heard to say that to several people. I think she intends the remark to be paradoxicle."

"To be what?"

"A paradox, sir, is something that is apparently abserd or impossible, but turns out to be true. Her ladyship was not referring to John Brown, sir."

"Oh?"

"She was referring to you."

For a moment he took my breath away. When the idea got through to me I felt immensely flattered.

"Well, I say, you know, that really is rather a complement, don't you think? I mean, here I am, with all my advantages, rather marked off by my birth, set apart all my life for a special task, and yet I manage to keep the common touch to such an extent that she can say that about me. I feel quite touched. She's right. I am ordinary. No one would call the Russian emperor ordinary, would they? Or the kaiser? She really has me summed up very well."

"I'm glad Your Royal Highness sees it that way."

"I do. I'm obliged to you for clearing up the misunderstanding. In fact I'm obliged to you for giving the other matter such a satisfactory outcome too."

I felt about my person for something with which to

show my appreciation of his very special services. It is one of the drawbacks of being royal that one has very little use for ready money, so one very seldom has any on one. Fortunately I have always found that people feel just as well rewarded by a sincere expression of royal gratitude. I clapped my man on the shoulder.

"Thank you, Lovesy," I said.

Bertie and the Fire Brigade

by Peter Lovesey

One of the favorite pastimes of the British while reclining in a hammock is to think up worthwhile jobs for the Prince of Wales. Everyone from the sovereign downward has his two-pennyworth, regardless of the fact that most of the occupations suggested are utterly unsuitable for me. I can't imagine how the idea got abroad that time hangs heavy on my hands. Between laying foundation stones and receiving visiting heads of state, I have precious little time for my social obligations, let alone earning "an honest crust," as one newspaper impertinently proposed.

However, since the rest of the nation indulges in this sport, why shouldn't I? I'll tell you how I could have earned a handsome living if circumstances allowed. As a detective. Given the opportunity, I would certainly have risen to high rank in the police, for my deductive skills as an amateur sleuth-hound are well attested, if not well known. And I could also have made a decent show as a fireman.

Yes, a fireman.

The great British public is largely ignorant of my pyro-exploits, as I call them, my adventures with the gallant officers of the London Fire Brigade. I don't mind confiding in these memoirs that I have attended fires all over London for the past twenty years. Frequently—when not attending to affairs of state—I can be found enjoying a game of billiards at the fire station in Chandos Street with my old chum, the Duke of Sutherland, another gentleman fire-fighter, while we wait for the alarm to be sounded. We both have the kit, you know: full uniform, with helmet, boots, and axe.

Oh, how I relish the ride on the engine, bell jangling, horses at the gallop!

Are you intrigued? Then I shall tell you more. I once triumphantly combined my skills as detective and fireman. It happened in the summer of 1870 when I was twenty-nine and "under fire" myself, so to speak. There had been some deplorable publicity in February of that year when I was called as a witness in a divorce case, to emerge, I may add, with my character unsullied, utterly unsullied. The husband who had been so misguided as to name me and several other gentlemen had his petition dismissed on the grounds that his wife was insane and could not be a party to the suit. The wretched newspapers, not content with the result, mischievously set out to stoke up republican sentiments. I remember shortly after being hissed in the theater and booed at Ascot. *At the races.* Mind, when a horse of mine won the last race, the same fickle crowd cheered me to the echo. I remember raising my hat to them and calling out, "You seem to be in a better temper now than you were this morning, damn you!"

A few days later, on the Friday, I was at my club, the Marlborough, enjoying a short respite from affairs of state in a foursome of skittles, when a message came for Captain Shaw, my partner for the evening. A fire had taken hold in Villiers Street, a mere quarter of a mile away. You must have heard of Shaw, the intrepid chief of the London Fire Brigade, immortalized by W. W. Gilbert in *Iolanthe* and stigmatized by Lord Colin Campbell in the most notorious of all divorce cases. Personally, I always had a high regard for Eyre Shaw, whatever may or may not have happened with Lady Colin on the dining-room carpet of the Campbell abode in Cadogan Place. The man is a dedicated fire-fighter, so dedicated, in fact, that he chooses to live beside the fire station in Southwark Bridge Road, a particularly unsalubrious area. His house, which I have visited, is most ingeniously fitted with speaking-tubes in every room so that Shaw can be promptly informed of fires breaking out.

Immediately news of the Villiers Street fire was conveyed, Shaw apologized for interrupting our game and called for the helmet he keeps at the club for just such an emergency.

"Sir, would you care—"

"I should take it as a personal affront not to be included," I informed him.

Ideally, I like to ride to a fire in full kit on the running board of the engine, but on this occasion we had no time to call at Chandos Street to dress the part, so we hailed a cab and made the best speed we could down Pall Mall to Trafalgar Square and into Villiers Street by way of the Strand.

An awesome scene confronted us. Villiers Street is a narrow, dingy thoroughfare beside Charing Cross Station, sloping quite steeply down to the Thames. It is always cluttered with coffee stalls, whelk counters, hot potato-cans, and wood-and-canvas structures festooned with gimcrack rubbish, and this evening the news of the fire had brought hundreds of sight-seers off the Strand, the station, and adjacent streets. The naphtha flares mounted on the stalls showed us a daunting spectacle from our elevated view in the four-wheeler, wave upon wave of toppers, bowlers, and greasy caps.

The cabman confided his doubt whether he would succeed in moving the vehicle through such a throng. The feat would not have been impossible, but it would have been deucedly slow in execution, so we elected to climb out and make our own way. Fortunately, the Chief Fire Officer is instantly recognizable when he dons his helmet and to repeated cries of "Make way for Captain Shaw!" we progressed down Villiers Street like Moses through the Dead Sea. As for me, I held on to my hat and followed close with eyes down and collar up, or we should never have got through.

Bright orange flames were leaping merrily at the windows of a large building almost at the bottom of the street and the Chandos Street lads were already at work with two engines. The proximity of the Thames meant that a floating engine had also been deployed.

Shaw at once sought out the man directing operations, Superintendent Flanagan, and established what was happening. I knew Flanagan passably well as a competent officer who could handle a hose more expertly than a billiard cue. Like Shaw himself, he was Irish, more than a touch pleased with himself (a weakness of the shamrock fraternity), but conscientious and a respected leader of men. I'd once met his wife at Chandos Street, and a prettier, more beguiling creature than Dymphna Flanagan never crossed the Irish Sea. She had that combination of raven hair and lily-white skin that is unique to Irish women. You can tell the impression she made on me because I seriously thought afterward of suggesting to some London hostess that she add the Flanagans to the guest list on an evening I was coming for supper. Finally, I abandoned this intention. I was willing to put up with Flanagan's brash manners for an evening with his winsome wife, but I felt that I couldn't inflict him on my fellow guests.

"Is anyone inside?" was Shaw's first question.

"No, it's empty," Flanagan told him as confidently as if the house were his own.

"You're sure?"

"Sure as the Creed, Captain. The owner died last Friday. There was a manservant, and he was dismissed the next day."

"Who told you this?" I asked.

"One of the stall holders, sir. They miss nothing."

"You say the owner died. The corpse . . . ?"

". . . was moved to the mortuary the same evening, sir."

"Who was he?"

"A retired bookbinder, name of Millichip. It's a pity he was moved from the house."

"Why on earth do you say that?"

"Curious to relate, Mr. Millichip was chairman of the London Cremation League."

"The what?"

He repeated it for me. "They advocate disposal of the dead by burning."

"What a heathenish idea!" I commented. "The Church would never sanction it."

"Ashes to ashes, sir."

Damned impertinence. I wish you could have heard the uppish way he said it, for the tone would have told you volumes about his bumptiousness. Captain Shaw quite properly put a stop to this morbid exchange. "If you'll pardon me, sir, you'd better redirect your hoses, Mr. Flanagan. The fire is starting to take hold on the top floor."

Shaw's assessment was correct. It never ceases to amaze me how swiftly a fire can spread. In spite of the best efforts of the crews, huge forks of flame ripped through the upper story in minutes, sending showers of sparks into the night sky.

"What the deuce burns as fiercely as that?" I asked, but Shaw had left my side to assist in the work of raising a fire-escape ladder, the better to direct jets of water onto the roof, where slates were already cascading off the rafters. I should have realized that a bookbinder might possess samples of his work, for it later transpired that the top floor was practically lined with books.

But I wasn't there, as most bystanders were, merely to goggle. I set to and organized a human chain to convey buckets of water from the river as an auxiliary to the pumps. I doubt whether any of my shabby helpers recognized me, but they deferred at once to the authority represented by my silk hat and cane.

For upward of an hour, we struggled to gain ascendancy. The falling slates became a considerable hazard, and I was obliged to borrow a helmet from a fireman who readily conceded that my skull was more precious than his own. As so often happens, just as we were getting control of the fire, reinforcements arrived from Holborn and Fleet Street. The stop, to employ a term we fire-fighters use, came twenty minutes before midnight. The house was a mere shell by that time.

Wearily, we senior fire-fighters gathered by the nearest coffee stall and slaked our thirst while the firemen were winding up the hoses. Flanagan looked ready to drop, and I told him so.

"I'm feeling better than I look, sir," he said.

Firemen work longer hours than the police or the army. Even a superintendent takes only one day off each fortnight as a matter of right. Of course he slips away when things are quiet, but he is constantly on call.

"What exercises me about this fire," I remarked to Eyre Shaw, "is how it started. If no one was inside, what could have set it off?"

He nodded, taking my point. The wily Captain Shaw hasn't much faith in the theory of spontaneous combustion.

He said an investigation would be set in train first thing next morning. I offered to take part, if not first thing, then as soon as my other engagements allowed.

My dear wife, the Princess of Wales, had retired by the time I returned to Marlborough House, or she would certainly have passed a comment on my appearance. As it happens, we have separate bedrooms, so it was not until breakfast that she tackled me. By then, of course, I'd bathed and changed my clothes and really believed she would have no clue how I'd spent the previous evening. She doesn't altogether approve of my pyro-exploits. Such is my optimism that I'd forgotten that Alix has a keener sense of smell than your average bloodhound. More than once it has been my undoing over breakfast, and not always due to smoke fumes.

"You really ought not to spend so much time with the Fire Brigade, Bertie. I can smell it in your hair."

"Oh?"

"If your Mama had any idea, she would be deeply shocked."

"Mama is shocked if I cross the road," said I.

"Where was the fire this time?"

I gave Alix an account of my evening and told her about the advocate of cremation who had unluckily been removed to the mortuary before his house burnt down. "If his timing had been better, he'd have had his wish. I wonder if one of his supporters put a match to the place in the belief that the body was still inside."

Alix commented, "It would be rather extreme, burning down an entire house and putting Charing Cross Station at risk."

"True, but someone must have started the fire. The servant wasn't there. He was dismissed the day after Millichip died."

"Who, by?"

"One of the family, I gather."

"Well, the servant must have been unhappy about losing his job so suddenly," Alix mused aloud, then added emphatically, "He came back with a match to deprive the family of their inheritance."

It's often said and often demonstrated that women are illogical. Obviously I married a notable exception. I wouldn't have thought of the servant as an arsonist, but Alix was onto him already.

I'm in the habit of taking a constitutional at 12:15, and that morning I directed my steps to the site of the fire, where I discovered Superintendent Flanagan and his deputy, First Class Engineer Henry Locke, in earnest conversation with a tall young man dressed in mourning.

"Your Highness, may I present Mr. Guy Millichip, the son of the late owner of this house?"

The young man's grip was clammy to the touch. You can tell a lot from a handshake. I should know; I've shaken more hands than you ever will, I'll warrant, gentle reader. A clammy hand goes with a doubtful character.

"My condolences," I said. "All this must be a fearful shock, coming so soon after your father's passing. Was he a sick man?"

"No, Your Royal Highness. It came out of the blue."

"A sudden death?" My detective brain was already working on possibilities.

"Yes, sir. His heart stopped."

"Isn't that always the case?" said Flanagan in his irritating Irish lilt.

Millichip glared. "I meant to say that the doctor diagnosed a sudden heart attack. The post mortem has since confirmed it."

"I see. And was anyone with your father when he died?"

"Only Rudkin, the manservant."

"Where were you at the time?"

"Of Father's death? In Reigate, where I live. I hadn't seen him for over a year. When I noticed the announcement in *The Times*, I came to London directly."

"And dismissed Rudkin directly?"

"He'll find other work. I gave him an excellent character, sir."

"Where is he to be found?"

"Rudkin? I have no idea. He resided here."

"Until he was dismissed?"

"Yes, sir."

"And now he has no address? You consigned him to the streets?"

"I had no use for his services and no certainty of being able to pay his wages, sir."

Here, Flanagan's deputy, Engineer Locke, observed, "You'll inherit something, surely? Aren't you the only son?"

Young Millichip shook his head. "I don't expect to get a brass farthing. Father made it abundantly clear that the entire proceeds of his estate would go to the London Cremation League." He spoke without rancor, as if remarking on the weather. Then he showed himself to be human by adding with a slight smile, "Their windfall has been somewhat reduced by the fire."

"Has the will been read?"

"Not yet, sir. The family solicitor will reveal the contents after the funeral, but I know what's in it. Father told me months ago when he drew it up. That's why we fell out. I was incensed. It was the last conversation I had with him. Those cremation people will blue it all on beer. They're bohemians for the most part, writers and artists—Trollope, Millais, Tenniel, people like that. They meet once a month in some plush hotel in the West End with no prospect of achieving their aims."

"If it isn't impertinent to ask, how much was your father worth?"

"A cool three hundred pounds, sir."

"That's a lot of beer."

When the young man had left us, Flanagan preempted me by commenting, "I recommend that we look for signs of arson."

"I should have thought that goes without saying," said I in a bored voice. "Clearly the servant must be found and questioned at once."

"The servant?" said he, as if I'd named the Archbishop of Canterbury. "I was about to suggest that Millichip must have set the place alight."

"Millichip? But why?"

"To deprive the Cremation League of its legacy. He's a very embittered young man, sir."

I wasn't persuaded. However, we had much to do. I proceeded to examine the building with Flanagan and Locke. The ash was thick on the ground, but so are shoeblacks at Charing Cross, so I didn't hesitate. It's fascinating to look at a gutted building with a man of Flanagan's experience. He had no difficulty in finding the seat of the fire, which was in the basement, close to the street, and he rapidly concluded that arson was the most likely cause. By picking at fragments of ash and sniffing his finger and thumb he was able to inform us that a paraffin-soaked rag had been used as tinder, probably set alight and pushed through a broken window by the arsonist.

"So simple, if a person is really bent on destroying a house," he said. "We had a similar case two weeks ago, didn't we, Henry?"

"That is correct, sir," Locke confirmed without much animation, for it presently emerged that the Friday in question had been his day off duty, and he had missed a spectacular blaze. As he'd also missed the Villiers Street fire for the same reason, Henry Locke had every right to feel deprived. Most of the calls the fire service deal with are chimney fires, which can be very tedious.

"An empty house in Tavistock Street went up like a beacon," Flanagan explained for my benefit. "We fought it for three and a half hours. It belonged to the eminent zoologist, Professor Carson. He left on a trip to the Amazon a couple of days before. The police are investigating."

"How could I have missed it?" I mused aloud, then remembered that a supper engagement had taken me to Gatti's restaurant on the night in question and to a private address thereafter. I was bending my efforts to *raise* a fire that night, so to speak, not to dowse one. "Well, the police have a straightforward task in this case. I shall instruct them to detain Rudkin, the servant."

I spoke confidently, showing my contempt for Flanagan's theory that Millichip was the arsonist and incidentally omitting to mention my reservations about the efficiency of the Metropolitan Police. Straightforward their task may have been, but in the event the raw lobsters required five days to find Rudkin, in cheap lodgings in the shabby district of Notting Hill. I had him brought to Chandos Street Fire Station for questioning on the following Thursday.

James Rudkin may have looked the worse for wear from his new way of life, but in deportment and speech he was still the gentleman's gentleman, with airs of refinement. I suppose he was forty-five years of age, dark-haired, with muttonchop whiskers going gray. He claimed to know nothing whatsoever about the fire. "This is calamitous. When did you say it occurred, Your Royal Highness? Last Friday? Was there serious damage?"

"Never mind that," I told him, eager to catch him out, for Flanagan and Shaw were sitting beside me, and I wanted to prove a point or two. "Where were you last Friday evening?"

"Me?" He piped the word as if to imply that anything connected with himself was unworthy of consideration. "You wish to know where *I* was, Your Royal Highness?"

Indifferent to the wretched fellow's playacting, I tapped the ash from my cigar and waited.

Rudkin hesitated, apparently collecting his thoughts. "Last Friday evening. Let me see. Oh, yes. I was at South Kensington, at the Art Training School."

"The Art School?" I said in total disbelief. "You're an artist? I can't believe that. How could you afford the fees?"

"Oh, I wasn't required to pay a fee, sir. They paid me. I was, em, sitting."

"Sitting?"

"Well, reclining, in point of fact, sir. The school advertised for models and I applied. It was force of necessity. I needed the money to pay for a night's lodging."

"I follow you now. What time was this?"

"The class lasted from 7 to 9 P.M., sir, but I had to report early to remove my clothes."

"Good Lord! You were posing in the buff?"

"It was the life class, sir."

I turned to Eyre Shaw. "At what hour did the fire break out?"

He coughed nervously. "Approximately 8:30, sir. Certainly no later."

That evening, I told the Princess of Wales that her theory about the servant had been confounded and in a manner acutely embarrassing to me personally. "Rashly I asked the fellow if he could prove this extraordinary alibi of his, and he said there must be twenty drawings of his anatomy from every possible angle. He couldn't swear that every one would be a good likeness, but I was welcome to inquire at the school. Imagine me—asking to examine drawings of a naked man."

"It wouldn't be advisable, Bertie."

"Don't worry, my dear. I may have been a trouble to you on occasions, but I'll not be caught looking at drawings of a butler in his birthday suit. I'm just relating the facts so that you can see how mistaken you were. Rudkin cannot possibly be the arsonist. It was such a persuasive theory when you mentioned it."

"I'm not infallible, Bertie."

I sniffed. "Regrettably, it seems that Flanagan—that bombastic Irishman from Chandos Street—is the one who is infallible. Young Millichip put a match to the house to prevent it from passing to the London Cremation League. I shall suggest to the police that they arrest him in the morning. Frankly, I'm not interested in questioning him a second time."

Alix continued with her sewing.

"It's a great pity," I maundered on, more to myself than Alix. "I should have liked to have solved a case of arson. I shall have to bide my time, I suppose. My change will come. It's becoming a common crime—every other Friday, in fact."

"Speak up, Bertie."

Alix is somewhat deaf.

"I said arson happens every other Friday. A slight exaggeration. A house in Tavistock Street three weeks ago, and the Villiers Street fire last week."

She stopped her sewing and gave me a penetrating look. "You didn't mention two cases of arson when we discussed the case."

"At the time, my dear, I hadn't heard about the Tavistock Street fire. I missed it. I was, em, otherwise engaged that evening ... putting the world to rights with the Dean of St. Paul's, if I remember correctly."

"Two houses set alight?" said Alix.

"Two."

"On Fridays?"

"Yes."

"Both started maliciously?"

"Apparently, yes."

"Was anyone hurt?"

"No, no. Both houses were uninhabited."

"Then let us suppose both fires were started by one individual. How would he—or she—have known that no one was inside?"

I said, "I'm damned if I know. One individual? What makes you say that?"

She ignored my question. "Presumably, the late Mr. Millichip's death was reported in the newspapers."

"That is true," said I. "His son read it in *The Times.*"

"And do you know the identity of the owner of the Tavistock Street house?"

"That was Carson, the explorer. He left for the Amazon three weeks ago."

"Was his expedition reported in *The Times*?"

"It may well have been. He's a famous man. I'll speak to the editor and find out, if you think it's important."

She gave a slight shrug and lowered her eyes to the needlework. Poor Alix. She never knows whether to encourage me in my investigations. But she'd said enough to stoke up my analytical processes again. I asked myself whether it was conceivable that some wicked arsonist was lighting fires at random. No, not at random, but by reference to *The Times*. If so, it would be devilish difficult to identify him. What facts did we have? He was a reader of *The Times*, presumably a Londoner. He selected houses that were empty and he favored Friday evenings for his fire raising. Would there be another fire this week, or next? If so, where?

There was a panic below stairs when I asked the head butler for the entire week's issues of *The Times.* Normally I never see a copy that has not been freshly ironed and then they tend to get creased and sprinkled with cigar ash in the course of my perusal. Lord knows what happens after I've finished with them. One thing was certain: the prospect of retrieving six copies and getting them fit for inspection caused my head butler's eyes to resemble coach-lamps, even after I assured him that ironing would not be necessary. In the end six immaculate newspapers were supplied from heaven knows where, and I set to work compiling a list of recently vacated properties. Within a short time I realized the scale of the task I'd set myself. The deaths column alone ran to fifty or sixty names each day. I therefore confined myself to names in the vicinity of Chandos Street Fire Station, where the two previous fires had taken place. At the end of two hours, I had a list of twelve residences that I considered prime candidates for arson.

I was so pleased with my detective work that I showed Alix the list. Somewhat to my surprise, she laughed. "Oh, Bertie, what will you do now—travel the district on a bicycle keeping watch on all these houses?"

"That isn't the object," I explained. "If one of them goes up in flames tomorrow night, I shall know for certain that my theory is correct. The arsonist selects the houses from *The Times.*"

"And then you can make another list next week," said Alix with a lamentable lack of sensitivity.

"What else do you propose?" said I chillingly.

"I make no claim to be a detective, but I would look for a motive, my dear."

"It's all very fine to talk in such terms," I protested, "but why would anyone put a match to a house? To see a damned good fire. Believe it or not, there are people who derive a morbid pleasure from watching a property go up in flames."

"Oh, I believe it, Bertie."

"They are known as pyromaniacs."

She regarded me steadily. "Yes."

"Then what is the use of looking for a motive?"

"There may be a more practical motive."

"I doubt it," said I.

But later, in bed—my own bed—I paid Alix's last observation the compliment of considering it at more length. Suppose there was a practical motive. Why set light to a building if it isn't for the undoubted satisfaction of seeing it ablaze? It wasn't as if some insurance swindle was involved in either incident, so far as I was aware. And there was no attempt to put anyone in personal danger; in fact, the reverse was true. The arsonist appeared to have gone to some trouble to select an empty house and so avoid an accident.

In the small hours of the morning, a theory began to form in my brain, a brilliant theory that I was perfectly capable of putting to the test. It encompassed both motive and opportunity. I could hardly wait for Friday evening to learn whether the arsonist would strike again.

He did not.

I had to wait another full week and compile another list of proprieties from *The Times* before this drama came to its conclusion.

Two weeks to the day since the Villiers Street fire, I took high tea instead of supper and arrived at Chandos Street Fire Station sharp at 7. Captain Shaw had not yet appeared and nor had the Duke of Sutherland, so after changing into my fireman's uniform I had a game of billiards with Superintendent Flanagan and beat him soundly. Then I put my proposition to him.

"If there's a fire this evening, I'd like to have command of one of the escapes—with your consent, of course."

He pricked up his eyebrows. Generally, I'm content to take a subordinate role in fire fighting. "Is there a reason for this, sir?"

Damned impertinence. I ignored the remark. "You have no shortage of escapes?"

"Oh, we have more than we ever use."

"Mine can be surplus to requirements, then." I added cuttingly, "I wouldn't want to hamper the work of the London Fire Brigade through inexperience."

He had the grace to mumble, "That's unthinkable, Your Royal Highness."

"Very good, then. And Flanagan . . ."

"Sir?"

"We won't mention it to the others."

"As you wish, sir."

George Sutherland arrived soon after and restored my *joie de vivre* in no time. He's an old friend and a marvelous eccentric who happens to own more land than any other man in the kingdom. The Shah of Persia (another notable eccentric) once advised me that Sutherland was too grand a subject and I'd be well advised to have his head off when I come to the throne. I never miss an opportunity to remind George of this.

The alarm came at twenty minutes past eight. A house at the Leicester Square end of Coventry Street was well alight. Marvelous! It was on my list. The owner had died ten days ago, according to *The Times*.

I told nobody the significance of the address at this juncture. I was playing a cautious hand, by Jove. I made sure that I was last in the rush to the fire-fighting vehicles. I watched two engines and an escape being whipped out, bells jangling. Flanagan and George Sutherland were aboard the first to leave.

My team of two firemen waited deferentially for me to step up to the driver's box, and I took my time, making certain that everyone else was out of the yard and would be clear of Chandos Street before we followed.

"All ready, Your Highness?" the driver asked.

I nodded. "Except that we shall not be going to the fire. Kindly drive to Eagle Street."

"*Eagle* Street, sir."

"Eagle Street, the other side of Holborn."

"I know it, sir, but I didn't know there was a fire there."

"Wait and see," I said cryptically.

We set off northward up St. Martin's Lane. People are pretty considerate when they see a fire appliance coming, and we rattled through to High Holborn at a good trot.

"Has the engine gone ahead, sir?" the driver inquired.

"An engine won't be required," I told him. Perhaps I should explain that an escape, such as the vehicle I had commandeered, is simply a cart with extending ladders. The fire engine is the vehicle that provides the steam for the pumps. It is unusual, to say the least, for an escape to attend a fire in the absence of an engine. You can imagine the look on the face of my driver. The look became a study in disbelief when we turned into

Eagle Street and there was no engine and no fire. Not even a puff of smoke.

"Shall I turn about, sir?" he asked.

"No," I told him. "Draw up outside number 39."

"That's Mr. Flanagan's address," he informed me. "Our superintendent."

"I'm aware of that. Just do as I say."

We trundled to a stop. There was no sign of a fire at 39, Eagle Street. Nobody was at the windows shrieking, or on the roof.

"Raise the main ladder," I ordered. "And make as little sound as possible."

The firemen exchanged mystified glances. Fortunately, they didn't dare defy me. They cranked the ladder upward.

"That will do," I presently said. "Now can you swing it closer to that large window at the top?"

I made sure that the top of the ladder didn't touch the windowsill, but it was pretty close. "Is it stable?" I asked. "In that case, I'm going up."

Watched by an interested collection of bystanders, I mounted the ladder briskly, as firemen do. I have an excellent head for heights, and this was only three stories high, so I went up almost without pause. I drew level with the window and looked in. This being a September evening, there was still a good light and the curtains had not been drawn. What I saw may offend some readers; it would have offended me, had I not been prepared. Indeed, I might well have fallen off the ladder.

This was the Flanagans' bedroom. There was a large double bed, occupied by the personable Dymphna Flanagan and a man who couldn't possibly have been Flanagan because Flanagan was fighting a fire in Coventry Street. Without wishing to be indelicate, I have to say that Dymphna and her visitor clearly weren't discussing Irish politics. They were naked as cuckoos. I should state here that I'm no prude, and I'm no Peeking Tom either. The reason I remained staring into the room for two more minutes is that I needed to be certain of the man's identity. I was waiting for him to turn his head. When he did, our eyes met. He saw me on my ladder, and I saw Engineer Locke, Flanagan's deputy.

I had fully anticipated this, of course. Friday—every other Friday—was Henry Locke's day off. He had been setting unoccupied houses alight once a fortnight in order to make sure that Flanagan was usefully occupied for the evening. And I had deduced it.

One cannot defend an arsonist, yet I must admit to some sympathy for Henry Locke. It's a frightful shock to be caught *in flagrante* by anyone, let alone the Heir Apparent in a fireman's helmet poised atop a ladder.

I descended, stepped to the front door, and knocked. Dymphna herself answered, having flung a garment over her head in the short time it took me to dismount from the ladder. She even managed a curtsy. Perhaps she hoped that I hadn't recognized her lover, for when I asked to speak to Engineer Locke she clapped her hand to her mouth. To his credit Locke then stepped forward. There was a distinct whiff of paraffin coming from his clothes—more confirmation, if needed, that he was the arsonist.

It was not needed, for he confessed to the crimes. Manfully he refused to implicate Dymphna in the fire raising, though I'm privately certain she was an accessory.

In November, 1870, Henry Locke pleaded guilty and was sentenced to penal servitude for life. You may think it a harsh sentence—as I do—for a *crime passionnel,* but that's the penalty for arson, and it *was* a dangerous way to court a lady.

Dymphna Flanagan parted from her husband soon after and took off to France with an onion seller. Flanagan lost all his bounce and retired prematurely from the London Fire Brigade in 1873.

To end on a rising note, Captain Shaw kindly offered the unemployed servant, Rudkin, a job as a fireman third class, which he accepted. When I last inquired, he was performing ably. All things considered, I would recommend the fire service as a satisfying career for any man with a sense of public duty and a wife he can trust.